KEEPER
OF THE
MILL

KEEPER OF THE MILL

Mary Anne Kelly

ST. MARTIN'S PRESS
NEW YORK

Library of Congress Cataloging-in-Publication Data

Kelly, Mary Anne.
    Keeper of the mill / Mary Anne Kelly.
       p.   cm.
    "A Thomas Dunne book."
    ISBN 0-312-13530-0
    I. Title.
PS3561.E3946K44   1995   95-34736
813'.54—dc20   CIP

First edition: November 1995

10 9 8 7 6 5 4 3 2 1

for Anne Marie
my sister, my friend

With heartfelt thanks to those who helped me with this book. To Tommy and Michael and Father Joe Keane. To Ilse. To Charles Rembar. To Ossi, Tereza, and Martin. To Patricia, Ivy, Hilde, Sister Diane, Hannelese, Mrs. Marino, Elly, and Sister Kathleen. To the Potter's Wheel. Thank you most of all to my superb editor, Ruth Cavin, and her assistant, Elisabeth Story, and in memory of Tony Smythe.

KEEPER
OF THE
MILL

1

―――――◆・◆・◆―――――

She dreamed of a translucent moon, round and up high
in a china-blue sky and a yard full of blowing white
wash in the wind. A reward, she acknowledged, awake, her
toes now on top of her husband's. A reward for some obscure metaphysical transaction well done.

Claire slipped out of bed and went down the old stairs,
glancing at the ballroom-sized closet she'd spent the day
before putting in order. She stood still at the bottom and
surveyed the quiet floor. It would never look like this again,
cleared of the children's toys, smelling of the fruit she'd arranged in a bowl on the table and the Murphy's Oil Soap
she'd massaged to a glow in the wood. The still unsettled
squall of dust she'd churned up in a frenzy lingered in the
stained-glass air. There it was. The housekeeper's tidy universe, infinite and miniature. She yawned and stretched.

Claire went into the kitchen and put the coffee water up
to boil. She sat down on a stool by her lamp with the big
tobacco-stained shade. If there was no morning sunshine in
her kitchen, blotted out as it was by the canopy of evergreen, she at least had this core of orange warmth she'd in-
vented for herself. Claire held on to that warmth for a moment, enjoying it before the others woke up, before the day
would formally begin, before Isolde would arrive and take
the joy out of all of it.

Isolde Donnerwetter would strew her expensive luggage all over the house and disapprove with a glance of all Claire's fine efforts. She'd make that puzzled smalling of the eyes that imagined, boy, what *I* would have done with this place! With similar eyes, Claire noticed the piece of pottery on top of the baker's rack. It really was a little too fussy. What she needed was a simple piece of pottery. Claire wrapped her old terry-cloth robe more snugly about her. It didn't matter what Isolde thought. She wouldn't let it.

They'd bought this house, Claire and Johnny had, expecting to stay for a short while and then move on, out to some more suitable neighborhood; only now, happy despite themselves, despite an overwhelming Third World immigration, even, in some cases, because of it, they lived very comfortably, thank you very much, in their plush and shady old house. There were benefits to hundred-year-old, ramshackle dwellings: front porches, back porches, cavernous cellars, and big, dusty attics for children to hide-and-go-seek in.

Claire had, at last, the enormous kitchen she'd always dreamed of and never would have been able to afford if they'd moved somewhere more appropriate. They had a great deal of property for the area, and without the drain of high taxes so many of their friends had to put up with. Friends who'd moved away to more idyllic, "safe" neighborhoods. To which they would certainly reply, "Right, but you've got to pay those killer private-school tuitions." "You have to die from something," Johnny would snort, and shrug. He liked to be near Brooklyn and she liked to be near the city, so it worked out all right. There were twenty-seven full-grown trees in their backyard. It was a good two lots, one opening onto Kew Gardens, the more highfalutin neighborhood with access to the woods, but a shortage of parking spaces, and the other resting in the dowdier but charming Richmond Hill, where you could park wherever you pleased on the roomy, potholed streets. What used to be a barn now served very well as a three-car garage. The broad, sloping hill in front of the house looked clear down to sleepy Myrtle Avenue. It would be quite something one day, when they got it fixed up and all that pachysandra pulled up and grass seeded in. It was as close as you could get to the country in the city. Already she had the backyard almost perfect. Claire padded softly over to the window and looked out. She leaned against the cold sill and watched a robin make his dour way through the snow-creased mud. Just give the grapevine another year or two and they could move the picnic table from under the pines. A nice bottle of that homemade red wine from Johnny's Italian precinct sergeant and some fresh mozzarella from Suino d'Oro on Liberty Avenue, well, these were the pinnacles of any summer evening. Then she could have Johnny move that whatever it was, that old thingamajig statue off to the side. She would put in a pattern of climbing blue slate in a trail up the side of the steep, viney overgrowth. When she got hold of some nice old blue slate, she would.

Claire padded softly over to the window and looked out. She leaned against the cold sill and watched a robin make his dour way through snow-creased mud. It wouldn't be long before spring was here, she shivered. Yes, she would clear away those shrubs. She would do it herself. She was good at that sort of thing, once she got her old jeans on and got going. Just yank the buggers out and before you knew it, they'd have their own prestigious entrance on Park Lane South. An arched trellis. With roses. Big, voluptuous, old fashioned, cream colored roses. And blue morning glory. The idea cheered her and she returned to the tasks at hand. There was a dishwasher Johnny had put in for her under the butcher-block board, but she hardly ever used it. How she had made fun of her mother for not using hers! Now she knew why she hadn't. When you had your sink at the window and a fair, awakening yard to look out on, this squirrel and that, all these birds and the thick virgin wood out the back brimming over, it was almost a pleasure to wash dishes. Well, it was a pleasure, she revised her thought. As long as you'd shackled the garbage cans well the night before. Those raccoons could get pretty ingenious when they caught the scent of last night's pistachio ice cream.

Claire washed herself under the cold-water tap while the coffee steeped. Plenty of elbow grease had gone into the gleaming gooseneck faucet. Hadn't they all told her it was useless and she'd best throw it out! They had. And now look at it. The icy cold hurt her narrow wrists but she didn't want to use the hot water and wake up the house, not yet. Let them sleep. Those pipes rocked and rolled like sneakers in the dryer when you gave them more than one job to do, and she didn't really mind the invigorating torture. It was good for the heart, wasn't it?

She crept up the ceremonial expanse of the stairway, with its disapproving urchins and gargoyles, letting her white fingers trail and linger along the wood. She stole past Johnny. There was only one massive, pelted arm of his to be seen, abandoned in sleep across the crumpled eiderdown. The air was particular with that foreign, tart man smell of him. Mine—she narrowed her eyes and acknowledged—all mine. She sucked it in and swept up her old green cozy turtleneck from the floor. There were underwear and warm socks that matched in a basket of clean rumpled laundry. On the way down, Claire looked in on the children. Their mouths were wide open. They were off in their dreams. Astonishing, she considered, how angelic those cutthroat blackguards appeared in their sleep.

Floozie the dog, never one much for mornings, barely lifted her head. She just thumped her snub tail in greeting as

4

Claire hobbled past, struggling into a pair of ugly rubber boots conveniently left by the previous owner, a Mr. Kinkaid. Mr. Kinkaid was a cantankerous, widowed old gent who'd happily—no, gleefully—signed the whole shebang over to Claire and Johnny and moved to a warm attic apartment down the block.

Claire found her navy pea jacket downstairs on a peg. The phone rang and she grabbed the receiver.

"What are you doing up?" a thick, cigaretty voice accused. It was Jupiter Dodd, she knew right away, *She She* magazine publisher, cranky and fast making his belligerent rounds, waking up the world and giving them a good yell before they were guarded enough to stand up for themselves.

"I'm just going out," she told him, cocking one ear toward upstairs, happy to hear from him. She was always happy to hear from Jupiter. He was her only source of income in a world with very little income nowadays. Of course, she could always finish off the basement and rent it out, but even that took money, and they didn't have any.

"What's up?" She tried not to sound like a fish on a hook.

"Any ideas for a shoot on Barbados?"

"Barbados?" Her heart leaped. She hadn't been to Barbados in years. "Let me think."

"You see, I knew you'd been there. I'm sending Hideoki with a half dozen Amazons. He's never been, and neither has the stylist. I told them you'd been everywhere and would have an idea."

"Oh," she said, her mind racing to find something to say that wouldn't let on her disappointment.

"It's been such a long time," she drawled. "What was the name of that place I used to stay? I'll have to look through my old appointment books. Can I get back to you?"

"No, I'm going out. I'll call you back this afternoon. Have you finished shooting those accessories I sent you?"

"Um, just about," she lied.

"Good. And please don't use that local stuff as background anymore. We're sick to death up here of Queens railroad trestles done up to look like the banks of the Seine."

"Right-o," she chirped stupidly and they hung up. Claire held the door so it wouldn't slam and made her way outside over the crackly drenched ice and mud. The sky was low and woolly behind the branches, and her breath came out in tight white puffs. There was a great show of padlock and husky chain on the garage door, but it wasn't really latched and any easy push scraped it open. You only had to watch out for splinters. Claire blinked carefully in the startling darkness. There was a smell of rust and old rubbery things. She always checked for raccoons before she went in, not wanting to corner one off guard.

Along the wall her maroon Columbia bicycle waited for her. Her gallant steed. She wheeled it out with doting care, making sure it didn't knock into the Chrysler Royale Johnny was restoring. Johnny was an undercover detective, but he really enjoyed working on what he called "masterpieces" like this. The bicycle he'd come across in a garbage heap in East New York on his way back from a drug bust. He'd thought she might like it. She'd seen it coming, limping up the driveway under his skeptical tutelage. She had loved it, immediately and effusively. Johnny was a little bit jealous of her bike, she suspected cheerfully, hopping on and wobbling away, kicking the door shut, straining not to lose control down the steep drive, setting the deep steel basket straight before she slipped the bulky mitt back into her pocket. Spring was here. She smiled at the tufts of crocus on everyone's snow-puddled lawns. Or would be any minute.

Claire tooled down to Jessy's candy store on Myrtle,

now actually Mohammed's Chapadi Emporium, but he still sold New Jersey milk and eggs and poppy-seed rolls and the *Daily News,* did Mohammed, so the early-morning regulars continued to gather there, and they still called it Jessy's, never mind it reverberated curry and there was a rainbow curtain of ladies' punjabis along the wall. Mohammed put on "News Radio" for them till nine o'clock, when he'd go back to "Bangladesh Top Twenty Hits." Then the sleepy Indian housewives would begin to tiptoe in.

"Good morning, Mrs. Claire." He displayed a set of enormously healthy-looking white teeth and gave a half-bow. Claire smiled tentatively back. Mohammed refused to believe Claire was not some wealthy heiress. "Such an important house, on top of the entire Richmond Hill," he would cluck admiringly, shaking his head.

"Mohammed," she'd admonish him, piling items into her ecologically correct net bag, "I am just another mortgage-impoverished Queens housewife and you only badger me to make me feel good, don't you?"

"Yes, 'tis true," he'd say, wobbling his head and holding the door open for her, "but you have visited my country, have you not?" He liked to remind her of this as she pedaled away, as if that made her the same just-flown-in from Delhi apparition in her freshly ironed and nevertheless wrinkled linen jacket. As indeed she once had been. Once. She sighed and carried on contentedly and pedaled up the potholed street, passing crazy Lydia Schuler as she bumped along. Lydia Schuler was harmless, just another burned-out, zigzagging pedestrian of Richmond Hill. Claire hardly looked as Lydia, nearing fifty, banged her head against the graffitied mailbox on the corner. Claire checked her watch. A quarter to seven. She had a couple of spare minutes before the family started to wake up. She'd stop off and bring a roll to Iris von Lillienfeld. She leaned her bike against the bent sycamore and went lightly up the steps of Iris's magnificently intact antebellum. It would take her a long time and a lot of grief to get over not having this old lady around to talk to. Originally a gruff enigma, Iris had become her blithe, if elderly, mentor.

Claire, charmed with her own thoughtfulness, rattled on Iris's relic-of-a-sea-horse knob. It lay sideways, and you had to turn it like the key in a music box.

Iris, meanwhile, stood with weary eyes, wispy sprigs of pale chin whiskers fluttering in the draft and a digestion gone merrily berserk. She stood behind the expanse of the refrigerator. Perhaps, if she stood very still, Claire would go away. She should come back later. Claire always did, no fear of that. You'd think she'd have the decency not to be so good so early.

"Iris!" Claire's imperious whisper carried through both helpless doors.

"Fool!" Iris groaned. She would wake the cat. He was so old, though, Lü the Wanderer was, one wondered if he heard anything at all at this point, or just read lips. He had to be twenty-seven, or twenty eight. Iris was afraid to wake him up and at the same time she was afraid not to. One day she would shake him and he would be cold and stiff. She didn't want to deal with that. She supposed it would be better, though, than him finding her cold and stiff. Who would look after the old fellow? Who would care that his teeth were very bad and he could only manage tapioca and the like? Iris moved with a decisive lurch out into clear view. Better Claire than the ASPCA.

"Ah. There you are! I was just about to worry."

Iris unlatched the inside door and let her in.

"I didn't hear the clock."

"You mean the bell." Iris was always mixing up common words. Iris moved away in case there was a lingering trace of booze about herself from the night before. Claire would get all worked up and sermonize. Little did she know that Claire had her own silent soldier of Bordeaux dying fast in the back of the crockery cupboard, justified primly by Tilset- and Appenzeller-loving veins and arteries that nowadays, thank God, the experts admitted, required such slosh.

"I've brought you a nice fresh roll," she said. She waited. Iris did not smile but turned her back and retreated past the grand piano to her bedroom. Perhaps she was not well? Claire hesitated. Iris came back out, her teeth installed, and rewarded Claire with a filmy grin.

"You're out early," she growled in her still thick German accent.

"I've got that friend of mine coming from Munich today," Claire reminded her, remembering herself. Her heart sank.

They shared an intimate grimace. Iris knew that Claire had had a whole other life over there in Munich and didn't much like dredging it up again. Well, she liked it but hated it at the same time. It was complicated. Iris understood because she'd lived other lives over there as well. You didn't switch entire continents when things were going hunky-dory. It was all right, though. It would be all right.

"Better you than me," Iris said, referring to Claire's company. Or any company, for that matter. Her own letter from Germany lay propped against the Tiffany lamp, along with bill receipts and unopened Hanukkah cards. She batted her eyes, struggling with fatigue. All night long she'd walked around the empty house, awake. She might as well not even go to bed till dawn, for all the good it did her. She didn't get a wink till then anyway. Iris nudged Claire out of the way and went to the sink to fill the kettle. Claire stood there indecisively. "Well," she said, "I suppose I'll head on home and get my crew up and at 'em."

"So soon?" Iris pouted insincerely.

"Tell you what . . . I'll stop back later. It will give me an excuse to get away. Just in case Isolde drives me nuts. Which she will."

Iris looked, from behind, like a kimonoed model for an art nouveau stained-glass window. Her waist-length hair had been rolled up for so many decades into the same Oriental chignon that by now it went that way itself, without any comb or barrette. Iris was a noblewoman, not only in character but by birth, and there weren't many whom she let get close. In fact, none. There was the grocery delivery boy, the liquor-store delivery boy, and then there was Claire. And Claire was so busy with her own life that she didn't notice how empty anyone else's was, especially not the life of someone whose face she was so delighted to behold. Iris always remained mysterious and dignified, even the more she got to know her. A Libra woman.

"Don't worry so much," Iris advised her as she left. "She will either love it or she will hate it. It's already decided by her mood. I know my Germans."

"Yes." Claire stopped halfway down the back steps, remembering Iris's vague confidences of Nazi persecution and her narrow escape from Bavaria. "I suppose you do." But she knew her Germans too, Claire did. She hadn't lived in Munich ten years herself without learning something of the "new" German. As far as that went, if the sun was shining, Isolde would be in a splendid state of mind, and if it was raining, she would be picky and nasty and fault-finding. Which was why you were always better off dealing with an on-vacation German than a German at home. Or maybe that was racist and ridiculous, and Claire held her breath in a sudden and absolute state of confusion. It was too soon. She never should have told Isolde she should come. The thought of the state of her cellar! Ah, well. She remembered the window boxes Johnny had made for her and painted forest-green. Really, one couldn't help being impressed with those. Anyone who had half a shred of imagination could see just what she intended there. Feeling better, she gave Iris von Lillienfeld a wave and pedaled home. This was good. This was lovely. She pedaled faster. At this rate, her stomach would be flat in time for bathing-suit season. For once.

She watched her house come into view with the same mixture of astonished pride and shame she'd feel running into her son when he was filthy and in dire need of a hair-cut. There was an awful lot of rusty tricycles, bedraggled doll's houses, and balls and bats scattered across the drive-way. She'd have to get them to clear the place. Promise them an excursion to Bishop's Comic Book and Baseball Card Store to juice them up. First impressions were so im-portant, and no one was more fastidiously clean than Isolde. Hadn't she taught Claire to scrub the bathroom tile behind the faucet with a recycled toothbrush and bleaching powder? Stood behind her, hands on her hips, until she'd got it right? Who'd been coming to visit, Claire's own boy-friend? Claire jumped off the bike and took the steep hill by foot. "San Francisco in your own front yard," Johnny liked to say. The phone was ringing as she came in the back door, and she covered the kitchen floor in two long strides to get to it.

"Claire? Oh, good. I wasn't sure what time it was there."

"Isolde? My God. What time is it? Have you landed al-ready?"

"Darling, I never took off."

"Wait, what? You're still at Munich Airport?" This wasn't bad. Now she'd have another whole afternoon to snazz up the basement, not just ram things into clandestine piles in overloaded cupboards.

"No, you don't understand. I'm home. I'm still home! I'm not coming after all."

"What?"

"Oh, Claire, don't sound like that. Your voice so forlorn."

"What do you mean, you're not coming? I bought new sheets and curtains for the guest room. You've got to come!"

Isolde's husky, whisky voice laughed long and hard. Then, "Claire," she whispered, becoming intimate, "I can't come down because so much has happened, and—I hope you're sitting down—I'm getting married."

"Married?"

"Tch. You don't have to sound so astonished. Yes, married."

"What? But how—"

"I know"—Isolde yawned across the broad Atlantic—"it's all still new to me, too."

"When, today?"

"Of course not today. He only just asked me. May seventeenth."

Claire looked frantically around her bright, cold kitchen. The door, unlatched, swung open in the wind. "Who? Who asked you? Wolfgang?"

"Wolfgang? Don't be silly. Who would want to marry Wolfgang? It's Blacky. I'm marrying your old kumquat, Blacky."

"What!"

"Oh, please stop shouting 'What' like that."

"You can't," Claire whispered.

"I bloody well can."

"Isolde, have you gone absolutely mad?"

"Yes, I suppose I have."

"What will become of you?"

They both said nothing, mulling together what would indeed become of her. Both saw, as if by magic, the same evening sunlit picture of an Isolde older still, sitting on an orange-and-white chair beneath a chestnut tree in a busy beer garden, holding her head of great dark hair in her hands, bemoaning her absurd, romantic destiny.

"Well, anyway," Isolde said finally, "I'll have my crow's feet done for nothing from now on."

Blacky, Doktor von Osterwald, was the busiest plastic surgeon in Munich. And this was a rather pointless, silly thing for Isolde to say because she had never paid Blacky once, and he'd had a hand in that stunning face many times already. For years. Even when he and Claire had been together. Claire remembered: Blacky had always been bringing them together. Claire had never worried because Isolde had been a good—what was it?—six or seven years older than she, automatically eliminating her from what Claire considered the "running." Now, of course, Claire was older than Isolde had been then. And that put a different slant on things. Claire knew now, for instance, that eye contact, more than any dewy youthfulness, had to do with sexual attraction, and she wondered what the two of them had been up to years ago, while she'd been off on an unsuspecting shoot in Vientiane or Villengilly.

"I don't suppose you love him," Claire heard herself say.

"Love?" Isolde snorted derisively, characteristically. "Certainly not."

So Claire knew, then, all at once, that Isolde not only loved him but was hopelessly, crazily in love with him. "That's all right then." She tried to sound chummy. It wouldn't do to let Isolde know she knew. Poor thing. "I can't believe you're not coming, though," she said, meaning it, suddenly seeing the days and the weeks before her free. Nothing in front of her but seeing the children off in the morning and doing the marketing and being there for them when they came back. And laundry, lots of laundry. Johnny coming and going. No real Johnny to look at and talk to, really talk with. Those days were over, she sighed, unhappy at last, wishing that Isolde still were coming and she could show off her brilliant sense of color and *Gemüt-lichkeit,* coziness, for hadn't she learned all that from Isolde? Hadn't it been Isolde's sneer in her ear she'd used in deciding whether or not to buy this or choose that? Yes, she admitted now, for she had no reason not to, it had.

"Of course you'll come," Isolde said.

Claire laughed. "I wish."

"What, of course you must. You'll stand up for me."

Claire started to whimper. No tears would come. They never did anymore. Her face crunched into a grimace of misery and a catlike sound eked out.

"What's that? What are you doing, blubbering?"

"I'm not, it's just—so happy for you, Isolde. For you both."

"Sure you are. Tell me, has that moron you married figured out how to steal some money yet? Oh, please, don't answer, don't defend him. I can't bear it."

"Isolde, please. Don't."

"All right. But only because I know you'll hang up on me if I go on, and I don't feel like redialing that dreadful, boring number. So what can I do? Send you the ticket? I will, you know." And for a moment Claire feared there was nobody else, no one to stand up for Isolde in her moment of—whatever it was she was going to accomplish—but how silly. Isolde, Munich's own party girl extraordinaire. Even if she went they'd hardly see her for the throng.

"I know you would, Isolde. I couldn't, though. You know that."

"*Ach. Scheisse!* The doorbell! I've got to go. It's that fool Wolfgang. I'll call back tomorrow." She hung up the phone. The mournful, empty ring of a gone connection sang from Claire's still trembling hand.

"What's the matter, Mommy?" Anthony stood in the

doorway, pajamaed and rubbing one eye with a fist. "Is it the dryer broken again?"

And outside the house, where Claire had been so sure that spring was on its gentle way, great white flakes came down in a hurry, the way they will do when they cover the house and intend, absolutely, to stay.

Breakfast started off well, pancakes and bacon and nectarines, the cozy excitement of a good fast snowstorm, not fast enough to shut down school, though, and Claire was left with a muddy, sticky floor and a pile of dishes in the sink. She sat, legs crossed, rocking one foot up and down while she finished reading the *News.* Floozie the dog kept her company. Something lovely was on the radio. Brahms, she supposed. She pushed the paper away and frowned, grappling with an ornery cuticle. She didn't know how she had supposed she could have provided a charming household for Isolde. Just look at this place. She sighed, the dog sighed, and she got up and put her warm pea coat on and her worn, but still very nice, navy-blue beret. The door banged shut and left the house the way it was in there, quiet and full of things and on its own. Her bike was in the yard. Luckily she'd propped it against the house, underneath the porch awning, and it was still dry. Floozie, never one to stay home once she was up, deposited a steaming yellow piddle in the snow and hopped up onto the scarf in the handlebar basket and they were off.

It was good packing snow, not slippery, and they tooled along, philosophically accepting their pelting of teeny doilies in the mouth, in the eyes, looking up at the tops of the heavy trees and watching as, little by little, the closed knots of buds were obliterated with white. A remarkable morning. And, yes, better that Isolde hadn't come. Claire pedaled down to Jamaica Avenue, but the five-and-ten wasn't open yet. She pedaled back; it was slower going this time. She decided to make a nice visit to church, noticed there was a Mass going on and so thought better of it. She hated to think how that early-morning crew would make shocked faces at her bicycle. She didn't know why. God wouldn't mind her bicycle at all, but never mind, she wouldn't go, she would do a good deed and stop in at Iris's. Cheer her up. She wheeled her bike brazenly into Iris's garage, transported Floozie up the steps, and wound the bell. There was a little forest of potted plants on the porch, looking very dear and Swiss and chilly. When Iris didn't come, Claire rattled the door finally and there she was, aggravated from the look of her and—Claire took a quick step backward—drunk from the blue, ginny reek of her. "Jesus," Claire said.

"Well, come in anyway," Iris said.

"No, I'm sorry I disturbed you, I—Iris! What the hell are you doing? Drinking at ten o'clock in the morning?"

Iris looked her up and down with a frayed, sad sneer, then turned her back and swayed unsteadily across the room. It was filled to the brim with antique tables and chairs and worn Turkey carpets and blown ruby glass and paintings in golden frames. There was the substantial coat of dust old people's houses have. Iris lowered herself to the edge of a tapestry wing chair and then fell, *phlump,* back against the cushions. She laughed.

"Whoa there, Nellie." Claire tried the seat across from her.

"I'm not so drunk," Iris complained. "I was for an hour or so, but now"—her eyes slid shut—"I'm just ready for a nap."

Claire watched her for a moment, reached across and patted her hand, then stood to go.

"You don't have to leave just yet," Iris murmured.

"Well, then I won't." Claire sat back down. She pulled a well-worn bisque baby doll from underneath her butt and got comfortable. "There's no one waiting for me at home till three o'clock anyway," she admitted. "And"—she shrugged—"Isolde won't be coming after all."

Iris's eyes clicked open. "What's that?"

"Yeah, and you won't believe why. She's getting"—she cleared her throat—"married."

"Married?"

"Yes. And do you know who it is she's marrying? My old boyfriend, that's who. The doctor." As this didn't seem to impress Iris too much, she added, "The one with all the money."

"Ah."

"I mean, they invited me to come. Well, she did. Isolde wants me to be her matron of honor. Of course I said no."

"Of course."

"I couldn't leave my family."

"Of course not."

"I'm so glad to be back in America anyway. Who wants to go there again, for God's sake?"

"Not me, that's for sure. You wouldn't get me back to Munich," Iris agreed, shivering. "Not for five million bucks."

"Ha. Five million bucks, I'd go."

"Not me." Iris shook her fragile head vehemently. She reached over to the nearby keys of the baby grand but flinched at the awful stiffness of her fingers. "Not again, not ever. And I've got reason to go, let me tell you."

Claire, past propriety, narrowed her eyes. "So tell me."

Iris glowered at the wet dog on Claire's lap but didn't answer.

"Come on"—Claire swept the back of her hand through the air—"don't you hold out on me."

Iris regarded her with limpid, froggy eyes. "What were we talking about?"

"About not going back to Germany and why you would have reason to after all."

"Oh, *ja,* I've got plenty of reasons. Hundreds of thousands of reasons." She snickered faintly.

Claire leaned forward hopefully. "You mean family? You still have family over there?"

"You know that I don't," Iris rasped, disgusted. "You know Hitler took them all from me before I had a chance, before I—" She stopped suddenly, and Claire didn't want to press her. The haunted look she'd seen come screaming from Iris's eyes came out of somewhere deep and derelict inside. Claire didn't want Iris to go back there. Not even to remember. Not even for a minute.

"You want me to let Lü out?" Claire nicked her head in the direction of the dining room, where the Siamese stood atop the burled walnut sideboard, a myopic and displeased old veteran on four rickety, but deft, bowlegs.

Iris came back. *"Ja,"* she murmured sadly, "you let him out and I'll get us something to eat."

"Good," said Claire, always ready, at any time, any place, to eat.

Claire warmed up nicely with a lot of oatmeal cookies and a fancy little lady's china cup of steaming chocolate. The windows, never clean, steamed over and rushed with the falling snow.

"More shoki?" Iris held the porcelain rose pot above Claire's head.

"I wouldn't mind another cookie."

"That you never say no to. Eh? *Was?*" She bent down, grabbed Claire's unsuspecting belly in her surprisingly strong hand and shook it heartily back and forth.

"Hey, knock it off!" Claire gave an embarrassed laugh and caught the affronted, capsized dog with one hand.

Iris, always resilient, was recovered enough now to indulge in reminiscence. It was her Uncle Oswald, she confided, who'd managed her escape from Diessen, a town in Bavaria. Her entire family was taken prisoner, and she would have been taken as well, but for a clandestine rendezvous with her girlfriends, Effi and Ursula. Effi was a common girl who'd been inadvertently responsible for saving her life by keeping her out late on a group date with a pair of shockingly drunken and irresponsible SA officers (that was one step below SS). The young Iris had been furious with her. She had sworn never to speak to her again and, as it happened, never would have, except Iris was to come home to an empty house rather than the furious father she'd expected. There had been no father there, no mother, no brother, no seven-year-old redheaded sister, wild for boy's games and soccer and marzipan and—*ach!*—Iris stopped for a moment while she mopped her cheeks.

They were all gone. Gone. The windows of the summer house had been left open, the way her mother always kept it for a good long while after supper. The smells of cooking should be swept away by the clean Bavarian wind. It was such a pretty cottage, Iris remembered. White stucco, with brown shutters and window boxes filled with red geraniums, and a low, overhanging brown roof. There was a wind that night. The curtains stretched in fluttering sheets across the polished rooms as the astonished Iris stood there gaping. No one was there to shut them now, no one to click their tongues and shush the little one off to bed, to shut away the cold, chill night. Uncaring, cold-hearted endless night.

"Iris?" Claire whispered, but she didn't hear her. Iris stood in the doorway of years ago, her useless key in one hand and her open purse in the other. A terrible rattling stole her back from confusion and shock to her Uncle Oswald's distorted face behind the parlor window. He was grimacing, signaling to her. *"Komm! Mach schnell! Komm!"*

He walked her hurriedly down the backway paths of the Ammersee, the lakeside, where nobody went at night. They stole furtively past the boathouse, where the old man slept with his crisp light on, past the garden house of shut-tight sun umbrellas and chaise longues on white wooden wheels. Teeth chattering, without even a small bag of overnight things, because Uncle Oswald had insisted, *"Es wird ja zu gefährlich,"* it would be too dangerous. They went first to his own cottage past the gazebo. She stood waiting for him, her arms at her sides as he fumbled through cleansers and pails and washrags under the kitchen sink. In a shoe box, scrawled with the word *Gift,*—"Poison," he found a tin of saddle soap wrapped in a muslin rag. He rammed this into his pocket, left everything as it was on the floor and raced, frantic, from the house.

She stumbled behind him, not believing, not wanting to believe the terrible nightmare that for her and so many others had now begun.

Claire moved uncomfortably in her chair. She didn't want to hear this, but she didn't want Iris to stop talking either. She tried not to show the shock on her face. She sat very still and breathed out and waited. Eventually, Iris caught hold of her voice and went on.

"He had come, my uncle, for the dessert. My mother, she made the most scrumptious desserts, shooing the cook from the kitchen and doing it all by herself. Oh, she was very vain about her pastry. Didn't want anyone else to get the credit. She was something, my mother. She was Jewish. Well, you know that. My father, he married beneath his station, as they say, but he knew, we all knew, especially my mother's family—they considered the marriage a step down for *her*—that no one was as good, as radiant with goodness, as my mother. He loved her so much. So much." Here Iris stopped and glanced at Claire. "Your mama always reminded me of mine. The same type. Capable. The same"—she hesitated—"grace and serenity. So. She would make these special desserts for my uncle and then he and my father would take their *Bummel,* their stroll around the lake. That was a special day. It was my mother's birthday. My father had presented her with her dearest wish, a Japanese maple tree. A dwarf. *Sehr teuer!* Very costly. We had a great ceremony planting it; my uncle was the shoveler. Ach, Ammersee was a beautiful place. Beautiful. Full of moonlight and the smell of Johannisbeere, black currant blossoms. It's a peculiar smell, that, like ammonia and sweet hay. Unusual. There was no moon that night. You could not see the *Zwiebelkopf,* the onion dome, on the Marian Münster, the Minster, down the lane. And so we walked and walked. I thought he was taking me to somewhere special. To a destination. It was years later I realized he might have had no idea where it was he was leading me. He had come just in time to see the SS take the family away. He'd shut himself up inside the tool shed and watched as they shoved and pushed my gentle family into their car. *Meine kleine Schwester!* Just a little Fräulein in white socks around the ankles, slipping always into her shoes.

"Then my uncle had stayed for me, praying no one had been left behind to wait for me. No one had been, of course. Why bother? They knew I would go to the *Polizei* in Diessen, in the village, to find out what had happened. And they could arrest me then. We were, you see, a law-abiding family.

"My uncle and I, we walked all night. All night. My uncle had brought with him the shovel. From planting the Japanese maple tree. It had been lying still on the ground, and he'd picked it up and carried it. He led me, stupefied, to

21

the outskirts of Munich. There was a *Lastwagen,* a truck, stopped on the side of the road. My uncle spoke with the driver. He offered to give him the shovel. He whispered. The driver didn't want to take us. Then my uncle started to act very strangely, poking at the man with his elbow. Winking. I was naive, but I knew what he was doing. He wanted the man to believe I was his *schatzi,* his girlfriend. My uncle, remember, was an old man. "But"—Iris shrugged meaningfully—"so was the truck driver. Finally, winking and snickering back, he let us come with him to Munich. And he took the shovel. He had it the whole time he drove, banging between his legs. He was pleased with that shovel. He drove a long time on country roads. I remember we passed Nymphenburg. We passed the palace. You could see the glint of gold everywhere in the very dark and the folded white wings of the swans, like small boats, gliding down and then up the canals.

"At last, my uncle told the man to stop. We must get out. It was not yet dawn, but already the light climbed in the distance. My uncle jumped from the door of the truck, but he was no longer young enough to move so suddenly so quickly. He was stiff, and he hurt himself as he landed. His hip. He pretended he had not, but I knew he had. He tried not to grimace because he thought I wouldn't let him continue if I knew he was in pain. I knew. But I let us conspire together to save my young life.

"We came to a village along the banks of the Isar. It was called Saint Hildegard's. Named for Saint Hildegard of Bingen."

"Saint Hildegard's!" Claire cried out. "I know Saint Hildegard's!" It was the charming inn and beer garden where all the "right" artsy people met and drank and argued and gossiped. Everyone knew Saint Hildegard's Mill. Not everyone could afford to go there, though. And if you weren't their sort, they conveniently forgot you and let you sit there stewing till you vowed never to set foot in the place again—which was just what they intended. Artists were always tolerated, though, and according to how promising they were, encouraged to loll about as long as they liked, signing their bills rather than paying cash. As a result, the walls were hung with beautiful, unusual paintings. The house was notoriously affable to taking payment in work rather than elusive cash.

"I remember the way it looked," Iris continued, too absorbed to notice Claire's excitement, "so quaint and misty in the dawn. A grassy meadow and a small, steep hill with a chapel, like a bell on the meadow. It was such a pretty place. My uncle knew somebody there. Or of someone. A man he could trust. We stopped. He gave this man at the *Mühle*, the Mill, he gave him *Geld*. Well, not money; stones—diamonds. At least one diamond he gave that man. I saw him take it out first from the boot-polish container. He turned to me as he took it out, as if no one, even God, should see what he had there. I saw the glitter of all the stones. Sixty stones. All blue-white and clear. 'Irislein,' he said to me, he always called me Irislein—his pet name for me—'your future.'

"He nodded to make sure I understood, and I nodded back. He told me this would keep me safe until he could come back for me. I should sew the stones into my clothes to keep them, when I could. And so he put me to wait beside a great tree on the hill. I sat there, cold with terror, but with joy and relief, too, for already I had learned, during that long, dark night, to cling to my survival. Even already I knew, with that cold box warming on my breast, that no matter what happened to my family—my mother, my father, all of them—I was prepared to go through anything, do anything, to live. I remember I cupped my bleeding feet inside my hands to comfort them. I saw the churning mill water under the lifting mist. The grass was sharp and short.

23

A bird cried out from the chapel roof, and let me tell you, I wanted to live."

Claire held her breath, and Iris rocked quickly back and forth. There was no sound but the clock. Claire thought perhaps Iris meant her to go, but she wasn't sure. She stayed sitting there. Finally Iris continued. "My uncle left me there a long, long time. I put my head down on the ground. Perhaps I slept. I don't remember. I remember looking up and seeing my uncle coming toward me with a very big, a huge, Bavarian man. Adam. Adam von Grün-wald. You could always tell what was a Bavarian. They are dark and round and compact. This fellow, though, he was massive. He looked at me on the ground like that, and"— Iris's eyes filled with tears—"he felt so *sorry* for me. He picked me up like I was a run-over animal. He carried me back to the Mühle, it was also a Gaststube, an inn, for artists mostly, and he put me upstairs. It was his mother's room. He put me in her bed, and he had this great big hand, and he"—Iris touched her withered cheek—"he stroked me softly with this big hand and looked into my eyes with his shrewd black eyes and he said something in Bayerish—Ba-varian. Who understood that dialect, gentry Berliner that I was? But whatever it was, I understood him and I felt safe, and I slept. He saved my life."

"And what happened to him?"

Iris sighed.

Claire leaned forward. "He took the diamonds, right?"

"He? He didn't take the diamonds. He hid them. He hid them good, too. For me, right there at Saint Hildegard's Mühle.

"He and I, we were lovers. He was, you see, the great love of my life." Iris smiled kindly at Claire. "Yes, even this old, ugly woman once was beautiful enough to be loved." One gnarled, arthritic finger flicked a years-gone-by-and-vanished pin curl from her livered eye. "You sit there young and feel immortal, Claire. I tell you I was once immortal too. And now, I live in time." She tossed her head. "We always thought we would go back together, get back there. It never occurred to us that we wouldn't. I never saw my Uncle Oswald again. They intercepted him that next day returning from Munich to Diessen. He died in Dachau. But then everything started to happen. The whole world turned, somehow, upside down. There was no going back. There never will be. I should have sewn the stones into the lining of my clothes, as my uncle instructed me to do. But I didn't. I left them, nice and safe there, hidden."

"What? But, you mean it's all still there?"

"Yup. But I wouldn't go. I couldn't."

"But, you mean you're really sure they're still there?"

"He told me he would hide them there for me. Keep them. They would never leave the Mill until I came back for them. He swore this."

"You believed him?"

"Oh, I believe it still."

Claire remembered the opulent green of the Mill in the spring. A green as green as a Tunisian sky was blue. Wouldn't Jupiter Dodd just love it as a background? She could even—her heart grew strong within her chest—use the dashing girls from Isolde's wedding party. "I could," she said out loud, "I could go."

Iris lit a small cigar. A Davidoff. "I'd give you half," she said. She puffed a fancy, contemplative cloud around her head. "Well. A third."

25

2

*T*wo *old former* models sat at the fresh-squeezed car-
rot-juice and yogurt kiosk in Munich Airport. They
both had married well and just now bundled their husbands
off to Zurich on the everybody-gray-suit, early-breakfast
flight. The ladies' legs were knotted around themselves, and
each bottom foot tapped out an agitated ditty.

"Wasn't that Claire Breslinsky, the photographer?" the
one said to the other.

"You know, I think it was."

"My God, she looks forty!"

"She is forty," the other one said. "Why shouldn't she
look it?"

I *solde thwacked Claire's* light luggage into the spotless
trunk of her silver 850 CSI BMW. Claire was very smug
about her light luggage.

"Directly to the Mill?" Isolde raised an eyebrow at her.
"Or shall we take a coffee on the Leopoldstrasse first?"

"Oh, the Mill, please." Claire displayed her exhausted
face. Isolde on the Leopoldstrasse would find innumerable
unworthy subjects to talk to, "tchotchkes" to buy, lunch to
linger over.

"All right," Isolde agreed, surprising Claire. Everything

was a fight with Isolde, and when it wasn't, you tended to be wary. But Claire's vision was both sharpened and softened by time and distance. She leaned her head back on the sheepskin headrest and let go, let the green fields of Raps, the onion domes and pretty farms, turn to a blur of chartreuse cushion on each side of the silvery autobahn. It was loaded with massive, well-kept trucks and spotless Teutonic vehicles. They wouldn't slow Isolde down. On the contrary, she drove at breakneck speed, her only speed, behind designer-black-and-golden glasses, weaving determinedly onward, never hesitating, shifting instinctively down, then up, prowling momentarily behind two giant riggers, then plunging suicidally forward between them, her pretty, slippered foot flat down and slicing through the steely middle.

I will not be afraid, Claire instructed herself, clutching the weary hand luggage on her lap. She reminded herself of the sink inevitably full of dishes back home. There were fates worse than death. What amazed her was that this all had happened so easily, had fallen into place the way things will when they are meant to be.

Her children were well stashed away; Anthony with his grandparents on a long-awaited, often-postponed and now finally realized trip to Disney World; Dharma was with her Aunt Carmela, Claire's sister. Carmela was slowpoking her way through an opulent grant from a feminist group and, Claire suspected, all this was right up Dharma's liberated little alley. Her heart tugged for a moment at the thought of the children's missing her, but she wouldn't be gone that long and then it would all start in again, wouldn't it. The dog was safely with her other sister, Zinnie, a New York City detective. That left only Johnny to worry about, and you know something, she told herself, remembering the suspiciously still-fragrant bottle of Chivas she'd stumbled over accidentally while rummaging around the cellar looking for her stuff, the hell with him. Well, maybe not the hell, but a little limbo wouldn't hurt either of them. And if it did, perhaps it was meant to. She took a deep, cleansing, deliberately young and defiantly free breath. "It's awfully nice of you to pick me up like this," she said.

"Blacky insisted." She shrugged. "Not like the old days, is it? With the cozy little Humphrey Bogart airport just outside Bogenhausen. This new airport is a hike. Twenty kilometers."

"Tch," Claire commiserated.

"And the benzene! You can't imagine what I spend a week on benzene. Of course you know everything is through the roof. These are terrible times in Germany."

Claire eyed Isolde's 22-karat Rolex. One of them, at least, had hit pay dirt. So it was Claire's abandoned pay dirt—at least one of them still had it. Claire glanced sideways at Isolde's been-around thighs. Still good, those thighs, brown and lithe from tennis. She was prettier than most women, taller than most men, and thinner than most human beings. Her shrewd brown eyes flashed with restless energy and life. Isolde was perfumed, important, and, Claire had not quite forgotten, impossible.

It hadn't been in the least difficult to get her to marry at the Mill, though. All she'd had to mention was where she'd read Kristina von Ekelsdorf was having her fund-raiser there this summer for the Bosnian orphans. Kristina was, after all, the hostess to outdo in Munich. Isolde, despite her efforts, never could hope to keep up. Now, with Blacky's money, well sir, there was no end to the possibilities. The fact that Claire had never really read that Kristina von Ekelsdorf was having the fund-raiser at the Mill didn't matter. Maybe when she'd read about Isolde's posh wedding there, she would. Claire felt quite like Brer Rabbit. She turned and gazed fondly at Isolde's beautiful profile glittering in the light. Isolde might be a professional beauty, but she was a beauty nonetheless. She was a priceless friend to have. There was no one, nor would there ever be, anyone like Isolde.

She wondered if she would do well to tell her about Iris and the diamonds. Isolde was so good at that sort of thing—what sort of thing that was, Claire was not exactly sure—but Isolde would doubtless be good at it. Claire might find herself lost without her prowess.

Reading just enough of her mind to misunderstand, Isolde said, "I hope you don't mind staying at the Mill?"

"Of course not." Claire smiled. How like Isolde not to remember the Mill had been her idea in the first place. Better that way.

"The *Gästehaus* at the English Garden was all filled up," Isolde continued. (That meant she'd booked it up with her more prestigious friends.)

"I prefer the Mill. Really. It's so romantic."

"Well, they're not always good with guests. They're so . . . independent. And they're so out of the way for you without a rent-a-car."

"Oh, I won't be wanting a car."

"They are expensive." Isolde's penny-pinching detector was always up.

Claire wasn't going to tell her Jupiter Dodd was footing the bill. She didn't like to admit to having sunk to shooting accessories. Isolde would think she was washed up. Well, she was washed up. And at the moment, she rather liked the feeling. It was the same as starting fresh.

Isolde eyed her shrewdly. "You're not going to go trying to seduce my fiancé, I hope."

"Wha—?"

"Because if I see even the slightest signs of flirtation—"

"Oh, Isolde, really!"

"Don't 'Oh, Isolde, really!' me! I know your sweet little two-goody-shoes routine."

Claire laughed. "It's Goody Two-shoes. And I'm flattered that you would even consider me a threat."

"I don't. I just don't like Blacky to think he's one up on me. He's a little—uh—piqued just now about all my admirers, as ridiculous as that is!" •

Claire pursed her lips. "How little you must think of me—to imagine I would come all this way to your wedding and then turn around and—"

"Oh, shut up! Everyone knows what a tease you imagine yourself."

Offended, stony Irish indignation fumed through the car. To think she'd almost been fool enough to share her secret about the diamonds with her! And—she snorted a firm burst of air through pinched and righteous nostrils—that would be the end of Isolde's getting her hands on the heavy bottle of Jack Daniels she'd lugged just for her all the way from the Duty-Free at Kennedy.

Isolde, realizing she had gone too far, or at least too soon, reapproached.

"I'm sorry I couldn't get you a better room at the Mill."

"What do you mean—can't I have a front room?" She imagined cooking smells and late-night noise.

"I'm afraid not. There's a crew staying there. You know how they're always putting artists up. This lot are film people."

"No, I didn't know," Claire said, happy again. Claire loved the movies. She would always be a fan. "What sort of film people? Hollywood?"

"Heavens, no! British. Temple Fortune and his entourage. They wouldn't like regular hacks to stay here. They fancy themselves the only aristocratic patrons of the arts in Bavaria."

"Temple Fortune . . . Temple Fortune . . . I know I've heard the name . . ."

"You remember"—Isolde swept a dismissive, heavily

braceleted arm past Claire's face—"he made that award-winning film in Marrakech, all Italian colors and Episcopalian dialogue, the one where the girl commits suicide at the end."

"Vaguely . . ."

"Oh, you know. He finds all these well-written pieces of literature where the grandson of the dead author's estate just lost a million-something in Monte Carlo and he offers him a piece of the profits. At least that's what he did on this one he's making now. I don't know. Funny you haven't heard of him. To hear him talk, you'd think he had this enormous following in the States."

"Who told you that?" Claire smiled. "Him?"

Isolde glanced at her out of the corner of her eye. "Yes."

"Oh, don't go by me." Claire yawned outright. "The only films I get to see lately are PG-rated or two years old, late at night on cable."

"Well, I wouldn't brag about it."

"No," Claire said, "you're right." This trip wasn't going to be about how ordinary her life had become. They were nearing the town. Bright, furiously awake Bavarians marched to their bicycles and trams and U-Bahns and cars. At the traffic light on Prinzregentenplatz, the fragrant aromas of coffee and warm sweet rolls wafted enticingly through open windows trimmed with white lace and red geraniums. Well-scrubbed, red-cheeked workers stood good and still at the red light despite the fact that no traffic passed. You wouldn't find jaywalkers lurking in this town.

Claire took a sharp breath in. "I *do* remember. There was an article about him in the *Trib.* It was a while ago, though. No. It was in the gossip column, and it was about his new star. I remarked on it because I tried to book her once. She was very short but very good. I wasn't surprised that she'd made the transition from model to actress, she had something interesting about her—intense. Anyway, I never got her because she was all booked up with Günther Sachs in Gstaad. Jesus. That was years ago. Mara, that was her name. Mara Morgen. So she's still with him, this Temple Fortune?"

Isolde shrugged, pretending she didn't know or care. She was as impressed with films and film people as Claire was, but she wouldn't have them outshadowing her own performance. Enhance, yes. Outshadow, no. "That's what I mean about you." She frowned. "You always get involved."

"Involved? Oh, really, Isolde! All I said was—"

"Yes. Where you don't belong."

"What *are* you talking about? Now you sound just like my husband."

"Ugh! Let's not bring him into this."

"On that we agree." Claire sniffed but said no more. She wasn't going to share her fears and jealousies about her husband with Isolde. Wistfully, she smoothed her skirt. One of Isolde's long black hairs had settled there. Claire shuddered. She pulled it furtively to the window and let it out.

"Rupert is in Switzerland, by the way," Isolde said. Rupert was the younger of Isolde's two sons. The older boy, Dirk, was at the American school. At least he was nearby. "He's up at Klosters," Isold added. Claire wanted to ask if Rupert still stuttered but decided against it. It made her too unhappy to think of Isolde's boys so isolated and far from home.

"Oh, and listen," Isolde warned, "don't mention the wedding to Hans von Grünwald, the keeper of the Mill."

"Why not?"

"Or to anyone else who works there, for that matter."

"How come?"

"Just do as I ask you, all right? He'll charge me double if he thinks the party I've booked is for a wedding."

"For heaven's sake! He'll know soon enough."

"I'll just pretend it was a last-minute decision and will fit nicely into the family gathering I've planned."

This wouldn't do at all. Claire needed the wedding as an excuse while she poked around. "But I'm supposed to be your photographer! What am I supposed to be doing, hanging around an old mill on my own for a couple of weeks?"

"Pretend you're recovering from a nervous breakdown. You might as well be." Her critical, snappy eye swept over Claire's jet-lagged state. "And since when do you owe Reception a raison d'être, anyway?"

"Hang on a second." Claire laughed. "I smell a rat. There's something else you're not telling me."

"No. Oh, all right, yes. If you must know, Hans von Grünwald has been desperately in love with me for years. I didn't want to actually tell him about Blacky until—well, the thing is, Blacky and Hans despise each other. If Hans knew I was marrying him, he'd never let me have Saint Hildegard's Mill."

"I think you're exaggerating. Who isn't in love with you and hasn't been that way for years? As I know men and their all-important businesses, it would hardly stop any of them from making a profit on the competition."

Isolde answered with a scornful face as if to say, "A lot you would know about men being desperately in love with you."

"I think—" Claire started to say.

"Never mind what you think. Just don't mention it."

There. That was better. They were both more comfortable with Isolde at the top. So had their relationship begun and thrived, and so must it remain if it was to go on. Claire didn't mind. She'd grown up under her sister Carmela's thumb and felt comfy there. However would she come off so virtuous without a meanie bitch around to make her look good? She was no longer the thoroughly arbitrary girl

Blacky had always summed her up as, but she had developed a finer sense of self in recent years, sparring with her feisty husband and the same belligerent sister who'd originally held her down. So she would sit still like a good little girl, but only as long as it pleased her. People did change, she noted smugly. "People do change," she said.

"They do not."

"You're wrong. They do. I have."

"No, you haven't. The people around you have, that's all." She reached over suddenly and took Claire's hand. "Why don't you forget about everybody in New York, Claire? Why not just forget them while you're here?"

Claire digested this idea and watched the busy, crisp part of town become the easy green streets and alleys of Schwabing and the English Garden. It was going to be a glorious day. Students lolled in outdoor cafés, and uninhibited young people stripped off their clothes along the lazy banks of the Isar. "Well," she said finally, "perhaps both. The people around me have changed, and that's changed me."

"There's a sophomoric observation."

"And these are different times." Claire ignored her. "For example, I grew up not knowing I didn't have to defer to men. The world has changed."

"*Ach!* The world never changes."

"Yes, it does."

"No, it doesn't. It just goes round in circles."

"*We* certainly do."

This seemed to satisfy them both and they traveled pluggedly on, the snow-capped Alps in the distance, the buildings growing sparse and the pines above and around them growing dense. They drove onto a small lane, and the sudden quiet was broken by a bird's call, warning, welcoming. They turned the corner then. Isolde stopped the car. The old Mill stood on a faraway hill, patient and once apricot, brocaded with ivy and bougainvillea creepers. There was the Isar below, spangling in a sinuous curve across the meadow. You could just make out the edge of the Roman Bridge behind the vast lawn stretched before them, green and cockeyed as a full-moon sea. One great chestnut alone on a tilted slope just before them shaded a winsome chapel.

"Saint Hildegard's Mill," Isolde said.

The air was wild and heavy with the distinctive scent of black currant blossoms, and Claire thought of Iris, remembered for her. Here it was that she must have rested. She could almost see her lying in her bedraggled party dress, those many years ago. Here was where it had begun.

Confused, she looked again. That *was* a woman lying there beneath that tree. A beautiful woman from long ago. A shiver ran up her spine. She reached, instinctively, for her camera bag.

"All right," came an irritated voice from the thicket, "now you've had your thorough look-see, would you very much mind getting on?"

Startled, Claire and Isolde scanned the foliage for the source of the voice.

"Or," it went on, and they saw him then, in his film director's khaki, many-pocketed camouflage vest, "we could write you both into the scene. Shall we do that then, Puff?" he said to the smallish, red-nosed fellow at his elbow. "Shall we write them in?"

"Pretty enough," the other one said, "clothes are all wrong, though. Wrong season."

"Wrong decade, I should think." Isolde took it all in and came right back.

"World War Two," the one referred to as "Puff" clarified for them, "so we're all right." He stepped forward, extending a hand. "Puffin Hedges is my name. And this is Temple Fortune."

"We've met," Isolde said. She nodded curtly to the notorious Temple Fortune, and the two of them took off, chatting each other provocatively up and down, doing their obligatory predator's dance. They'd recognized each other as worthy adversaries, neither admitting to being overly impressed with the other but insisting each admire the traits that made the other famous.

"Tell you what," Puffin Hedges interrupted finally, with his busy headwaiter/homeroom-teacher authority. "You two run along, and we'll get back to work, and we'll all meet up later for tea." He waved to their slowly-becoming-annoyed film star still out there under the tree. She was being powdered by the makeup person on one side while a young man was reading her face with a light meter on the other. Gamely, she waved back.   .

Isolde roared off down the road with an appropriate cloud of dust. Boy, her squared-off shoulders seemed to shimmy and brag, did they get a load of me!

Claire didn't say a word. She let her cotton sweater tumble from her warm arms.

Temple Fortune had been a shock. Although he'd spent the entire episode flirting outrageously with Isolde, Claire hadn't missed the moment's hesitation when he'd laid eyes on and over her. He might have been speaking with Isolde, but Claire recognized the pained sucking in of breath as his eyes swept Claire's generous breasts and hips. She almost felt his eyelids lower with desire. A warm, rosy flush had crept recklessly up her married cheeks. Her body, she realized shamefully, was not as committed to family life as she was.

Not only that, but she had seen Temple Fortune before. It was so long ago, she'd been a different person; a little girl, really, just starting out on her own from her parents' house with a bright mess of pimply girlfriends to the Keith's Movie Theater, not to miss the arrival of the British Invasion rock group. They weren't *the* rock group, but they were popular enough to draw the prerequisite mob of screeching teenagers, and Claire had wriggled through the crowd to the front by the police barricade just as they were disembarking the huge airport bus.

They were adorable, all of them, but there had been one who'd looked directly into Claire's gaga blue eyes, held her glance, swept her brazenly with hooded, merry eyes, made a face as if to say, "If only . . .," winked philosophically and was bustled off with the rest of them to the stage inside.

Claire had stayed warm and pink for weeks. She'd bought every album and learned every song. When he'd sung lead, she'd lain reverently down on her bed and relived that magical moment they'd shared, only she'd take it farther—sometimes she'd pretend they held each other longingly, hopelessly, backstage. Sometimes he found out magically who she was (from a theater manager who doubled as a CIA agent, she supposed), and sent for her from England, where she would suddenly appear in a cashmere suit on a steamship gangplank, to be swept off to his parents' estate (on the moors?).

Claire laughed out loud.

"What?" Isolde said.

"No, nothing." Claire shook her head. So the famous Temple Fortune was not Temple Fortune after all. Or if he was, he was someone else as well. At least his name was not so fancy. Still, she would never forget it. He was, or had been at one time, the adorable, guitar-playing Douglas Dougherty.

You don't fantasize adolescent love to one man's collage of fan-magazine photos for more than two years and not recognize him—what? Twenty-something years later? Claire shuddered to think how many years had gone by. She flipped the sun visor down and peered into the makeup mirror. Yuck. She snapped it humbly back up, and the car swerved into the white pebble drive. They got out of the car and she had a good stretch. There was a bunch of freshly painted white chairs and round tables by the door. A sort of runty collie-mutt lifted its sleepy head, yawned and went back to sleep.

"Always reassuring to know you've got a good guard dog to keep you safe," Claire remarked to the decrepit old woman sitting at one of the tables wrapping knives and forks into paper napkins.

"Oh. He'll let you in, all right. Just don't try to leave. He won't let anyone leave."

"Thanks for the warning."

"Keep that crazy dog away from me!" Isolde froze behind Claire. "He almost bit my arm off last week!"

"Were you leaving?" Claire unclasped Isolde's hand.

"Yes."

"That was your first mistake. Never"—she winked at the old hag at the table—"try to leave." But the woman had forgotten any communication between them and gone back to her work.

Claire inhaled the fragrant air. The Mill was edged in billowy pink rhododendron and white lilac. The tulips were done and poppies beginning to bud. Rounded paths were riddled with chamomile and lily of the valley.

Whoever the gardener was, he or she was passionate. It was wonderful.

From the upstairs window trickled the sound of somebody playing the piano. The music stopped abruptly, and there was the muffled garble of argument. A door slammed. There was, Claire was delighted to see, a maypole glinting jauntily in the sunshine. A man with an intricately wood-carved cane came to the open front door. A sporty-looking, beefy, absolutely-in-charge fellow with not much of his fine blond hair left. He was no longer young, but not old either. Adam von Grünwald's son? Claire wondered. She watched him carefully. Was this the son of the man Iris had loved so much? He was so fair. He'd been wearing a white apron over his spanking blue-and-white-checkered shirt. He threw it off and strode over with a trace of a limp. He was huge. His cane, Claire noticed, sported a hand-carved bird's head at the top. He swirled it with a drum majorette's flourish. He had bright-blue, shrewd peasant's eyes that went almost stupidly besotted the minute he turned them on Isolde.

"Oh, Hans," she said offhandedly, "here is Claire Breslinsky. She'll be staying with you. From New York."

"Ah! *Direkt aus* New York? Manhattan?" He gave her hand a hearty shake.

"Actually, no. We come from Queens. We—"

But Hans had already turned his attention back to Isolde. Every backwoods Bavarian knows you only have to cross the Queensboro Bridge from dazzling Manhattan and you've entered the mud puddle of cultural oblivion. Hardly a German hasn't already been to New York on a charter, stayed at the Plaza, shopped at Bloomingdale's, eaten vinegar dumplings in Chinatown, marched up Madison, jogged through Central Park, and gone home, job done, one more must-see city under their belts, *meine Liebe.*

Hans swung Claire's suitcase over one strong shoulder and linked the other arm with Isolde. "Evangelika," he snapped at the old woman, *"Mach mal schnell!* Hurry up!" And he and Isolde disappeared into the cool darkness of the Mill.

Evangelika, nonplussed, snorted and spat onto the gravel before she followed him in. The yard was still. Only the film crew in the near distance tinkered with their long lenses. A quite big bird pecked away and breakfasted happily on a long line of freshly buried sunflower seeds.

Then a beautiful girl, about eighteen, slipped from the back of the inn to the side where only Claire could see her and, imagining herself unobserved, dropped her small head of heavy, Gretel-like braids into her hands and wept.

She was so young and so fair that Claire's first impulse was to call out to her, or run over and comfort her, the way you would run to a brokenhearted child. But the moment passed. Claire knew well enough that people didn't like to be caught suffering. She turned and took her camera bag and went inside.

It took a moment for her eyes to adjust to the darkness. Rough beams supported the low-ceilinged room in restless patterns. The floor was so old it tilted. Claire felt strangely dizzy. It was like finding yourself below on a pirate ship.

Hand-painted tiles and plates and steins lined a shelf stretching around the top of the room. Exquisitely simple pottery pieces graced the shelves just above eye level. There were clocks of all sizes, each from years ago, all ticking at a different speed and blending into a delicious busy hum. Each table had creamy-white linen and a cut-glass vase of forget-me-nots. Oils and watercolors in museum-quality frames filled every available space.

"Hello," Claire called, but there was no one there. She walked down the hallway to Reception. This was a great dark room with a huge polished desk. They really didn't cater to guests here, did they, Claire thought as she was standing there. She walked through to the kitchen. Two women sat beneath gleaming copper pots and plaited straw flowers. Behind them in the chimney, last night's fire had been swept and the tiles scrubbed. The old one, the one Claire had seen outside, Evangelika, slovenly but sitting erectly at the long pine table, continued, mantra-like, to wrap her cutlery and stack it into perfect piles. She scarcely looked up.

Herbs grew in every window, with the other green of the backyard looking in. Up the hill from there was the path to the Roman Bridge. It really was from Roman times and, Claire knew, had played a great part in many battles. Hildegardians were quite partial to their romantic, crumbling bridge.

The other woman was hand-writing menus and arranging them on spindle wires on a wicker dessert trolley. She was a bristling woman, the sort who never could stand Claire. Claire never knew why, but she always sensed it right away. The woman wore a tailored gray suit and a string of good pearls. She had that rosy, creamy complexion, marless and seamless, that almost requires pearls.

"Kann ich Ihnen helfen?" the woman asked, and then, summing Claire's nationality up with a quick, irreverent sweep of her shrewd, brown, smallish eyes, "May I help you?"

The way she said it, with tight-lipped disapproval, led Claire to feel she ought not to be in there at all, this was entirely off limits. Claire couldn't resist putting one antagonistic foot into the forbidden kitchen. "I'd like to check in," she said.

The prim and properly corseted one stood up to her full height, which was not a lot taller than when she was sitting down.

They confronted each other. The soft, flowing lines of Claire's wardrobe were admittedly "designed" by Evar, the kindly Indian man on Jamaica Avenue, but she always started out clean and well ironed. And if not ironed, then hung scrupulously and swiftly from dryer to hanger.

This woman's taste in clothing bordered on the compulsively dry-cleaned. She even wafted a sort of right-angle myrrh as she bustled past in her shantung suit, indicating with a rude flick of her hand that Claire should follow. She was a bit well endowed, but you'd better not notice, dared the haughty, ramrod posture, the raised fluffy eyebrows and the pursed pink lips. Her sensibly heeled shoes clicked past Claire. Claire's eyes met those of the scrawny, elderly woman in the slovenly house dress. Her eyes said nothing.

Neither, Claire decided, would hers. She turned and followed the woman to the front desk. The woman snapped open the leather-bound guest book. "Passport," she demanded and was not pleased when she realized Claire had put it in front of her.

When she was finished, she stood up and marched away. "You will follow me," she ordered.

"*Jawohl,*" Claire said, grinning, then frowned appropriately when the woman turned back to glower.

There was a certain sort of German, Claire knew, who didn't care much for *Ausländer,* or foreigners, even if they did earn their livelihood from them, so Claire didn't take the woman's disdain personally. This one, Claire realized, was younger than herself. It was always a bit of a rude awakening to identify bossy, authoritative figures as younger than oneself, but there you were; the world flies by and you find yourself who you used to want to be.

"Will you be taking your breakfast in your room?"

"May I have it out of doors?"

"I will notify the kitchen. Weather permitting, naturally." She scribbled doggedly. "Otherwise, you will find your breakfast in the East Room." Distracted, she pulled one earring off, then the other, and caressed each downy lobe. Her ears, uncovered—Claire tried not to be seen noticing—were trumpet-like and ugly and, ultimately, compelling. "My name is Fräulein Wintner. If you have any problems, you will come please with them to me." She regarded Claire with a lifted face, her unfortunate ears once again safely parked away. "And not disturb the family."

"Okay." Claire followed Fräulein Wintner's bobbing head of crisply bouffanted, honey-colored hair. They made their way up the polished wood stairway and down the wide, old-fashioned corridor to the last room.

"Who's that playing piano?" Claire asked.

"I'm sure I don't know," Fräulein Wintner lied. "Here

you are, *Fräulein.*" she handed Claire the lacy iron key. "We trust your stay with us will be enjoyable." She smiled without warmth.

"And I hope," Claire couldn't resist saying, "you'll enjoy having me."

The woman turned without a word and Claire stood there, alone at last. There were two windows, one in each corner, both open to the morning breeze and softly framed with white priscillas. A powder-blue wooden bed, with a high, clean white eiderdown and two Goldilocks pillows, was tucked in invitingly with a white chenille spread. On the floor was an Afghan carpet, and on the pine nightstand a white ceramic lamp, a bowl of fruit, a nosegay of wild-flowers, and a box of Swiss chocolates. There was a straight-backed pine chair and an ornately painted pastel wardrobe—alive with roosters and pomegranates—and footed with lion's paws, their toenails lacquered a heavy-duty salmon. On top of that were even more pillows and a straw basket of freshly dried baby's breath. Heaven—Claire smiled to herself—absolute heaven. She shut the door, kicked off her shoes, and lay down on the billowy softness of cool sheets.

Someone ran, clop, *clop-clop-clop,* down the length of the hall. *"Aber du hast mir versprochen!"* ("But you promised me!") Claire recognized Fräulein Wintner's plaintive voice call out before she fell, like pelting darkness, off to sleep.

The telephone jangled Claire back from a netherworld of melodic dreams. She fumbled around for the antiquated phone on the wall, the unsettling music of her dream becoming real and only down the hall. "Hello?" she said and cleared her throat.

"Good morning!" The brisk, metallic twang of Jupiter Dodd came through without the usual cross-Atlantic delay. "Oops. Is it nighttime there?"

"No. You just caught me napping. I think it's late afternoon. What's up?"

"Hold on to your hat, sparklin' eyes. Matt McGee was up here yesterday—"

He didn't have to tell her who Matt McGee was. Everyone who'd ever worked in the world of advertising knew that name. His agency had been on top for as long as Claire could remember, and he specialized in mega-accounts only.

"What was he doing up at *She She?*" she asked idly, getting up and peeking out the window. There was an old black Mercedes with running boards in the driveway behind the greenhouse.

"Well, I'd like to tell you he came up solely for Davey's new campaign pitch." He lowered his voice. "But I'd be more honest by saying I think it was the gorgeous new lawyer we've got—anyway, he was up here, so of course I utilized every moment, chucking slides at him from the fashion thing with Hideoki—he was looking for locations for the new Harris cigarette campaign he landed, and whose slide do you think he picked up on? That solitary old, dog-eared slide you sent me of Bavaria in springtime to convince me to let you shoot the accessories there. It just happened to be in the same manila. You remember? The crowd of healthy German kids on the green hill?"

Of course she remembered. She wouldn't have been able to afford her flight or accommodations without *She She* footing the bill.

"Well, Matt McGee went nuts; said this was exactly the sort of thing he was looking for—fresh without being tropical—he's fed up to here with tropical—make a long story short—he wants you to shoot the campaign. Claire. Back in the big time. Sky's the limit! Hire whoever and whatever you want. Jesus. Maybe I'll come over myself, once you get things rolling. Have they got a fax where you're staying?"

Jupiter rambled on. He was so caught up in his own ex-

44

citement, he didn't notice Claire's lack of enthusiasm.

She held the receiver tightly and closed her eyes. "Jupiter," she finally got a word in, "I hate to tell you this, but I don't do cigarette campaigns."

Silence at the other end. "What does that mean, you don't *do* them?"

"Just that. I can't—I *won't*—shoot cigarettes . . ."

Jupiter was still. She could hear the commotion of his chaotic office around him. Then a resounding, quacking laugh jarred the line and wheezed to an amused finish. "Ahhh, dumpling. You really had me going there for a minute, you know that? You're bad."

"I mean it, Joop. I won't use my"—she hesitated to use the word talent, then figured what the hell, that's what it was she was using—"my talent to further that addiction."

"You're joking."

"I'm not."

"I'll force you."

Claire groaned. "You can't. I made this decision years ago. I just won't do it."

"But you used to shoot tons of nicotine. I remember! What about the Maldive thing with the flying fish? That was some of your best work!"

"Yes," she admitted sadly, rubbing her eyes, "I remember. I'll bet you used to do a lot of things you wouldn't do anymore yourself."

"So what?"

"So what? Jupiter, you sound just like my son!"

"You ought to think about your son. That's just who you should be thinking about, and that steep private-school tuition you're always complaining about."

"You're right. I am thinking about him. How am I supposed to justify glamorizing cigarettes and then stand there one day and tell him not to smoke?"

"Claire. Grow up."

"I have grown up. That's just what I have done. Why do you think no one smokes in New York anymore? Because they've stopped advertising gorgeous people smoking on TV, that's why."

"Listen, Claire. People don't not smoke because of stopping advertising."

"Now you listen, Jupiter. If you or I didn't believe in the monumental force of advertising, neither of us would have gone into it."

"If you don't shoot the cigarette campaign, you can come right home. I won't pay you for any of it."

"You can't do that."

"I can and I will."

Claire's heart sank. "Thanks a lot, Jupiter."

"You'll shoot it, then?"

"Hell, no. I'll just have to come home sooner than I expected and start paying off the trip myself."

They both waited. Finally, Jupiter said, "Look. All I ask is this. Look around for a couple of locations and just think about it."

"But I told you—"

"Don't talk, just listen. I'll call you back tomorrow. You can give me your answer then."

"It will still be the same."

"Then you still have until tomorrow to enjoy yourself on my money. Good-bye."

He hung up, then so did she.

A very bad feeling overtook her. She knew it well. It was that old schemer, Temptation. It sure would be nice to have a lot of money to play with.

She went back over to the window and looked down at the old-timer Mercedes. Man, oh man. They didn't make them like that anymore. She wondered whose it was. Above her head a floorboard creaked. Claire shivered. The afternoon had grown cooler, and she went to look for her soft

46

gray sweater. She found her brush with it and went back to the window, tugging it through her auburn hair.

That lovely young girl who'd been crying was down there, quite recovered, it seemed. She held on to a kitten, stroking its fur, while she chatted to a fellow her own age, about twenty, in the doorway of the greenhouse. He was dressed roughly, and his big hands dropped from his pitchfork when the girl turned and walked off, the pebbles crunching under her narrow feet. He kept watching and she kept walking, swaying, knowing he still watched. This poor fellow doesn't have a chance, Claire thought wryly, pleased not to be that treacherously vulnerable age anymore.

She must call Iris. She picked up the phone and was told by the ever-surly Fräulein Wintner that all transatlantic calls must be made from the desk. She should give her name and number, hang up the phone, and Fräulein Wintner would ring her back when she got through. Claire sat on the bed, trying not to suspect she'd have been better off staying at the modern Americanized Sheraton after all, when the call came through. "Hello?" She cupped one ear and called. "Iris?" This connection was not as clear as the first had been.

"Hallo?"

"Iris?"

"Mfphph.—ullo?"

"It's me, dear. Claire. I'm here. I'm at Saint Hildegard's Mill."

"Oh. Clai-aire!"

"Can you believe it? I'm actually here. Iris, it's beautiful! The flowers—"

"The flowers are blooming now here, too," Iris shouted defensively.

"Yes. Yes, well, I just wanted to let you know. I have a lovely room."

"Don't forget to look in the clock."

"No, I won't. I'll look everywhere. I won't forget."

"And don't trust a soul. Now, beware of those who take the joy from what you love. Don't forget, it all looks nicy-nice on the outside, but something festers there."

"All right, I won't forget."

Iris's voice cleared. It changed. "Claire?" She sounded young again and full of yearning. "What do you see?"

Claire went to the window. "It's . . . everything green. An old man far off walks the hill. There's a stream."

"And the tree?"

"Yes, the tree is still here. I see the tree." She listened kindly to Iris's reminiscent silence.

"You won't not call again. Claire?"

"No. I won't. I promise I'll call you soon. If Johnny comes over, uh, just tell him I love him."

"All right." Iris wasn't going to be the one to tell Claire that that tart Portia McTavish had shown up on Johnny's doorstep as soon as she was gone.

"I've got to go. There's a wonderful smell of *Schwein-shaxen* in the air and I'm starving."

"Go now. And have a beer for me."

She laughed. "All right," and they hung up. The extension somewhere else was hung up as well. A golden Bavarian beer. Her mouth watered and she turned to go when she saw Blacky, Isolde's intended, her dear old lover and enemy Blacky, strolling from the chapel on the hill and heading toward the Mill.

He certainly was a fine catch, she conceded, his notorious black hair having electrified to a leonine halo of pure white. He wasn't that big, but he always seemed to be, with those great shoulders and his barreling neck. Women adored him. They always had, she remembered ruefully, watching him pick his way over the messy remains of the gardener's compost. He had a way of rubbing his meticulously clean hands together at the start or finish of anything. They were rammed, at the moment, in the pockets of impeccable linen trousers. He looked bad-tempered. Why ever had she left him? she wondered, admiring his upsetting yellow eyes, and suddenly she did remember, she remembered exactly why she had left him.

It was in the early days when they'd both just returned from India, and he was busy setting up his practice. She'd gone with some models to see the African ballet that was in town for a week or so and afterward had gone backstage with the rest of them. Well, they'd had a grand time and gone off to the clubs to show those Africans just what a jolly town Munich was. It got very late, and Claire decided to get back home. Blacky would be returning from the hospital shortly, and she wanted to be there when he got in.

It turned out he already was home when she got there. She still remembered everything, strangely enough, right down to what he and she were wearing. She could see it all in front of her, as clear as a film. Anyway, there he was, and there she was, and she kissed him and started to tell him about what a marvelous time she'd had, and he said, "How did you get home?" and she said, not even thinking, "I hailed a cab on Maximilianstrasse, only one of the dancers wanted to go back to his hotel and asked if he could share mine, so of course I said 'Sure,' and I dropped him off first; that's why you got in first, I guess." She hadn't noticed Blacky's stony silence until she turned around and looked at him. "You don't mean to say"—he'd blinked uncomprehendingly—"that you got into a taxi with an African ballet dancer on Maximilianstrasse?"

She held her blouse crumpled in her hand. "Yes. Why?"

"Where any of my patients might have seen you?"

"Oh, Christ, Blacky. Just listen to you!"

"At this hour of the night?"

She couldn't believe he was so upset. He refused to forgive her. He wouldn't even speak to her at breakfast the

49

next morning. She told him he was being childish and racist and she was a grown person and would do as she wished.

Well, by the time he'd come home that night, he'd pretty much cooled down (realizing, she supposed, that his practice would survive and no one of major importance had seen her getting into the cab), but she, who'd had a thoughtful, self-righteous and pretty pious afternoon behind her, was just getting started. Now it was he who couldn't believe how upset she was. They fought all the time. In the end, surprising both of them, she'd left him.

Claire looked down at the handsome, older fellow there on the drive in his own country. It hadn't really been the African who'd separated them, she knew. He'd only been the excuse. Blacky, feeling himself watched, looked up and into her eyes. He is kind and good, she thought, smiling. That's what he is first. Funny she should think it last.

Old Father Metz sat in the Mill kitchen sipping his weekly allotment of coffee from Evangelika. He felt more comfortable down here, away from the intensity of the family and their exorbitant, bourgeois furniture. And that piano. You always had to sit through some exquisite piece painstakingly eked out by that maniac, Cosimo. And they watched you, watched your reactions. If you weren't tapping your foot and outwardly enjoying yourself, one of them would prod you and inquire if you were.

He didn't mind coming—Hans von Grünwald was Saint Hildegard's most generous contributor and must be coddled, for who else was there?—but Father was always relieved when the strenuous hour was over and he could relax in the peace and quiet of Evangelika's open animosity and delicious pound cake. The gaunt, empty spaces of the old kitchen never failed to remind him of his own happier origins, his strict-but-loving grandmother's farm out in War-teweil.

Herr von Grünwald would, each week, deposit him here in the kitchen while he went to attend to the business of writing him out a check. Each was more comfortable away from the other, and so the procedure took a while. Father Metz's back was turned to the cat. He was allergic. The cat knew this and preened herself sadistically nearby.

Fräulein Wintner bustled in. She banged the milk pitcher recriminatingly in place on the hardwood table.

Evangelika barred her way, leaning over and pouring poor Father Metz another cup of her ferocious coffee.

There was no sign of Herr von Grünwald. Ah, well. Father sighed. Anyway, he was not looking forward to trying to start up the car. It was having one of its less enlightened days. If he waited long enough, Friedel the gardener would be done with his pruning and could give him a good push. So. He would go quickly to the bathroom, have one more slice of cake and linger a while until Friedel was done. He'd told his old housekeeper he'd be back in time for the Angelus. He couldn't wait all day for Herr von Grünwald, after all. If the keeper of the Mill would come to church on Sunday like everyone else, as his own children Cosimo and Stella Gabriella did, he wouldn't have to drive himself out here each week like an errand boy.

Father Metz had just mopped his lovely hands dry with a soft white Turkish towel when Fräulein Wintner stood before him in the vestibule.

"Father"—her voice trembled, yet she looked him sure enough in the eye—"will you hear my confession?"

"*Ach, Fräulein*"—he brushed his wisps of silver hair from his haggard face—"if you can't make regular confessional hours on Saturday, that's four to seven, I will be happy to see you anytime up at the Rectory. As long as you call ahead."

She opened the door to her own quarters and remained persistently there, silhouetted by the overheated pinks and beiges of her privacy. There were rugs over furry rugs and canopies on her bed and lamps. Fräulein Wintner might have sprung from the same sparse and plain beginnings as he, but her life would be as comfy and pearly as a successful housekeeper's could be. She trotted in front of him and tumbled a bunch of downy rose pillows to the floor where, he was amused to suppose, she imagined she would kneel at his feet.

Evangelika clattered reproachful pots and pans down the hallway in the kitchen.

"You know"—he lingered at the still-open door and smiled warmly—"I can't help feeling we would both be more comfortable in the conventional confessional."

"I know." She sat on the very edge of the soft hassock. The starched sides of her prim skirt stayed out, and the flesh-colored fastenings of her garter belt were almost to be seen. She lowered the top of her body enticingly forward. "But wouldn't you want to know just how wicked I have been?"

Old Father Metz's housekeeper looked up, jarred from arranging his tray. Was that the Angelus? Already? It couldn't be. He ought to be back by now. She rose decrepitly and looked the long way down to the Mill. It was the Mill bell ringing, not theirs. What was that—she tried her other glasses—dangling from the rope?

Claire hesitated. She loved the sound of bells. There was just time enough to sit outdoors and feel the last push of the sun on her skin. A clock was on the sideboard outside her room. Claire touched it with tentative fingers, then picked it up and turned it upside down. It was a neat, small clock. She tried her Swiss Army knife on one of the screws, but the blade wasn't nearly fine enough. There would be no room for a lot of diamonds in there at any rate. Iris said there had been sixty stones. Claire heard something and furtively put the clock down. She pattered down the waxed wood floor, past the shut doors, locked her moon-pale hand onto her pocket lint and jangled the new loose, exotic change. She whooshed down the stairs excitedly, savoring this clean, toilet-watered, just-ready-to-go-out rush when a swinging pendulum of dark shadow went back and forth past the window at the landing of the stairs. It looked—it was a man, upside down, his feet caught up in the bell ropes. He was swinging.

She stopped and gripped the wall. He *was* swinging. He looked— She waited, rapt, for the next time he would pass. She heard his skull crack against the tower wall.

His upside-down eyes, horrified, swept by.

His spotless blue-and-white-checkered shirt went back and forth with him inside it, holding him, entirely like baggage, dead.

Through the hallway raged a woman's screams. Claire never knew they were her own until she heard them stop.

3

The first one to reach Claire was Blacky. He swung around the corner, nimble as a fireman, and took her in his arms until he saw what it was.

"*Herrgott!*" he cried and let her crumple to the floor. Up the lighthouse-like stairs he lurched, pausing at the halfway window to see if he could jimmy open the shutters. They were crusted shut from years of paint. He gave up that idea quickly and raced the rest of the way to the top. He tried to tug Hans's body up from there, but he had no luck.

Puffin Hedges, lighting Mara Morgen's cigarette in the garden down below, saw what was going on, dropped his lighter and ran up to help. Between the two of them, they made a little headway, but then young Cosimo appeared behind them. When he saw who it was upside down at the end of the rope, he went mad. He shrieked. The men tried to calm him down and get him to help them haul Hans in, but it only seemed to drive home harder what had happened to his father.

Cosimo, his mouth in a horrible "O," held himself captive with his long beautiful hands and batted his head against the wall. Blacky, fearing the already unstable young man would throw himself out the belfry arch after his father (there was only the knee-high ironwork guardrail), let the dead man go, told Puffin to take the other end of

Cosimo and help get him down the stairs. But they couldn't get hold of him. Cosimo was furious with strength. His head was turning bloody from the wallops. In the end it was Evangelika who got him going, walking him down the stairs, whispering that his father wouldn't *want* him to hurt himself, he had to be there for Stella. He had to help Stella get through this. Someone would have to tell Stella.

The next thing you knew, everybody ran up. The gardener, the film crew, everyone. Claire wriggled Cosimo through the little mob until she got him to the landing. Stella Gabriella stood quietly in front of her lighted room. Her eyes were lit from within and removed, her lips were dry and parted, her heavy braids open, and her hair tumbled down her back. She had just removed her crystal necklace and she held it in her hands. She looked as though she was waiting for them, as though she knew what they would say.

"There's been an accident," Claire rushed to tell her. "It's your father. I'm afraid he's dead."

Cosimo yowled and fell into Stella Gabriella's arms. Stella flinched, but the expression in those eyes didn't do what Claire expected it to do. It was as though her reaction itself was a hesitation, as though the real reaction went obediently off into a silent drawer, to be taken out later and fingered, like a scarf.

The rest of them were edging their way down the stairs with the body.

"Let's get him inside," Claire suggested.

They walked Cosimo in. *"Leg dich hin,"* Stella told her brother sternly, and he did as he was told; he lay down on the bed, his face rigid in grimace, the now silent tears running down both sides of his face and into his pretty ears.

Isolde filled the doorway. "What's happened?" she demanded.

"It's Hans." Claire rushed to her. She put her arm

around Isolde's waist and led her from the room, a finger to her lips. "He's fallen. From the belfry. He was tangled in the ropes. Oh, Isolde, he's dead."

"Dead? He can't be dead. I was just with him. We—" She stopped herself and looked at Claire. "He can't be dead."

"I'm sorry, Isolde. I'm afraid he is."

Isolde pushed her away and ran down the stairs to follow the crush already moving to the ground floor. Cosimo bolted up. He and Stella trampled past Claire and ran down as well. Claire stood there in the doorway of Stella's surprising room. It looked sparse, Japanese. Claire felt shocked, frightened. Everything was out of control. Somehow, with Cosimo in the bed, she had had the silly notion that all was well. The child was in bed, everything would be all right. She turned, sensing herself watched, but there was no one. She ran down the hallway to the top of the back stairs, just above the kitchen, where they'd taken Hans. She didn't know whether to go down or stay put, wanting to help but not wanting to intrude. And then she was drawn to the activity. She tiptoed down the stairs, touching the steady safety of the walls, old and painted blue. There were so many people, it wouldn't matter if she went in or not. She slid in.

Hans was laid out on the table, Father Metz was administering the Last Rites. All you could hear were the loud clocks ticking and Father's Latin murmurings.

Everyone was silent in the presence of death. All the doorways and windows were filled with the curious silhouettes of the guests, standing still, their hands holding on to their cheeks or their mouths.

"Ah! Everyone here! Jolly good!" Temple Fortune clumped in, the refreshed and landed gentry complete with elbow patches and the squire's billycock. He swatted his hands together and rubbed them back and forth and stomped his feet. "The light's lovely just now. Let's push on for the next scene, shall we?" He stood still. "Hello, what's up? You all look—" And he stopped at the sure sight of the corpse on the long kitchen table. "Begorra!" he cried in his otherwise tucked-away mother's own tongue.

When the police and ambulance had come and gone, both guests and help sat together, stunned and chatty in the beer garden. Blacky had tranquilized Cosimo, and put him back to bed. Stella Gabriella was upstairs with him still. All the rest of them stayed outside in the last rays of leafy warmth. Old Evangelika, shocked herself, was kept busy transporting drinks, for everyone wanted a stiff one. No one knew what to do. Puffin Hedges, reverent with death, suggested they all pack up and leave, head for another hotel. "But we're just in the middle of shooting the last scenes," Temple Fortune protested.

"It would be the only decent thing to do," Puffin Hedges insisted. "Think of the family."

"Well, I won't hear of it," Temple Fortune said. "It's not as though we're family friends. We're paying guests."

"Sizable-fortune paying guests," Puffin added. "Still, I guess it wouldn't do them much good to take away their income." He sat in a splendid bit of yellow light, alternately opening his portable backgammon kit and then closing it up. The Shetland collie-mutt stood underneath the spot where Hans had died, and the poor fellow wouldn't be budged. There he stood in full view of them all, legs planted apart, baffled but steadfast. He wouldn't come when Evangelika called him in, not even for his meal. No one hollered at him, the poor old fellow. His master was gone for good now, and no one knew what to do for him but let him be.

Evangelika was so rattled she wasn't keeping note who drank what. The serving girl, Gaby, a tense little Bavarian butterball in earphones and a dirndl, nervous and easily rattled on a good day, had been so discombobulated by what had happened that she'd flumped onto her bicycle and taken off, pedaling home to her *Mutti* and the safety of the village. "More like to get a good start spreading the news," Evangelika snorted, disgusted.

Claire felt sorry for the old woman. Here she was, long past retirement age herself, and there she went, doing for everyone else. Well, that's it, Claire decided, all this looking after others kept you from dwelling on your own problems, kept you strong. On the other hand, she noticed the old woman falter on her way back to the house. Claire got up and went over to her. "Can't I help you?" she asked.

"Na, na." Evangelika wagged her head vehemently. *"Ich mach schon alles,"* she insisted. She could handle it herself.

"Yes, I've noticed how you single-handedly run this place," Claire admired. She remembered that the old woman spoke English, even though she pretended not to when it suited her. Claire didn't want to insult her, but neither did she like the idea of a collapsed Evangelika as well as a dead proprietor. Those steins were heavy. She noticed Puffin Hedges behind her, helping himself to the goose-liver pâté.

"Mr. Hedges"—she tapped him on his costly heather-and-moss tweed—"would you mind helping me carry out these steins? Then I can get the trays of cheese and *Wurst* she's laid out. I don't think the poor thing can manage." Puffin Hedges looked at Claire as though she'd addressed him in Cantonese. Such an idea was preposterous, the pale-turquoise eyes above that red nose indicated. "Be a dear"— he smiled—"and handle all that yourself. We'll see to it you're taken care of when we tally up. There's a good girl."

For a moment she thought he was about to include a hurry-along pat across her bottom. She would have sputtered a defiant reply, but she was so taken aback that she went numb. She'd get him back for that one, she resolved, but in her own way and time, and properly.

When Blacky saw what she was up to, balancing and lugging heavy stuff, he jumped up to give her a hand. Temple Fortune noticed the aristocratic doctor there, gravely rolling up his white sleeves to pitch in, and he joined them at once. The three of them worked swiftly and companionably until the hefty loads of food and drink were nicely arranged on a group of tables pushed neatly together by the two men.

Claire couldn't help enjoying herself. She liked getting things done in a flurry, herself at the helm. For once Isolde was shocked into submission. She sat smoking her Merit cigarettes and looking wiped out. Her starched outfit defied her withered attitude and stood out from her like a costume on a hanger. Her magnificent hair only drizzled down over her shoulders. Claire wondered, for a moment, how much Isolde had cared for Hans von Grünwald after all.

Well, Claire wasn't going to pretend to herself she felt any sorrow. She'd only just met the man and hadn't much liked him. That wasn't true, she'd liked him well enough, she supposed, she'd just been put out when she noticed he hadn't been much taken with her. At least she would help give the poor fellow a fine send-off, something any Irishwoman knows just how to do. Funny the way a death will make you appreciate life, she mused, gathering up the small bouquet of lily of the valley Evangelika must have been working on when all of this happened. She was just about to carry the pretty thing out with the condiments when something decent, a sense of reserve, stopped her. She put the flowers down on the empty table and left them there, then said a hushed Hail Mary for the poor and maybe now still-hovering and (who knew?) listening spirit.

"What I don't understand"—the film star Mara Morgen

was batting her cigarette about for emphasis before continuing in her charming, heavy accent outside—"is *why* would Hans get himself tangled up in a bell rope up there anyhow? I mean, what was he doing up there? Why was he there?"

Friedel the gardener gave an annoyed wave of his hand to ward off her intrusive smoke from mingling with his own. "Haven't we all just been asked the same questions by the police? I mean, isn't it enough?" He'd been coming up the drive when all of this had happened and didn't see why he should have to answer anything.

Fräulein Wintner held her arms and squeezed herself in disbelief. "This cannot be happening." She shook her head. Blacky went over to her and looked, concerned, into her eyes. You never knew who would flip out next. The least likely people would suddenly do such outrageous things.

"It is his property, you know," Friedel reminded them in stilted English. "He did have a right to be wherever he chose, didn't he?" He put his mud-creased fist gently, but firmly, on the table.

"What's he doing here?" Puffin indicated Friedel's presence at their table.

"Hans might well have gone up to check those shutters for a scraping," Blacky suggested. "They're crusted shut; I noticed it when I tried to get them open. He might well have been inspecting what needed repair. And then got tripped up in the coiled ropes and fell. I'm sure it was something as simple as that."

With his priest and his mistress waiting for him foolishly down below, Father Metz mused sardonically to himself. He finished up the lovely golden liquid of his beer and shook his head. Life was fleeting. It was good for all these fancy hedonists to realize that. Guiltily, he looked toward the door. Stella Gabriella, Hans's daughter, poor soul, ought to be relieved from the torments of her brother. God knows what he was torturing her with now. Blaming her, perhaps. He ought to go up and see. The truth was, he was frightened of Cosimo. He stood carefully, never liking to parade his corpulence in a crowd of artists and swells and despising himself for caring. He minced his way across the garden, shook his wrinkled sleeves down over his wrists, and went into the house.

Isolde glared at Blacky. She hated the way he would run over and assist any little poppet who needed help or felt the slightest bit ill. It really was an unappealing side to him. "Check his property!" she sneered at Claire. "Hadn't we, Hans and I, just been having a cozy little chat upstairs when Hans suddenly thought of something, asked me to wait a moment and he'd be right back, that was just what he'd said. '*Warte doch ein kleines Momentli, gell?*' he said, asking me to wait a little moment and kissed my hand and turned and went. He never came back. I'd supposed he'd spotted Blacky or Friedel on the drive and hesitated to return to me. He was, if anything, discreet. And now this. It's unbelievable." She shook her head vehemently. "Unbelievable."

"You did mention all this to the inspector, didn't you?" Claire whispered.

"What do you think I am, stupid? They'll think I pushed him!"

"Oh, but Isolde, you must," Claire whispered urgently back. "What if they find out later and hear you didn't tell them. It will look awkward for you."

"And what will it look like now?" Isolde smiled grotesquely at Mara Morgen while she hissed to Claire. "Upstairs! Me alone with the victim a week before I'm supposed to marry his enemy?"

"Enemy? Surely you mean rival. And what is this, 'victim'? Good Lord, Isolde, it was an accident! And why *wouldn't* you be upstairs, looking over the rooms he was to provide for your guests."

"Really? That isn't what Blacky will think."

Claire looked around the table. She contemplated the two dazzlers, the famous fair Mara and the notorious dark Isolde. Isolde was the one who held you, Claire noticed, foolishly, loyally pleased. But it was true. Isolde was the one with good health and dash. Big white teeth, big everything. A juicy woman. Mara had the bone structure all right, but her skin in person was drab and sallow, mottled. She had the unfortunate habit of hunching over and fumbling through her vast handbag for something to grab hold of. Something glazed about her slanty, exotic gray eyes. You had the feeling she slept while she was awake. She had the merchandise, all right. It just looked, under scrutiny, used. Poor thing, Claire thought, not knowing why, and shivered. Claire looked over at Blacky. How strange that their first meeting after all these years should be accompanied by tragedy. The memories of their happy times had filled her thoughts all month. And they had been happy then. Young and free and happy. They just hadn't known it. They'd just been self-absorbed enough to imagine themselves miserable. Flying off to Venice for the weekend to recover from their overly theoretical, empty arguments of existentialism. What they'd needed, she realized now, were some yowling kids to fill up their vacuous days and nights. They'd had too much too soon, she and Blacky, and not enough suffering between them beforehand to absorb it and compare it with. She looked over at Blacky and found him looking good-naturedly back. Unfortunately, Isolde's eyes, suspicious and watchful, were pointed toward her too, so the smile she made back was merely congenial and toothless.

"All right over there?" he called out across the huge

table. Claire smiled again, this time warmly. If there was nothing wrong with her feelings, she had every right to expose them. She got up and went into the Mill. What she needed was a cup of coffee.

In the kitchen, Evangelika was weeping. Claire rushed over, then stood helplessly by. The old woman sobbed into a linen dish towel. When she was finished, she blew her nose into it and threw it on the floor. *"Nehm die Scheisskartoffeln,"* she barked at Claire and pointed, which means "Take the shit potatoes," but which really meant "Thank you for being here, even if you are a useless American."

Claire went wordlessly back outside with the enormous bowl of vinegar-and-parsley potatoes on a tray and put it down.

"You know," Blacky was saying, "there *is* supposed to be a treasure at Saint Hildegard's Mill. So the story goes." Claire froze. She tried to look interested and uninterested at the same time.

"Really?" Mara peered at him. "How fascinating."

"Hans could have been off looking for treasure," Puffin proposed. "That would explain why he was up in the belfry."

"What sort of treasure?" Mara pressed.

"A treasure with a curse, no less," Puffin said.

"What fun!" Isolde said. "I knew there was a ghost. I never knew about the curse!"

"A ghost, too?" Claire smiled.

"What rubbish!" Fräulein Wintner said. "Wartime gibberish. Made up to keep the marauding peasants away from the pottery."

Isolde looked up at Claire. "You know there really is some valuable pottery here. Not that you'd know it from the look of it. Old dusty stuff. Right up your alley."

"Thanks a lot," Claire said. A man walked up the curved path toward them, meandering into the lengthening shadows. He came up past the beautiful black car with running boards. It took a few moments for Claire to realize it was Temple Fortune, crunching the drive pebbles with long strides, his slender hands loose and swinging, the burgundy cashmere scarf he seemed to wear always still tucked casually in his breast. Did he consider himself delicate? She liked his hair, she thought, brown and soft. A little long, it was true. A little too attractive to every half-baked romantic female. She couldn't imagine anyone looking at him and not thinking he was, well, gorgeous. That was the idea, she supposed, annoyed. Until now, she could only watch him from afar. If he got too close, she was careful not to let her giveaway eyes meet his. Nor he (or did she imagine it?) hers.

He came along, and for a moment she forgot who she was; forgot, for that matter, who he was. She half-expected him to walk directly toward her, to her chair. It was almost with a jolt that she watched him stop and lean over Mara Morgen.

Mara Morgen, the film star, seemed nervous and, Claire thought, hardened since the days when she was Munich's most-sought-after face. Well, all those cigarettes wouldn't have helped. And the high life in Europe was a hard life. Especially, she imagined, with a man as attractive as Temple Fortune to keep up with. Claire felt her own face liquefy and disassemble when he got close. He made her lose her structure. She could feel her features melting and wobbling out of position just when she would have liked them to stay put. They refused to reorganize. A dreadful state for a grown woman to be in. Claire panicked. A dangerous state.

"What's this?" Isolde saw finally what had been set down in front of her.

"It's just some food. I thought you might need something."

Isolde pushed it away with disdain. "I couldn't eat a thing."

Ashamed of her appetite, but famished enough to overlook it, Claire seized the mouthwatering *O-Bazda* and dug in. This was a disgusting-looking, but curiously exquisite-tasting, mixture of battered Camembert, chives, paprika, garlic, and butter on sturdy rye bread. She then helped herself to a healthy draft of Isolde's stein. God, that was good. She felt better right away.

Puffin Hedges was performing an epic of film-business amusement with Temple as the hero, to distract them all. Fräulein Wintner burst into a fit of hysterical laughter.

It occurred to Claire that all of what was being said was directed at, and for, Blacky. He was, she realized now as she never had done in her own self-important, independent youth, profoundly wealthy. Suddenly he, Blacky, demanded in a loud voice, "What sort of a name is Temple Fortune?" He didn't quite slur his words, but everyone knew he'd had enough.

Temple Fortune smiled calmly back. Obviously this was not the first time this question had been put to him.

Puffin, as was his effete English schoolboy way, answered for him. "Temple Fortune was the address we were staying at in London when we had our first break with film, isn't it, love?" Temple answered with a wink, enjoying this. His eyes, green as money, smiled calmly back. He liked to recall those happy first days of success and hard work. "It started as a joke, you know. Sort of a giggle. But it caught on, didn't it? Yes, yes, those were the days."

"I see." Blacky wobbled his head at them belligerently. "You named yourself after your neighborhood." He turned to Claire. "That would be like you calling yourself Richmond Hill, wouldn't it?"

"Yes." She laughed uncomfortably. What was up? Apparently she was too impressed with this film business for Blacky's liking. He might be in love with Isolde, but he liked it best when all the gals were in love with him. "But that's no more silly than naming someone Mr. Rosary Beads. That's what the Germans did, after all, making the Jews take names of common objects. *Rosenkranz* means 'rosary beads.' Hello, Mr. Rosary Beads."

"That's not the same thing at all."

"No, but it's certainly as silly," Claire said sweetly. She liked to remind him every chance she got that he shared the lion's blood. It never shut him up, but she enjoyed indulging so sanctimonious a compulsion.

"No worse than Puffin Hedges, eh?" Puffin jabbed Fräulein Wintner with his elbow. "Not even we remember how that got started. We were pretty spaced out in those days, eh, Temple?"

"Well, you look like a Puffin," Blacky said.

"So what's your name, then?" Claire said to Blacky. "Clearly Redundant?"

"But my real name is Almut," Puffin confided morosely. "Harry Almut Brown. Beat that if you can. I mean, we just *had* to do something about that."

"Maybe I *should* have changed my name to Richmond Hill," Claire, compulsively arbitrary, said, mulling it over. "I can imagine me quite famous with a name like that."

Temple smiled at her and she smiled back. A dizzying rush swept through her.

Mara Morgen narrowed her eyes at Temple Fortune. "You didn't tell me when you talked me into coming here that we would have a murder, too." She said it lightly but accusingly.

"Mara!" Temple Fortune said.

"Yes, Mara!" Puffin Hedges' eyes darted back and forth from one to the other, then across to Blacky. "What a hideous thing to say!"

"The poor dolt slipped," Temple said. "Even the German *Polizei* said so."

Aside, Puffin said, "And there's nothing as suspicious as the German *Polizei.*"

Mara shrugged. "It could have been murder. Murders have been known to be made to look like happenstance."

Temple stood with his hands on his hips. "Well, we'll know in a few days. They'll have an autopsy, I imagine. Someone's bound to come up with the theory he was after those sixty blue-white diamonds."

Claire tried not to choke.

"That doesn't have to prove anything," Mara pressed. "He could have been pushed. *Tzack!*" She thrust the air before her forward, gaining everyone's attention. "Although that guardrail is so low it would be easy to fall even if you weren't pushed."

Isolde mopped her perspiring face with someone else's napkin. "You ought to be whipped," she said, narrowing her eyes at Mara.

"I'd like to see that." Puffin's eyes sparkled.

"Hans was no poor dolt," Mara continued in her unruffled, accurate, if thick-accented, English. "He was a very capable megalomaniac."

"What we used to call," Puffin murmured, "a bully."

Temple had positioned himself behind Mara. There he stood, wobbling her chair with his foot, a pained look on his face. "A little consideration for the dead, if you don't mind."

"Oh, right," Puffin said. "Wouldn't want to be chucked off the premises. Especially now we're so close—"

A knife-sharp look from Temple stopped him from completing that thought. Claire wondered what he'd been about to say.

"I wish that dog would come away," Temple said despairingly.

"It's very upsetting," Mara agreed.

They all looked over at the dog standing there in the drive.

"Come, old boy. Come, fellow." Temple slapped his thigh, expecting to be obeyed, but the dog stayed still, his tongue out and panting, his eyes heartrendingly glued to the spot from which Hans had fallen. There was a collective sigh from everyone.

"What will happen now?" Puffin Hedges wondered aloud.

Hearing no one answer, Fräulein Wintner ventured, "There will be a service at the Nord Friedhof, the North Cemetery. Then he will be cremated and buried."

"What? Both?" Claire asked.

"My God, he's barely cold!" Temple clucked.

"Well, that's the way we did it with his wife, Imogene, when she died," Fräulein Wintner cried defensively. "Didn't you just ask what happens now?" Fräulein Wintner seemed to be coming apart at the seams.

"Of course we did, dear." Puffin patted her hand. "You just pay him a never you *do* mind."

"Tell you what," Blacky suggested heartily. "We all could do with another round. My treat."

No one moved or said anything. Everyone was still very much in shock, Claire supposed, for all their snappy retorts. No one refused a drink, either.

"What an unbelievably terrible thing to happen on such a beautiful day," Blacky muttered. "A catastrophe."

"Yes," they all agreed, looking out over the soft green hill Hans would never see again. Friedel the gardener stared madly into his beer. He gripped the table edge. He looked, Claire feared, much like her son did a minute before becoming sick. There was something endearing about the fellow, in his rumpled overalls and muddy clogs.

"Such flowers you have here," Claire addressed him.

"So beautifully thought out! Is it Stella Gabriella who takes an interest in the garden?"

"Oh, no indeed," Fräulein Wintner interrupted before Friedel could answer. "Fräulein Stella is much too absorbed in her pottery. That's all she cares about. She has a kiln in the house out back, you know."

"Doesn't she do that Japanese-style pottery?" Puffin asked. "What's it called? Raiku? Raku?"

"I know she prepares her own mud," Fräulein Wintner informed them with a mixture of resentment and pride. "That's not typical, you know. She is"—her face took on the concentrated effort of quotation—" 'of the pure form.' There's a lot of them out in Diessen, a town out on Ammersee, the lake. Famous for potters. Like a cult, they are. Ever after the quest for the perfect pot. Fräulein Stella is their most important potter."

"It's Cosimo who does the garden," Friedel finally managed.

"A right lunatic he is about the roses, too," Puffin added. "Almost bit my head off when I tried to put Mara in the middle of them. Remember, dear?"

"It wasn't as though we'd have harmed them," Mara complained.

"That's right," the lighting man added. "We was ever so careful."

"A lunatic," Puffin kept on. "Flowers and the bloody piano, nothing else."

"Oh, well." Temple Fortune shrugged. "He's very good at both, isn't he? Marvelous, really . . ."

It is true, Isolde agreed silently. He was superb. She wondered if he would be recovered enough emotionally to play for the wedding.

Claire gazed at Temple Fortune. She liked a man who saw no need to justify a life of passion. He smiled boyishly back, ducking his head shyly and meeting her, only for a moment, with his eyes. They both looked guiltily away.

"What's this?" Puffin Hedges pursed his lips. He didn't miss much. "So Claire—it is Claire, isn't it?" he interrupted this disturbing involuntary pink they both had and peered at her from across the table. "We hear that you are a photographer."

"Ah," said Claire, not knowing what else to say.

"Really? What is your sphere?" Mara raised her chin and squinted unflatteringly, as though small glasses might be perched upon her perfect nose at other, more private, times.

"Oh," Claire murmured, "the unusual."

"Well, this is certainly extraordinary enough." Puffin made a lemon face and batted collusive eyes at Mara. His tone was baiting and unpleasant. "Perhaps you should be photographing this!"

Blacky moved disapprovingly back and forth in his chair. Irked but interested, Claire moved forward. "What do you mean, 'this'?"

"Well"—Puffin lifted both palms into the air—"us."

Claire smiled convivially back. "I am afraid I don't photograph the sensational." She savored the expression on Puffin Hedges's face while this sank in. "What I am after is"—she stopped talking again, long enough to ask herself what it was she was after, then looked exactly at him and said—"still life."

"Oh." Mara Morgen peered grimly at Temple Fortune. "Fruit in a bowl."

"No, not that. More like life caught standing still. And beauty. Whatever that is."

Mara, sensing Temple's interest quicken behind her, lanced back, "Oh, *beauty!* I would imagine one would give up that sort of thing, comes a point."

Surprised at such ardent venom, Claire remembered when she too had reacted to the green-eyed monster.

"No," she replied kindly, "more like the first moment I saw you, on the green, under the tree, motionless in your pretty costume. My first reaction was to shoot you."

Spontaneous laughter at the double meaning replaced the uncomfortable silence, and conversation resumed. Claire congratulated herself on handling that well, if unknowingly. She'd meant only to be honest and kind. She wouldn't want to make an enemy of Mara. Not yet, anyway.

"Funny he should die like that," Puffin Hedges ruminated out loud. "He'd just been telling me this morning how he wanted to—"

Mara, who'd been watching Claire shrewdly, interrupted Puffin with, "You are not the Breslinsky who used to shoot layouts in *Teuer*, are you?"

"Yes, I am," Claire admitted, not wanting to be old enough, but delighted that someone should remember her better work, something other than the advertising stuff she was so often connected to.

Mara continued to eye her suspiciously. "That wasn't you, though? The Breslinsky who did 'The Women of India' series?"

"You flatter me by remembering," Claire confessed.

"Remember?" Mara's buoyant enthusiasm obliterated her earlier mistrust and skepticism. "I just never knew you were a woman. I used to wait for things of yours!"

"Uh-oh," Puffin joked, "disdain to cahoots. Now we've got trouble!"

"No, really. I used to look for your work. You used to be great."

"Well, I'm not dead yet." Claire tried not to look decrepit.

Puffin squinted at her with suddenly motivated interest.

"It is a great pleasure to meet you," Mara said, extending her small hand across the table.

71

Embarrassed and happy, Claire grasped it and shook it heartily. She felt absurdly grateful.

This was all too much for Isolde. "Hans!" she cried out suddenly and buried her face in her bejeweled hands. Blacky knocked over his chair in his haste to get to her. He wrapped her up in his jacket and sort of lifted her by her shoulders. She was, however, too much for him, stronger and bigger, and she stayed right where she was, taller now but still right there, everyone watching and clicking their tongues. Fräulein Wintner commiserated with the appropriately woeful moanings.

Someone began to play piano upstairs. Hanging out at Iris von Lillienfeld's had honed Claire's classical-music-appreciation skills. On her less arthritic days, Iris was as delightful as any composer she chose. Schumann's "Arabesque." Claire recognized it at once and lifted her eyes to see Temple Fortune just pulling his own reluctantly away from her. She felt herself elevate with joy. Stella Gabriella, the daughter of the house, appeared at the open doorway beneath the music.

Stella was so enchantingly lovely, so luminous, with an ethereal grace that went beyond grief, so spellbinding, that they all stopped talking and gaped. Friedel sprang to his feet as if at attention, prepared to do her any bidding.

There was something alarming in the way she stood there. "Es war Cosimo," Stella declared. (It was Cosimo.) She cradled her arms, as in a dance. If any of the women at the tables had any illusions of imagining themselves quite something, they had only to look now at young Stella Gabriella standing there in the harmonious lavender dusk to know they would never dare to be so vain again. She looked smaller than before, like a jewel. Still no one spoke. Enraptured, they waited for her to say something. Claire thought Stella was about to sing. Instead, she lifted up what she had in her hands and held it out to them. It was something horribly alive.

"Oh, Lord," Blacky cried. "She's cut off all her beautiful hair!"

Claire slept the next day and night away, then was up before dawn. It was chilly and still. She pulled her warm cable-knit pullover over a long skirt and put on her Frei boots. Claire kept her camera bag under the bed, an old habit picked up in vile Far Eastern hotels where thieves dropping in had sometimes only moments to sweep the room before the chambermaid returned. Any edge, Claire still maintained, was a good edge. She slipped an extra camera battery from the side pocket and laid it in the ashtray on the dresser. You always went low when you needed it most.

Now what was that? She cocked an ear. Piano. Again? At 5 A.M.? It was morning, wasn't it? She panicked mentally. Jet lag could do strange things to you. She went over to the window and opened it, marveling at the clean, effortless ease of the Teutonic window frame, nothing like her weather-warped ones at home, which required the prerequisite bang with a fist, then a lightning-fast out-of-control *whoosh* where you practically found yourself thrust out of it. No, it was morning. The lightening in the sky came from the east. Schumann's "Rheinisch," she noted. Nicely done, too. She wondered how long the Mill would stay in business, though, with the proprietor waking the guests up before dawn with his eccentric license. She grabbed her camera and some film and crept down the quiet stairs. No one but Cosimo was up. She went out. The dog was still there, lying down but in the same spot. Claire went over and held out her palm for him to sniff. The dog raised his head slightly, then dropped it back down, listless.

"Poor kid," Claire whispered and walked on away, past the still-standing-there old-timer car, up the drive and then eagerly out over the field and the damp, soft hills, strewn blue with wild forget-me-nots.

The sun came grudgingly up behind thick clouds, and the air was filled with birdsong. The golden weather of her arrival was past, but it was refreshing to be out and about like this, no stopping to feed and dress the kids, no worry if Johnny would put on the new socks she'd laid out for him or just rummage around to select his old favorites from the hamper.

She stopped at the top of the hill and took some shots of the Mill. It looked almost like a watercolor in its puddle of mist. "Nice," she said out loud. She had loaded the camera with high-speed black and white. She was always happiest shooting black and white. Inevitably, she got carried away and finished the roll. Faintly she heard the rich sound of a man whistling. She looked this way and that. Far off to the other hill, there was somebody walking. "Who would be out at this time?" she wondered, picked up her long lens and captured him, an old fellow. It was the same walking figure she'd seen there the first day she'd arrived. Christ, was it just two days ago? It felt like two weeks had gone by.

She shot him just for fun. She would show this one to Iris, the fond whistling man on the hill, just above the old tree she'd described there. Claire sighed. She wasn't much looking forward to going through a mill full of clocks, as Iris had suggested. Why hadn't she told her there would be so many clocks? She didn't suppose anyone would hide a bag of diamonds in a tree, not for fifty-something years, they wouldn't, but all the same she thought she'd have a look. If nothing else, she loved a big old tree.

The hem of her long purple corduroy skirt was soaked wet by now from the high, dew-sodden grass, but she didn't mind; she felt invigorated and alive. For no reason, she started to run.

The gray-green world stood still around her as she swirled like an animal across the field, her camera banging at her hip. She reached the tree, out of breath and exhilarated, and put her arms around the trunk, touching the bark with the tips of her fingers, wanting nothing, wanting everything.

There were no diamonds here. Just an elderly tree with an elephant's memory. She laughed out loud. With her head still thrown back, she caught sight of a man from the corner of her eye. She jumped. He jumped. It was Temple Fortune.

"Bloody hell!" he lurched and cried out.

"Why don't you watch your step?" she panted. Her chest heaved from the running. "You scared me. I thought you were the Whistler."

"The Whistler?" He looked over his shoulder. "Sounds like a Fritz Lang film."

"What are you doing here?" she said.

"I might ask you the same thing."

She raised her chin at the scene before them. "I would use this angle if I were you," she suggested, admiring again the view of the Mill.

"So now you are recruiting visuals for me." He smiled. Or was that a sneer?

"Far be it from me." She sneered (just in case it was) back.

They both hesitated.

"It's going to rain," she said. They were so close and breathing so heavily, she caught hold of his scent. Their eyes met with a liquid collision. They smiled daffily at each other. "Vetyver," she concluded, recovering first, realizing where she was and that she'd run into the very one she would have hoped to; only now, his playful, exquisite presence was so physical to her that she imagined he could see right through her and read her wanton thoughts. Without another word, she ran off, away from discovery and back to the safety of the Mill.

It was not only that she didn't want him to know her, it was simply that she was so enjoying this rare and almost forgotten feeling of lust that she was afraid it would end if he said the wrong thing. And he must almost assuredly say the wrong thing. Who could live up to an adolescent fantasy? Who knew the script but her? It was as if she kept him at a distance, she could keep him forever, an erotic intoxication prolonged at arm's convenient length.

In the warm dark kitchen, Evangelika leaned over yellow egg yolks in a hollow of flour. She had one part of the long table set up with her rolling pin and a cold dish of water. A bowl of black cherries waited brilliantly.

"Strudel?" Claire mopped her damp face with her hanky.

The rain came down outside.

As Evangelika didn't answer, she walked on in.

"May I watch?"

"No," Evangelika said.

"I can pit," Claire bargained.

"What were you doing, snooping around out there before everyone is awake?"

"What, me? I was taking pictures. Photographs. That's what I do." Abrasive old bat, she thought.

"Ah. Another fancy one."

"I'm not so fancy," Claire defended the drabness of her life. She looked at her own unmanicured and work-worn hands.

"Sit over there, then," Evangelika sniffed, pointing to the farthest spot from her. "Just don't let me find out you

76

were up in the attic looking through all those old photograph albums he had up there. I have enough to do without strangers coming in here and messing everything up." She turned her back. "Just got things in order."

Claire took her stool happily. She found a knife she liked in the table drawer, a short sharp one, and got busy. The next thing she would be sure to do would be to go look through those photograph albums in the attic.

Dying for a cup of the delicious coffee she smelled brewing on the big stove, she thought she wouldn't press her luck. She'd get a good pile of cherries pitted before she asked. I hope he sees me like this, she caught herself wishing. Such a visual man as he was, to come across her sitting there prettily, industriously turning her fingers a ravishing beety pink, her hair silhouetted by the cheery stove.

Father Metz stood, tired, weary, in the doorway.

I am out of my mind, she congratulated herself. I have a husband I love and little children who need me. Well, what of it? It wasn't as though she had done something wrong. But she had, she had done something innately wrong, and she knew it. Just as surely as though she had done something really, because these feelings were more real to her than anything she'd felt for a long, long time. She had not said "Pooh, pooh" to the excitement of Temple Fortune's presence. She'd given every part of her being to enticing him. She had closed her eyes and prayed, "Yes, bring him closer." She had opened her mouth and breathed, irrevocably, in. If destiny wouldn't punish her for that, she knew herself well enough, she would do it for destiny.

4

So *Claire spent* the morning in subdued self-recrimina-
tion, purposely avoiding the film crew, instead taking
the tram into Schwabing to visit her old haunt, the Café
Münchener Freiheit on the Leopoldstrasse. This had been
her university, after all, the classroom of her younger days.
She still saw nothing wrong with having whiled away year
after year discussing films, headwaiters, politics, and religion with European hotheads and moody intellectuals. It
had done her good.

She wandered down the Leopoldstrasse, then sat herself
happily down at the Münchener Freiheit, its broad white
umbrellaed tables smattered with regulars even in the chilly
grim light. Chess players hard at work held on to their
heads. Puddle lakes reflected the curlicue rooftops. An
enormous plastic monkey-bars spiderweb in primary colors on the broad lawn kept children busy as their mothers
sat on the sidelines, smoking, watching. This was lovely.
Nothing to do but think and eat. Now where, Claire could
wonder at last, would she stash a bunch of diamonds at the
Mill? She could think now, away from the place. She'd been
too preoccupied with Jupiter not paying her expenses. It
wouldn't hurt to order breakfast, two eggs in glass (nicely
poached—not too much in either direction), a crispy
Brötchen with butter and apricot jam, a small glass of tart,

pulpy orange juice, and a pot of strong foamy *Milchkaffee.*
Who needed romance, she mused, when food was such a
comfort?

"That can't be Claire Breslinsky," someone said.

"Well, it is," she replied before even looking up. She expected some long-lost eyeglasses client or model and was
surprised when it turned out to be Blacky.

"May I join you?"

"Sure," she said, not sure at all. Isolde's animosity was
never a remote possibility.

"Sitting here thinking over what happened the other
day, are you?"

"Trying not to, really. Just enjoying being in this place
after so many years. The main problem with living in
America, as far as I'm concerned, is the lack of sturdy bread
and street cafés."

"Really?" He wriggled his bony bottom onto a cold seat
and lit a Marlboro with a Cartier. "I'm told one must stay
in SoHo when in New York. No lack of either there."

"Yes, well, you would want to."

"Sorry?"

"Stay in SoHo. When you and Isolde marry. You're much
too grand to stay with me." She said this jokingly, but all
he said was "Oh." He ordered a fruit-and-nut muesli from
the nurse-white waitress, then thought again and added the
Frühstück komplett. They lapsed into their haughty si-
lences. Finally he said, "Well, what do you think of the
scandal?"

"I don't know what to think," she admitted, glad, suddenly, to have someone gossipy with whom to discuss the
bad business. "I'm not too concerned about von Grünwald's death, though. People die every day. It has nothing
to do with me." Realizing she sounded harsh, she added,
"It's very sad for the children, of course."

Blacky barked a laugh. "Just the opposite, I should

think. Once they get used to the idea. He stood between them and everything they wanted, Hans did. He didn't like music or art, and that's all the two of them *do* like. For him it was a waste of time. Flowers. Forget flowers. Or Stella Gabriella's primitive, dirty-looking little pots, that's what he called them; he said she went out of her way to make them look measly. I know, because I heard him. All Hans liked was money. That was it. All his bluff hale-and-hearty didn't do much to disguise the cold and mean behind it all. Not once you got to know him."

"But he must have realized that music and flowers are what elevate any mundane atmosphere to a place that would bring in *more* money. I mean, he seems to have known what he was doing."

"That was his wife, Imogene, the children's mother. She wasn't artistic either. Just knew how to manage Hans. Don't know where the kids get it from. Fanatic about the church Imogene was, I think. The only thing those two had in common was their greed. Loved money. Funny how you can be that religious and still cling to money. Maybe, then again, she just wanted to be sure that her children's futures were secure. She was small, very pale, and blond, Imogene was. Stella Gabriella favors her side physically. A tall, slender girl. They say she chose Hans because he was the only one in the village taller than her. They didn't get along. She was always picking away at him. Of course, he had his side of the story, too. Hans once told me the only thing he could ever do right, in his wife's eyes, was bring in money. Imagine feeling that way! No wonder he was so greedy. Then there were other problems. You know that Cosimo is insane."

"Honestly? Certifiably insane?"

"Bonkers."

"Gee. I knew he was troubled. Anyone can see that. But he shows such genius, doesn't he? Everything he does is so superior to other people's ways of doing things. I mean, the way he plays. And then the way he's done the gardens. It's ingenious."

"Some would say obsessive."

"Oh, come on. You of all people should appreciate the nearness of obsessiveness to great art."

"Oh, it's a great art now, is it?"

She put her napkin down. "What is it with you Europeans—art isn't great unless it's dead and in a book or on a wall?"

He laughed happily. "One forgets the sheer naive directness of the American until one comes bumper-to-bumper with it." His muesli arrived and he dug right in. "It does one good," he said with his mouth full.

"Good." She shrugged, returning to her own breakfast, really liking him for the first time in a while. He had a sort of patriarchal tenderness that only bloomed when you insulted him, but one would have to do it justly. He was scrupulously clean. Scrubbed pink and shiny from his leonine dome to his brightly polished, well-kept and elderly cordovan shoes.

"Did you know Temple Fortune before this?" Claire asked, trying her best to sound merely conversational.

"No. Well, I'd heard *of* him, of course. But Puffin is the power behind the throne. He's the one with all the connections. Temple Fortune is just the talent. They just hit it right as a team, those two. Temple Fortune might be dressed up and preened and pruned, but he was just a down-and-out Irish immigrant filmmaker—slash—musician when he met Puffin. Jack-of-all-trades, master of none. Rock and the inevitable Roll, if I remember the story correctly. Course that was a long time ago. As good a way out of the ghetto as any, I suppose. It was that or the IRA. And we know where that will get you. No, Puffin Hedges is the one you want to know."

Maybe you, Claire thought. "It's rough about your wedding on the seventeenth," she changed the subject. "Bad luck, eh?"

"Don't worry about Isolde," Blacky snorted. "She'll turn it around to her own advantage."

"If anyone can, she will," Claire agreed. "Tell me, why did she decide to marry you?"

"Good move. Nothing better she could do at this point. Who wants an old diva?" He leered at her, as if to say, You see how horrid I still am, heh, heh.

"Phh. She's not old."

"For a diva she is. What does one *do* as a diva after one's prime?"

Claire looked more closely at this Blacky fellow from her past. Never had she heard Isolde criticized so disrespectfully. Still, she was sure that flippant tone would be subdued if Isolde were around.

"Surely not open a bistro," he continued, "much more fun to be a society hostess. Say," he added mockingly, "didn't you and I used to have fun?"

"Yes, we did. Now we're quite good friends. Don't tell me you're one of those fossils who believe men and women can't be friends!"

"They can as long as the one not wanted doesn't make a fool of him or herself and blow the facade."

Was he warning her? "Well, that's not the case with you and me," she assured him. "At least our break was civilized and by mutual consent." Claire sniffed and mopped her mouth with the heavy pink napkin, remembering in a flash the angry words and melodramatic scenes that had shocked even her. Oh well. "What's the story with the beautiful Stella Gabriella?" she asked.

"Beautiful is right," Blacky sighed. "I don't think I've ever seen anyone more beautiful, have you?"

"No, now you mention it, no."

"The funny thing is, though, I've never wanted to sleep with her, as knockout as she is."

"Hm." Claire would never cease to be amazed at men's unfathomable vanity—as though such a possibility would ever present itself! "Well, she is rather young," Claire said kindly.

"What I mean is"—Blacky rolled his fists and drummed the table with a frightening clobber—"she makes me horny as hell, but not to sleep with her. Do you get what I mean?"

"Jesus. You're not coming on to me, are you?" She pretended to be shocked.

"Well, no."

Claire laughed.

"What I mean is"—he patted his nubby fingertips together—"she provides this atmosphere of spiritual passion. A sort of plane of otherworldliness. Well, it just fills me with guile, lust."

Claire thought of Temple Fortune's hungry eyes. The way he'd looked at her. Taunting and wicked, as though he would eat her from her innocent plate.

"I know what you mean, I think. All that goodness fills you with mischief. Makes you feel wicked."

"*Genau.* Exactly."

"Now who's older? Stella or Cosimo?"

"Oh, Stella. He'll do anything she tells him."

"So do you think she'll keep the Mill as it is, or—"

"Convert it into a potter's haven for her potter friends?"

"You must admit it wouldn't be a bad idea."

"Mmm. The thought has possibilities. But there's no main force there to get it going. Just these two balmy kids who've never had to earn their livings. I could see the whole place going to seed. I mean, Stella might be the most beloved potter in Bavaria. What is it they call her, 'Ludwig's national treasure'? But even a national treasure needs tourists to pay the gas and electric. She doesn't strike me as the type who'd know how to engender business."

"No, you're right. That melodrama with her hair was indicative of, I don't know, instability."

"It was downright weird."

"Yeah, weird unless it was, you know, sort of a symbolic setting-free some people go through when a parent dies."

"But as eccentric as those two may be, they're not stupid. I can't see them giving the place up."

"Well, no. It is their home."

"They've always lived there?"

"Yes, and think of the treasure."

Claire went white. "What treasure?"

"There's a treasure hidden in the Mill. Didn't you hear them the other day?"

"But surely that's rumor. Gossip."

"That's not what Isolde thinks."

"Really? When did she tell you about the treasure?"

"Christ, woman, you were sitting there with us."

"Yeah, but I was distracted."

They remembered Hans von Grünwald's cold, dead body lying on the kitchen table, and they both shook their heads sadly, sobered by the enormity of death.

"One thing doesn't figure," Claire pursued. "If Hans was such a tightwad, wouldn't it follow that he'd encourage Stella's pottery? Seeing as she's so good at it. And already recognized, as you say. It must be bringing in money. She must get some sort of grant or something. Doesn't she?"

Blacky pursed his merry lips. "Money is one thing. Lots of money is another. You know yourself, being recognized as good doesn't guarantee financial success. Now marriage, on the other hand, and to the right person . . ."

"Do you mean Hans wanted to marry his daughter off to someone rich?"

"Rich and noble."

"Who?"

"Oh, I don't know." He shrugged, perplexed. "I just heard that there was trouble there. Hans had a sort of unhappy childhood, I gather. No father, more or less. Adam von Grünwald was a sort of bad-tempered cripple after his stroke."

Claire watched Blacky's cheek twitch. He'd grown up without a father himself. Almost everyone his age in Germany had.

"And," he continued unself-consciously, "the mother *was* a simpleton. Hans's mother, I mean. Kunigunde."

"Really? Really simple or pleasantly simple?"

"Two steps above moron. Sat all day out there in her garden with her roses."

"Doing what?"

"Drooling."

"Tch. You love to annihilate."

"Well, how should I know? Anyway, between the no father and just as well as no mother, he had not much ability to be the social prince. He just sort of festered here."

"Sad."

"Yes. He loved money, though. It took the place of family, I imagine. That's one thing that went right for him."

"He was good with money, then?"

"To put it mildly. It wasn't him, though, really. It was the Mill itself. And timing. Saint Hildegard's was always a functioning watermill. You know, for grain. They made bread, *Brötchen* in the village. Little breads. Not those wishy-washy little American things *you* call rolls. The plump, delicious crisp ones Bavaria is so famous for. Saint Hildegard's region always was known for tasty *Brötchen*. There was always a want for more. And of course Saint Hildegard's is so physically splendid. Every artist who was any good at all was welcome to come to the Mill and run up a bill. Pure method to his madness, naturally. They wound up paying up with paintings and sculptures that eventually surpassed in value any bill they'd run up for food and drink. He has a wonderful old cook."

"He did love his children, though."

"Oh, yes. One felt he loved them, in his way. He only didn't quite know how. He hardly paid them any attention. They pretty much floundered around as well, just the way the father had done, living at the Mill, going to the village school. What sort of life can that have been?"

"I can't say it sounds completely horrible."

Blacky stirred what was left of his muesli thoughtfully. The area was filling up with Sicilians and astrologers, models and exchange students. "It's the dog I feel sorry for," Blacky said.

"Me too. Whatever happened to their mother?" Claire asked.

"She died of cancer. Ovarian, I think. About fourteen years ago. He made her life a misery, they say. In the end he wore her out. Their mother was rumored to be a Jew. Did you know? Even though she was blond. People forget how dark Adam was. Cosimo is a throwback. He could certainly be Jewish. He looks Jewish. With that nose."

"Really. Well, it's not like being an alien."

"It is if you live in Munich. Of course, it's advantageous taxwise. Postwar Germans are so energetically repentant."

"Are you saying they shouldn't be?"

"I'm saying that they *are*. One dares *not* wonder, nowadays, if the Jews don't whine about the war too much. It's illegal. Still, a lot of people do."

"Oh, God. Where's my waitress?"

"Had enough?"

"Of you, yes."

"Come on, stay. I'll change the subject."

"I'm not going to fight World War Two with second-generation Nazis," Claire sputtered. "Not all over again!"

He laughed and laughed. When he wheezed to a halt he

reached across and covered her hand with his. "Oh, come on, stay. I'll be good. Now stop counting out your pathetic little mound of marks. I say, you still are a feisty little Yank. Do they all jump to conclusions the way you do where you come from? Or is it a female thing? I'm only voicing out loud what everybody thinks and doesn't say."

"Interesting how the only time I hear that one is in Germany. And I was just starting to forget all the things I couldn't stand about you."

"You'd better not." He smiled. Blacky's eyes glittered with some remembered passion. He lit yet another of his poignant cigarettes.

"I used to do that, too," she said.

"What?"

"Light a cigarette just as I was about to feel something . . ."

"Oh, I love my ciggies," he defended his red box, patting it.

"Yeah, I did too. They were my best 'chums,' cutesy names for pals that held my hand and stopped me crying anytime I was just about to feel something. When I actually got pregnant and had to stop, I cried and laughed for months. I felt all those things because there was no little 'chum' there to stop me."

"Oh, God forbid. I'd better keep on smoking then. That sounds dreadful."

"Just warning you, Blacky. If you have any idea about hanging out with me, I won't stop. I am vigilant."

"I can take anything for two weeks."

She looked at him quizzically. "How do you know how long I'll be staying?"

"You said so the other day."

"I did?"

"Say, are you paranoid?"

"I guess," she said, wondering for the first time why

she'd spent so many years in this café, this congress of lo[v]ers. Now, wait a minute. They weren't necessarily lose[rs]. They just weren't Germans.

"There he is!" Blacky swatted the air.

Claire looked out over the sea of faces and came to rest on Puffin Hedges standing at the periphery of the tables, scanning the sea of faces himself.

"Puffin Hedges," Claire said.

"Well, that's why I'm here," Blacky said. "To meet him."

"Oh," she said. "He's well named, isn't he?" Claire said as Puffin sidestepped his way through the tables.

"What? Puffin? I should say so."

Puffin caught sight of them, wrinkled his forehead happily upward at Claire's being there too, held an invisible telephone in his hand and a finger aside of his nose to indicate the one minute it would take him to make a phone call, and then he disappeared into the café.

Claire wondered if it would be Temple Fortune he would telephone. Well, of course it would be. Whom else? They were butter and bread. Would Puffin be a good little man and mention she was there?

"Hello," Puffin said, and sat down.

"That was quick," Blacky said.

"He's already left," Puffin said. He ordered Pernod.

"Why can't you order *Birnenschnapps* or Bacardi like every other alcoholic snob in the city?" Blacky turned his eyes to Claire. "So affected." He shook his head. "And where's Fortune?"

"Off to London," Puffin said primly.

Claire's heart took a spill. "Oh?" she said. "I thought the film wasn't finished."

"We're not done," Puffin sighed. "We're lamenting the ruin, as it were. Not really. Well, we are, but that's not why he's gone. We still have to shoot the 'rightful heir gets his due' shots. And Mara's close-ups. That won't take long. No, Temple's off to dine the Empress Dowager and rattle her burly pearls above our soup."

"Pearls after swine?" Blacky said.

"Yes," Puffin said. "These shoes are killing me. Killing. My poor tortured tootsies." He looked pleadingly at Claire and patted his pockets. "I say, you don't think the help at the Mill nicks stuff, do you? Can't find my money clip."

"Well, we wish him luck," Blacky said, ignoring his ridiculous question.

"Will he need it?" Claire said, wanting, really, to ask when he'd be back. And who was this Empress Dowager?

"We all need luck, Claire," Puffin said, "but we know what you mean, don't we, ducky? Temple needs no more than his charm to move many a feminine mountain. Anyway, we'll know Monday night."

Monday? Claire lamented. This was only Friday. She envisioned the suddenly long and dreary weekend ahead. How would she spend it?

In almost immediate reply, the sun shone brilliantly through. Left and right, people sat up straight. Disappointed faces changed and even creased with hope. In that one dramatic moment Claire could see the days she'd first arrived in Munich, the uncharacteristically sunny, leisurely days and the holiday atmosphere that had accompanied them. The reason she'd stayed. Even the nights had been soft and navy-blue and starlit, never going black. Everyone was young and making lots of money, zipping off to Ibiza and returning just as happily to the whirlwind of beer gardens and the river's playful edges. Claire smiled to herself at the memory. She had lived here for ten years. This faraway glockenspiel town was part of her life. Whatever happened to her, or didn't, she had happened to this. And she was part and parcel of it, as it was of her. When everything was at the end, if she had the luxury of looking back, this privilege would always be hers.

"In my horoscope," Blacky read from the *Abend Zeitung*, "it says that life's sorrows are not its misfortunes but its fears."

"Is that what you've come to in your old age, dear?" Puffin said. "Directing life from horoscopal dictates? How desolate."

"Not desolate at all. The older I get, the more I rely upon the wisdom of the sorcerers. Pass me the sugar."

Puffin puttered the bowl across, relinquishing its pudgy shininess grudgingly.

"Guess what happened just before I left the Mill."

"What?" they both said, ready for anything.

"Father Metz—you remember Father Metz, the cumbersome priest with the unfortunate teeth?"

"We know who you mean." Blacky nudged him impatiently.

A plan began to formulate in Claire's mind. She would shoot Stella, send the slides to Zoli, the model agency in New York, and by the time Stella was primed and dined and made a star—for there was no doubt in Claire's mind she would become a star—Claire would have her stuff ready and sell it to Jupiter Dodd and *She She* magazine. She would have helped herself and Stella. Stella would surely go for the idea. She would when she found out how much money a top model made. Enough, certainly, to keep the Mill open. And that would be what she wanted. Wouldn't it?

"I don't like priests," Puffin was saying. "They're unnatural."

"We all know what you like," Blacky sniffed, "and that might be considered unnatural by some."

"You don't know anything. But proceed," Puffin urged, unoffended.

"It was your story," Claire reminded him.

"Oh. So here we have this priest, standing at the back gate all done up like the bellhop of death, purple stole and what-have-you. I walk up, I say, 'What's up?' Friendly, mind you, passing the time, as the two of us are face-to-face, but he doesn't answer. He just stands there gaping into eternity."

Claire laughed at Puffin's suddenly excellent cockney accent.

"He was saying his office." She sipped her coffee knowingly. "They don't all answer when they're at that."

"No, he wasn't. So listen. Now I'm riled. Now I've got to have my 'Hi hello an' 'ow do ya do,' you know what I mean? So I say, 'Think it's going to clear up, parson?' "

"They don't call them parsons, the Catholics," Blacky scoffed.

"Whatever. Know what he says? He goes . . ." Here Puffin turned his cheek in a vaudevillian aside and recited in the priest's own reedy voice:

> " 'A tree
> has been felled.
> Its leaves
> are still alive
> its fruits
> are still ripening
> and birds
> are still on its branches.
> A tree
> has been felled.' "

"Why, that's very nice," Claire said.

"That's Rainer Maria Rilke." Blacky shimmied about in

his seat, proud of his Germans. "Now there's a fine tragic picture." Puffin was nothing if not entertaining.

"Thank you. So I say to him, 'That's lovely, parson. What's it mean?' And he looks at me like he just woke up and he says, 'We've just buried Herr von Grünwald. Hans. It's over now,' he says."

"Buried him?" Claire said.

"That was quick," Blacky said.

"That's exactly what I said." Puffin smacked the table, and Blacky's sausage jumped from its plate.

"What about the wake?" Claire said.

"If there had been one, you would have slept right through it," Puffin said to her in his normal accent.

"People don't do that sort of thing nowadays," Blacky said. "I was thinking more of an inquiry. And what did he mean by 'Its fruits are still ripening'?"

"Of course they do too have wakes," Claire protested. "The family needs that time to grieve before they give up the body. It's traditional. And the fruits are the children, living on, you know."

"One gathers it still is traditional," Puffin sniffed, "in the colonies."

"What do you mean, inquiry? There were no suspicious circumstances. He fell," Claire said.

Puffin and Blacky said nothing.

"Unless you two know something I don't."

Blacky plucked at the coagulated Hollandaise with his fork. "It's a curious business."

"At least no one's sorry he's gone." Puffin sighed. "I think I will have some lunch. How's that *Leberkäs mit Kartoffelsalat*, I wonder?"

"I feel so sorry for the young girl." Claire shook her head sadly. "She seems so desperately unhappy."

"Yes, poor thing." Puffin clicked his tongue. "All that money and no desire to spend it."

"At least now she won't have to marry whoever it is her father wanted her to," Blacky said.

"Maybe she'll marry me," Puffin said.

"There's a thought," Blacky said, "then you won't have to send Temple off to wine and dine rich widows who might refinance and co-produce for you.

"Poor Temple Fortune," Claire said.

"I'm sure he doesn't mind," Blacky said.

"He does this one," Puffin said. "She's stout as a house and old as the lamppost and smells of Arpège. A lot of Arpège."

"But I would think there would be plenty of backing for good films right now," Claire, appeased, said. "I mean, aren't there? It is a good film, isn't it?"

"Oh, it's a good film all right. Temple wouldn't do something that wasn't good. There only isn't such a great market for 'good' films that don't have a gimmick. *Venus, Cupid, Folly and Time* not only doesn't have a gimmick, it also doesn't have a shoot-out or a car chase. It's, you know, personal crisis; one of those things. The fellow wants what he deserves. The girl deserves better than she's got."

"What happens exactly?" Claire pulled her sweater over her head. "To the girl."

Puffin had a way of pursing his lips before he answered. "She is numb, the girl. She gets the chance to love."

"Good for her," Claire said.

"But only at risk to all she holds dear." Puffin winked.

"Uh-oh," Claire said.

"And our star looks like something the cat dragged in. *And* we still have the last close-ups to shoot."

"Now, now . . . meow, meow," Blacky said.

"Well, it's true. You only have to look at her. She's a ruin."

"Perhaps if she were able to rest for a few days," Claire suggested, remembering the resiliency of her own models when left to recuperate on their own for a day or two in a foreign country. Women needed time to recover from jet lag and lunar stress. It was amazing what a little time and good faith could remedy.

"*Tch*"—Puffin waved his hand in disgust—"she's had time. We've put off doing the close-ups time and time again. She still looks like hell."

All at once the Alps lit up and seemed nearby.

"Tell you what I ought to do," Blacky ruminated, "take a drive out to Diessen, that potters' town that's so pretty. Isolde said that's where they're having the potters' festival. You know, that little village on the Ammersee, where Stella goes. Everyone will be there. I might as well go. Now the weather's gone nice."

"Diessen?" Claire's eyes lit up. That was where Iris von Lillienfeld's story had begun. "I'd love to see Diessen. May I come along?"

"Excellent idea," Puffin joined in enthusiastically. "I must have salt water. Is it salt or sweet?"

"It's sweet, I think," Claire said, not knowing at all.

"Bloody hell. My car's in the shop," Blacky said.

"Don't go dodgy on us," Puffin said. "Take it out."

"I'm having the tires rotated. It's got to be done."

"Lame excuse," Puffin accused. "What about you?" He turned to Claire.

"I'd be happy to drive," she said. "But it will have to be someone else's car. I haven't got one. Unless . . ."

"Unless what?"

"Who belongs to that old Mercedes in the drive at the Mill?"

"Oh, that. That's old Father Metz's jalopy. He uses it to get back and forth. It never goes anyway."

"It goes," Puffin corrected, "it just doesn't start. If he doesn't park it on the hill, he has to have somebody give him a push, that's all."

"We could park it on a hill," Blacky supposed.

"What makes you think he would lend us his car?" Puffin said.

"He would if I said I'd like to buy it," Claire heard herself say. "We could be taking him out for a test run."

"Him?" Blacky said disapprovingly. "Cars are shes. She's a good old girl. She's on her last legs. Everyone knows that."

"Oh, this one is definitely a fellow. A sort of Otto von Auto, if I know my old buggers," Claire insisted, dying, for some reason, to get behind the wheel.

"Exquisite idea," Blacky decided. "We could have a picnic. Get away for a bit."

"He might really not want to sell," Claire thought out loud.

"Yes, he would." Blacky peeled an Israeli orange and passed it around. "He would jump. He wants a nice, new, blue for Our Lady Audi, with seat belts. Something that starts up in winter."

"I'll bet all he needs is a nice new starter," Claire said.

"Oh my dear," Puffin said, "your Otto von Auto needs a whole lot more than that. He needs a three-week head-to-toesies lube totalment at the Spa Mercedes in Stuttgart."

"In other words," Blacky said, "he needs nothing that money, money, and more money couldn't cure. Just what Father Metz doesn't have." He buried himself in the paper.

"But there's no reason Father Metz has to know that we know that!" Puffin said.

"No, he *should* know that we know," Claire said. "Then he'll lower the price."

"What price?" Puffin said. "We only want him for the weekend."

"That's true," Claire said. "I get so carried away."

They looked kindly at her, these two men, understanding her, liking her very much indeed. They were happy to take her over, invest their important weekend in hers, for she had something the other women didn't. She was safely married, safely mothered, safely familied in her own country and would make no further claims on them once her allotted time was up. They approved of the life she was loath to refer to, the untidy children, a bad-tempered husband, and God-fearing parents.

Claire, for her part, liked them too. She'd always been aware of the way her eager optimism and love of life rankled people, especially women. These two didn't mind at all. And they chatted with a fastidious irreverence she found adorable. Claire would laugh and laugh, and they, eyes shining with so appreciative an audience, would go on and on. No, she was a splendid girl. She didn't need them at all.

"Now, Claire," Puffin admonished, noticing Claire's thoughtfulness, "don't go getting pangs of guilt about taking advantage of an old priest. He would want us to go to Diessen. We could take the girl, Stella. Get her out for a bit. That's where she's always headed. It's where she likes to go. She has to take two buses and the trolley."

"We could take Mara, the movie star, along as well on our drive in the country," Claire suggested.

"Oh, jolly. Now we've got one hysterical mourner and one horrendous has-been. Just put them both in the backseat, please. I'll sit up front with you," Blacky said.

"Mara wouldn't come," Puffin assured him. "Temple wouldn't like it."

"Is he that possessive?" Claire asked.

"Not possessive. He can't stand her. He just doesn't want it leaking out what a mess she is."

Claire was almost ashamed of the relief this remark afforded her. She went absolutely expansive with goodwill.

"Well," she said, "all the more reason she should come, then. It will do her good. Diessen is one of the cure spots, isn't it? Good mud. Good for the blood. Good for the soul. How come Temple Fortune cast her in a leading role if he can't stand her?"

"Oh, those two go back a long way," Blacky said. "She was in his first commercial hit, you know."

"Well, that's not why," Puffin said. He lowered his voice. "Our backer wouldn't put up the money if she wasn't going to star in the film."

"I didn't know that," Blacky said.

"Neither of them will want to come anyway," Puffin said. "It will wind up just the three of us. Better, don't you think?"

"I don't know," Blacky said. "Isolde mentioned going. I like a mob. Maybe Isolde *will* come. Just her cup of tea. And she has her own car." He thought of those plush leather seats. He could ride back with her.

"I'm sure Isolde has tons of things to do." Claire lamented the whole day she'd lost sleeping. She remembered the reason for which she was supposed to be in Germany. "And who knows if you can still have the wedding at the Mill? You might have to find another place."

"Nothing to stop us now," Blacky said. "We're having it straightaway."

"Already! You can't have a wedding so soon! It will have to be next Saturday."

"This is not America, Claire," Blacky reminded her, "with printed invitations and entire cows rotating on spits. We'll simply call everyone up and put a tent on the lawn. Tch. It's a pity, really—von Grünwald would have jumped at the chance to have our wedding there. Just the sort of old money/new money thing that goes down so well at the Mill. Outdoors. *Trachten* or tux."

"That's the traditional Bavarian dress," Claire explained to Puffin. "It's considered formal wear in Munich, de rigueur for the opera. It's charming."

"I wonder if we could get everyone to wear this *Trachten.*" Puffin thought out loud. "Get some background stuff for the film, edit it in back in London."

"Not a bad idea," Claire said, imagining a layout for *She She.* Isolde would love to see herself in the editorial pages. Sort of a combination editorial/society thing. Everything black and white and then water-colored. She felt the surge of creative energy pick her up and put her right on keel. Nothing could destroy her now. This was the plane on which she belonged. Preoccupied. Generated by her plans. When it fit and she knew it was right, there was nothing better. Well, nothing except her children. But this was hers. This was her separate virtue of selfishness. She would shoot something at the Roman Bridge. The wedding party. Ideas raced in front of her.

"You know what I wonder?" Puffin said. "I wonder," he laughed, "if Isolde gave von Grünwald a little push." His pale-blue eyes glittered with conviviality.

"If she did"—Blacky reached for the check—"it was not the most inconsiderate thing she's ever done."

Otto von Auto tooled elatedly along the sparkling Mittlerer Ring. Claire was at the wheel. She loved the dashboard, reminiscent of what she imagined were her parents' courting years. A Nick-and-Nora-Charles dashboard, full of craftsmanship and dreams. The seats were more than a little doggy and the springs exhausted, as Puffin kept pointing out. Porsches and huge modern Mercedes flew alongside and sped past, but Otto von Auto maintained his dignity. Keeping his even, full-out throttle at thirty miles per hour.

Puffin Hedges sat beside Claire, and Mara Morgen sat beside him. Blacky had gone ahead with Isolde. They hadn't been able to find Stella, but Mara had been easy enough to get to come along. Without Temple Fortune on hand, the film crew pretty much fell to loose ends. Mara was happy not to have to sit another day out with them, pretending to be busy. She liked Claire, and photographers are so important to actresses. Claire had made sure to bring extra film along. Mara wasn't in that bad of a state. At least not full-length. And in her form-fitting leotard, Mara had the slender, loping, strong back and high ass of the cheetah. The same small head and long legs. Claire could always backlight her through a couple of rolls and see what turned out. Plenty of hung-over starlets had been backlit out of oblivion. Mara's pale skin was pulled taut against the cheekbones the camera so loved. Claire watched her watch herself in the side-view mirror. Mara would pout and narrow her eyes nearsightedly at her own image, softened by the mottled mirror. She crossed eyes with Claire and didn't mind at all. It was just this sort of cool, professional narcissism a photographer looked for. It saved so much time slicing through coy false modesty.

Mozart was on the still perfectly good Blaupunkt.

"Stop the car! Stop the car!" Puffin cried.

"What is it?"

"It's Stella!"

"Where?"

"There." Puffin pointed to a small gathering of people waiting at the tram shelter. It was Stella all right, blond hair crookedly hacked off at the nape of the neck. She was standing there holding a basket with nothing in it, gazing morosely into space.

She didn't see them. Claire eased the car over to the curb and flagged her down. Stella reacted very dully, Claire thought, as though this were an everyday occurrence, running into people one knew at an obscure intersection on the way to the town where one was headed. She almost refused to see them. Claire opened her door and got out. Stella's face lit up. She snatched once, absentmindedly, at her neck, reaching for the hair no longer there, and dashed over to the car. The other people waiting at the tram stop glared at Claire as though she'd taken something valuable from them, as indeed she probably had.

"We're headed for Diessen. Want to come along?"

"I'd love to," Stella said, and climbed in.

"I thought you were Father Metz"—Stella smiled radiantly at them, including them all in her glow—"coming to track me down. I'm so glad you're not."

"Don't like him either, eh?" Puffin said.

"I like him very well indeed. He just goes to such trouble to see that I'm all right. And I am all right. Really."

"We're all very sorry about your father," Claire said, wanting to get that out of the way. She wasn't comfortable with Stella's cool acceptance of her father's death. It was so unlike what her own reaction would be.

"How lucky for me that you're off to Diessen," Stella said.

"We got the idea from you," Puffin admitted.

"How did you get Father Metz to loan you his car?"

"Long story, that." Puffin met Claire's eyes in the rearview mirror. He turned to Stella. "We were going to stop somewhere outside Diessen and have some lunch. Would you point out a friendly spot? Somewhere charming and pretty?"

"Oh, but you must come with me, then. I'll put you to Aidenried overlooking the Ammersee. It's a beer garden, but you may bring your own fare."

Everyone agreed that this was a good idea. They relaxed. It was always nicer to know where you were going.

They drove along, through the flat countryside and then the pleasant rolling Alpine foothills. It didn't take very long to reach the more picturesque farms and country homes. Puffin pointed out the historical highlights of the area.

When the sun was high in the sky, they saw the town of Diessen nestled prettily in its own green hill. The facade of the famous rococo Stiftskirche stood out and greeted them like a great ship. A red sailboat swept the glittering lake. Church spires and maypoles stuck out here and there. The houses had solid wood balconies, painted sugary pastel colors, under broad overhung roofs.

Claire could well imagine Iris's family strolling down to the lake and taking one of the sturdy rowboats out. Church bells pealed out noon. Every church tower held a clock, and every clock pointed to twelve. Not exactly like home, where even the bank hadn't had a working clock in years.

They were all quiet for the *Glockenspiele,* or bell playing. Claire smiled to herself, remembering how Iris always mixed up those words: *Glocke,* or "bell," in German, was so like "clock" in English. Iris was forever telling Claire to go answer the clock or to look at the bell when she wanted the time.

Was that what Iris had meant when she'd told her to look in the clock? Could she have meant to look in the bell? Of course. Suddenly, Claire couldn't wait to return to the Mill.

"Hey!" Puffin Hedges cried. "What are you trying to do, get us all killed?"

"Oops," she apologized as she slowed the car down, wedging it through the narrow alleys lined with flower stalls. If the diamonds *were* in the bell, they'd more than likely still be there when she got back. "I didn't realize how fast I was going," she said.

"Yeah, I know your type," Puffin said. "When they stop us you'll say none of us were driving. We were all in the back."

Stella directed them up the very long hill toward a leafy marketplace of stalls for potters. They met there every May, gathering from all over the world to display and sell their wares. Claire parked the car along the road with the cars of the other tourists, and they left it there ready to receive the combination of admiration and jeers a car with running boards was sure to garner. Claire patted the voluptuous turn of the front end. "Good boy," she told the old metal. "Good job."

"Yeah, well done." Puffin Hedges flicked the rusty bumper with the toe of his boot and raised his eyes sarcastically to heaven.

Claire and Stella each took up one of the baskets Evangelika had packed for them, but Puffin proposed they leaven them till later. "No need to trudge around loaded down." But Mara had her great pocketbook. She always had to have her bag. They were all in fine spirits and galloped ahead. Claire made sure the car was locked, then changed her mind and left it open in case someone wanted to come back first for something to eat.

She fell into step with Stella, slipping film and lenses into different pockets around her many-pocketed vest. She was glad to get this time alone with the girl.

They walked up the slope together silently. Whatever men they walked past gaped openly at Stella. They couldn't help it. She was just that stunning. Claire couldn't wait to shoot her and told her so. "I only restrain myself from taking your picture because of your mourning," she added, hoping she'd be pleased. And yet, somehow, there was something about Stella that made her know she wouldn't be. She walked along, her shoulders back, not answering, reminding Claire of the women of the Kuchi tribes in Afghanistan. They were fierce and magnificent and, occasionally, toothless, but wildly photogenic with their remarkable faces and blazing colors. It wasn't anything they said or did (who knew what they said or did?) but an air of self-possession that Claire never failed to pick up on and respect. And they very adamantly did not want their pictures taken.

"Don't tell me"—she turned to Stella—"you don't want to have your picture taken, do you?"

They stopped beneath the grove of willows.

Stella smiled kindly at her. "No, no, I don't."

"I didn't think so. Would you mind telling me why not?"

"Uh-oh. Now I feel on the spot."

"Please don't. I'm sorry I asked. Forgive me."

"No, it's all right . . ." She sighed. "I might just as well tell you. I am going to join the order of the Sisters of Saint Catherine of Siena."

"You're kidding!"

"No." Stella, now quite used to being mocked for this idea, said quietly, "I am not kidding."

"But that's wonderful!"

Now it was Stella's turn to look surprised. As yet, she'd not told anyone of her decision who hadn't met the idea with shocked denial.

"You must have had dealings with nuns before," Stella said.

"Twelve years of Catholic school," Claire said fondly. "Josephites."

"Ah."

"I'm disappointed," Claire said, "but not surprised. Not really. As a matter of fact, it explains a lot. I mean, I couldn't figure you out before. Now I can."

"But why disappointed, if I may ask?"

"You won't believe this, but I had you lined up for my new superstar model."

"You're not the first," Stella said.

"No, I guess I wouldn't be." Claire picked up a stone and flung it into the field. She felt exasperated. She wondered if Jupiter Dodd's offer really would be such a plunge into immorality. There didn't seem to be any other way for her to make any money. Maybe she just ought to grow up,

103

give up her naive ethics and get down to pitching in with the mortgage payments. It wasn't as though the kids were babies and needed her at home all the time. All at once she remembered Stella in the doorway to her room with her glittering beads in her hand. They'd been rosary beads, of course! How stupid of her not to have picked up on that, she with a mother who had rosary beads for every occasion: her everyday's, her Sunday best, her rosaries for the wake, and her hand-me-downs from long-ago aunts in Ireland— sparkling puddles beside her Sunday missal in her night-table drawer. Right in there with the holy cards of the dead she'd known and would again upon Resurrection. Claire laughed. "I was remembering you with your beautiful rosary beads. I should have known then."

"Those were my mother's and her mother's before her." She looked more closely at Claire. "I have upset your plans?"

"Oh, that's okay. I should know better than to make plans without consulting the subject."

"Or in this case, the object."

"Touché."

"Never mind. Everyone else does. Did."

"You mean your father?"

Stella reached for the tall reeds along the side of the road. Instead of yanking them out, she caressed them lightly with the palms of her hand. There was the hot sweetness of white lilac trampled on the road.

"What was your father like?"

"Ah. My father. My father was tough. He was tough. He intimidated everyone. Cosimo. Me."

"And yet, now that I'm speaking with you, you don't seem to be intimidated by life."

Stella tilted her head mischievously. "But?"

"Oh, I don't know. Removed." All the nuns Claire had

known, and she'd known so many growing up, had all been so no-nonsense and down to earth.

"Nothing wrong with removed," Stella said.

"No, not in the line you're going into."

"This will shock you perhaps, but I am not sorry my father's physical self has departed. I can find no feelings there but release." She stopped and turned to Claire, challenging her with her waiting. Then, just as suddenly, she seemed to crumple. To give up. "It's my brother I worry about." She let go a long sigh.

"You're afraid the world will eat him up alive?"

"My brother is too good. If it weren't for him, I would have left the secular world already a long time ago."

"Are you that much in a hurry to enter religious life?"

Stella Gabriella's face took on that beatific sheen "society" considered unhinged.

"I can scarcely wait," she murmured.

"To be removed?"

"To sit undisturbed in His presence."

"Just how does that work? I mean, until you can sit undisturbed?"

"I give the wrong impression." She plucked at her face.

"What about your pottery?"

"I can still work my wheel behind the cloister wall. Work is prayer, too. We are an order of handworkers."

"And then, what? Like the Mother Superior sells the goods for the poor?"

Stella laughed. "To put it bluntly, yes."

Claire hesitated. "I take it your father didn't like the idea of your going into the convent."

"Yes, well, I think it's more difficult for men to accept that sort of thing." She sounded defensive.

"You mean your mother wouldn't be as upset?"

"Men have a naive way of believing in the physical, the

tactical plane as the only reality. Women realize the futility of accumulation." Claire thought *that* was naive. It's women, after all, who make shopping a life work. "My mother was my dearest friend," Stella continued. "She knew what my vocation was. Even helped me to see it." Stella craned her neck to straighten her spine. "She is never far from me, my mother. She knew I always wanted the religious life, doing for people. You see, my mother was, shall we say, delicate. She wasn't worldly."

Claire remembered someone calling her simpleminded. No, that had been the grandmother. Adam's wife—Adam's wife was supposed to have been simpleminded. Hans's mother.

"So how will it go? Is there a waiting period, to see if you like it?"

"What happens first is a physical and mental evaluation. The convent wants to be sure you are coming *to* something rather than away *from*. Then there is a mental aptitude test and an interview by Council."

"And then?"

"Well, there are two years in the Novitiate. The first year is the Postulancy. In the second year one is a Canonical Novice. After the Canonical year, you take temporary vows. These are renewed each year until final profession. Usually six to eight years after you enter."

"And your mother wanted you to do this?"

"No, she didn't want me to . . . but when I confided to her my vocation, she was . . . how shall I say? Joyous. She was joyous."

"She wasn't saddened that you would never have a family?"

"Oh, but I shall have a large and wonderful family." She smiled pointedly.

Claire nodded. "Stella? May I ask you a personal question?"

"Yes."

"Did your mother love your father?"

"Oh, I'm sure she loved him. Especially when they were young. Only later, as I grew older, I felt her shrink from him. He was not religious. My mother, very." Stella held her elbows and raised her shoulders up.

"Oh." Claire strained her eyes to see how far up the others had gone. A local resident, his house along the road, had rigged up an ice cream counter behind the clematis vine and was selling ice cream. There was only one flavor left, strawberry. Claire bought them each a cone, wondering as she did why, oh why, noblesse never failed to oblige.

"Delicious," Claire slurped, aware of her sloppy gluttony compared to Stella's refined, catlike licks. "If you go into the convent—"

"*When* I go into the Novitiate. It's quite settled."

"Yes, *when* you go in. Sorry, I didn't know it was definite."

"Mother Superior has accepted me into the Novitiate. Finally." She glanced quickly at Claire. "The same day my father fell, actually."

"What—you mean, your father knew you were accepted before he fell?"

"No, I hadn't received my mail until after. It was just as well. He was so against my entering that had he known, I might have attributed his fall to his anger. His being upset. I wouldn't want to have that on my conscience."

"Yes, I see what you mean." She noticed Stella's ladylike nibbles had progressed to a more uncharacteristic kidlike slurping.

"What will happen to the Mill? I mean, who will run it, now your father's gone?"

Stella licked her fingers with this new abandon. "That," she finally said, "is something I don't know." She stopped walking again, adjusted her basket, held her flat belly with her palms, composed herself, taking a deep breath and then another. "I only know it won't be me."

She talked, Claire thought, not disapprovingly, like a recovering AA member. "Stella, what was it you meant when you said, *'Es war Cosimo,'* 'It was Cosimo,' what did that mean?"

Stella dropped her pale lashes. "I was upset," she said.

"Yes, but what did you mean?"

She looked defiantly at Claire. "He told me to—"

Just then, before she could say, she stopped. "Ah," she said, "Doktor von Osterwald!"

"Where?"

"There." Too polite to point, Stella raised her chin in the direction of a tree bent low to a ninety-degree angle where a gathering listened to a calliope player. Blacky hadn't seen them yet. Claire experienced the old feeling of safety whenever he was around. "You'll never die when I'm around," he used to promise her. "I won't let you," he would say, and she'd loved that. What better way to feel with someone than immortal? She still loved him for his blasphemous bravado. There was no one more self-secure than Blacky. Which was why, she supposed, women literally flocked to him. Even now he was surrounded by a group of women. And why, years ago, she had admitted to herself, she couldn't bear to share his life. Blacky wore the simple, elegant sports jacket of the German professional. Claire pushed her lower lip stubbornly out and walked toward him. She was long past thinking the problem was with her or him. They were who they were. Blacky was, simply, a phenomenon, and that was that. Her life was certainly more magnificent for having known him.

"Hello." She grinned.

"Hello." He pushed his gleaming glasses upon his nose in a characteristic movement.

Stella left them to go talk to some devoted-looking potters in the main tent, after promising to meet them later at Aidenried.

Blacky and Claire strolled together through the marketplace. Claire had to restrain herself from lusting after all these magnificent pots and pieces of *Töpferei*. She didn't have to worry about buying anything exorbitant, she was on too tight a budget for that. But it was hard not to go nuts. And she would have to bring back souvenirs. In the end she chose some small, inexpensive, plain clay bells on long straw cords. They delighted her. They simply would, after all, persevere. She had one for each of her family and one for Iris. Then, oh well, one more for Mohammed at the newsstand. There was one odd-shaped one at the back, rejected by the avenue of tourists and restricted to the corner. She picked it up by its delicate cord. There was something decidedly Oriental about this one. Balanced but off-center. *"Ich nehme dieses auch,"* she informed the redheaded lady wrapping her lot, picturing it hanging outside her kitchen window, glistening with rain or sunshine, reminding her forever of this moment.

Blacky battled her hand and paid the woman, exasperating Claire. She didn't mind really. She was relieved.

"Happy?" Blacky inquired as they trotted away with her package.

She nodded.

"You always did like little acquisitions." He shook his head wonderingly. "It was the big ones that bothered you."

She stopped walking. "What does that mean?"

"What? It doesn't mean anything. It's just an out-loud observation."

"Hmmm. If I say it sounds demeaning, you'll say I'm indulging in paranoidism."

"Such an easy street of escape."

"A street I fear we've walked along before."

They looked at each other. "Let's stop," he said, stopping. "Shall we sit here?"

"All right."

He leaned across and inspected her face. Other people peered deeply into your eyes. Blacky scanned your face and skin tone for his reading of you.

She laughed. "Do you remember McLeod Gange, the Himalayan village where the Tibetan refugee camp was, where the Dalai Lama's private doctor would take stool and urine samples for a quick diagnosis? And his tools of research were his eyes and nose?"

"Yes."

"You remind me of him more and more."

"He was a splendid diagnostician," Blacky reflected, pleased by the comparison. "So! You seem to have held up pretty well, despite everything."

" 'Everything,' I suspect, means my marrying Johnny."

"If that's what you consider any upsetment in your life . . ."

"It's what I think you think is upsetting . . . I think it was very broad-minded and generous of Johnny to allow me coming here. I mean, after all, you are my ex. How many men let their wives go traipsing halfway around the world without them?"

Blacky stretched. "At this point, what's the difference?"

Claire laughed. "You got that right."

"There is that small droop here." He traced the skin below the side of her mouth. "I could do a quick tuck right here"—he pulled the skin taut beside her ear—"take off ten years in ten minutes."

"Jesus, Blacky, I earned those ten years. Do you mind?"

"What about work, Claire?" He frowned, concerned. "Why haven't you been working?" Good old Blacky. If he didn't get her one way, he'd get her the other. They both knew her body of work in Germany had been like paintings by Spitzweg, Germany's Norman Rockwell. Golden-yellow and idealized. She'd always portrayed them as they'd wished to be portrayed, her Germans, down a pre-Disney cobbled alley, up a pretty Berchtesgaden ski lift. A resurrected German, cleansed by his father's war of organized and brutal corruption. No smug and hideous skyscrapers of greed snagged her vista of Alpine wonderland. No, they were purified and *gemütlich*—cozy—antique, successful, harmless. They sat at the same hand-embroidered tablecloth of blind placidity she had imagined she'd despised. How she had successfully managed to avoid the modern, more intricate reality was beyond even her and a tribute, she knew, to her trusty escape mechanisms. And she was still turning over in her mind what he'd said about . . . at this point, what was the difference? What the hell was that supposed to mean? She was no longer in the running? Is that what he thought? Well, if she wasn't, that was a pretty insensitive thing to say. How was she supposed to feel? No wonder she had left him. "I am working," she said finally, sullenly. "I just did some promising stuff around the Mill. Beautiful, I think." She remembered the solitary figure, the man wandering through her pictures. She would be interested to develop those and see how they turned out.

"Oh, landscape. But what about people? It's people you do so well."

"I was rather hoping to get that at the wedding." She looked emphatically at him.

"And I'm sure you will." He patted his knees impatiently. "But that's all society stuff to a photographer of your girth. I was thinking more of political subjects. Real stuff."

Claire sighed the same weary sigh she had always sighed with him. Blacky had repeatedly tried to get her to do wartorn images, and she had always fought him. She was terrified of being shot or blown up. He, on the other hand, loved a good war and vacationed often on the outskirts of any battlefield, dropping in at the local hospital to contribute his skills. He really enjoyed that. I am not a photojournalist, Claire had argued seven thousand times. "I'm not a photojournalist," she said again this time.

"So instead you're a housewife in Queens," he said.

"A homemaker! A homemaker in Queens who is not a photojournalist."

"Yes, but you would be such a good one," Blacky insisted.

"But I don't *want* to be a photojournalist!" she shrieked, turning heads.

Claire had always been a little theatrical at heart. Blacky combed an unhurried hand through his hedge of hair. He gazed out into the sunlit stalls and people talking. His face had taken on a well-bred pinched and long-suffering expression. A young man with a cleanly shaven head had set up a stall and was harassing passersby with the idea of deporting foreigners as a solution to the German's woes. He was quite humorless, and his presence cast a bleak draftiness on the scene.

"These are bad times in Germany," Blacky said.

"Not for you, though."

Blacky looked at her over the tops of his glasses. "*Ach.* That was beneath you."

"Oh, you're right," she agreed. "I'm sorry. I'm probably just jealous that you're rich and I'm not."

"You could have been." He turned away.

"Oh, don't go giving me that poor you-deserted-me routine." She eyed him shrewdly. "You left me long before I left you."

"I never would have left you," he choked.

"Yeah, right. What about that French girl in India? What

was that? Remember?" Claire saw again the indigo silk blouse that spectacular girl had worn. She felt her lips tighten in savage jealousy. "You wanted her to come along with us in our van! *Our* van!!" She pounded her still-outraged chest. She cleared her throat, calming herself. "I was never enough for you."

"She had a lump!" Blacky sputtered.

"Oh, they all had lumps! There were plenty of ugly girls with lumps. I don't remember you bothering about any of them."

"*Ja.*" He nodded his head approvingly, remembering too. "She was unfortunately not bad. There was something irresistibly devilish about her."

Claire laughed. He had Isolde now. That should take care of that. Blacky wasn't only plastic surgeon to the photomodels and society ladies. His main work, as he saw it, was reconstruction of breast-cancer patients. You couldn't fault him for that. And any disloyalty to her had always been merely physical. There had never been, before or since, anyone who'd so staunchly understood and defended her creativity. He'd never thought her aim should be financial, as Johnny did. He thought it was enough that she be good.

"Dear Blacky." She reached across and covered his hand with hers. "I really am so happy to see you."

"Very pretty!" Isolde, perfectly timed, marched toward them.

Claire took her hand back. Only not so swiftly as Isolde would have liked.

"*Hallo, Liebling.*" Blacky stood and gathered Isolde's elbows into his hands. She let him kiss her cheek, then glared at Claire.

"You've been busy, I see," Isolde said to her, eyeing her package and meaning something else.

Claire threw up her arms and sighed. She kissed the fuming air beside Isolde's cheeks. "We were just talking about old times," she said.

"How nice." Isolde snapped her compact open and shut, taking in, in that moment of glittering reflection, the magnificence of herself in anger. Consoled, she collapsed on the bench. "I want that Gaudí-like vase at the end of the tent row," she commanded. "Do you want to go look at it?"

"Isolde, whatever you want is fine with me. You know that."

Isolde and Claire looked at him. It was really true. She could have whatever she wanted. They looked at each other. Subdued, Isolde said, "I think I'll just go buy it, then."

"Yes, do, *Liebling*," Blacky said. "Then come right back here. We'll wait. Have them send it. Tell them to send it to the Mill."

They watched her sashay importantly off.

"Why send it to the Mill?" Claire asked.

"We'll be staying there. At least there will be someone there to accept it when it comes."

"You'll be staying at the Mill? Why?"

"We've found we rather like it there."

"Oh."

"Isolde doesn't want to stay at my place, and to be frank, I can't stand hers. So many hangers-on always underfoot."

"Oh." They would no doubt be just as underfoot at the Mill, but never mind.

"We'll stay there till we find a new house."

"Ah."

"Since Hans is dead, there's no reason not to. Is there?"

"I guess not. Hey, you don't have to explain to me. Tell you the truth, I think it's the prettiest place in Munich."

"So do I." Blacky lit a cigarette with that contented air of major acquisition Claire knew only too well.

She looked at Blacky carefully. "You're not thinking of buying the Mill?"

Blacky lowered his upper lip.

"Blacky, he's barely cold."

Blacky shrugged. "Life goes on." He coughed. They all had a cough, these Germans.

"I can't believe you."

"Why not? They can't afford to keep it. At least I would restore it. Not turn it into some cultureless American hotel with coin-operated rattle-beds."

"You used to love rattle-beds."

"Yes, well. You see my point."

"What about Stella and Cosimo?"

"Stella will be gone. She wants to join some Catholic nunnery here on Heilige Hügel, Saint Catherine of Siena. They make pots as well as beer. All the cloisters around here are famous for their beer. Maybe that's what America needs. A good winery for their nunnery."

"Or at least," Claire agreed, "some good nuns for their winery. Oh, and I already know, I mean about Stella joining the convent."

"You know?" He looked at her in astonishment. "Aren't you effective! I thought we were supposed to be top secret about it. Who told you?"

"She did. But what about Cosimo?"

"Oh, well, Cosimo can stay with us. With Isolde and me."

"I thought he was mad."

"Well, yes. He is, quite. But I would never throw Cosimo out. I like him."

"You mean he would just continue to live there? Doing what?"

"Doing exactly what he does now, *verdammt noch mal!* Playing his piano. Gardening. Certainly such assets are worth room and board. I think"—Blacky's head vibrated in an unfamiliar, older-person way—"Cosimo is like poetry. I don't know. It's not much good to anyone, but"—he looked at Claire intently—"without it we are nothing more than robots. Yes, robots." He gazed out over the blue lake. "I owe his father at least that," he said.

"Why do you owe him anything?" Claire asked, puzzled. She had a hard time picturing Blacky allowing Cosimo his serenades at four in the morning after he owned the place. "I thought you two were rivals." Hadn't Isolde said Blacky despised Hans?

Blacky laughed. "On the contrary. Hans wanted Stella to marry me, or me to marry Stella."

Claire was stunned. "Of course." She knew Hans wanted someone titled and with money to marry Stella. "I don't know why I didn't think of it. But then why did Isolde say—"

"Oh, Isolde loves to think everyone is in love with her." He said this mockingly.

Claire looked at him closely. As far as she knew, this *had* always been the case. And not just in Isolde's mind.

"Never mind," he said more gently. "If it makes her feel better to think that." He shrugged. "Let her. What does it hurt?"

Claire smiled, but she wasn't so sure. She had seen Hans's adoring face when he'd welcomed Isolde that first day she'd arrived in Munich. That was not the expression of someone making someone else feel good.

A gust of wind brought with it the smell of nearby black currant blossoms. They both inhaled.

"Blacky," Claire said suddenly, "would you know where the old forester's house would be? It should be right in Diessen."

"I suppose one could find out," he said. "Whatever for?"

"Someone I know lived there once, long ago, before the

116

war. The smell of currants reminds me of something she said."

"Before the war this was mostly holiday homes for the rich," he said, as if that would eliminate anyone she would know.

"Yes. Well. Can you think of anyone we could ask? Oh, wait." Claire returned to Iris's living room and her tale of escape. What had she said? Something about a church nearby.

"Do you know what the smell of black currant blossoms reminds me of?" Blacky reminisced.

"No, what?"

"Turkey. Remember?"

"I certainly remember Turkey." She smiled back, not connecting the smell with that land at all. "Didn't we finally find a new windshield for our van in Turkey? The one I crashed in India?"

"Of course not! How can you think that? That was Iran! Herrgott, how can you confuse the two? You never took notice of anything! Not anything!"

Suddenly she remembered. Iris had said there had been no moon that night, you couldn't even see the . . . the . . . Marian Münster, that was it. "Marian Münster!" she cried out loud. "That was it!"

"Was what?" Blacky was still furious about the windshield Claire had crashed out driving through a roadblock north of Rishikesh. It had taken months to get another. Baffled, he pushed his glasses up angrily.

"Oh, let's go there, can't we? I just know I could find it from there."

"Find what?"

"The house. The house Iris von Lillienfeld was happy in."

"I'm not coming with you on one of your Catholic guilt seminars. Remember in Turkey you made me sit with you on that godforsaken bench, where the Mother of God was supposed to have landed? Do you remember?" he demanded.

"Yes, I remember. It was one of the nicest moments we had. And it was the three Marys. Our Lady, Martha's mother Mary, and Mary Magdalene was there too. They'd been condemned to certain death, sent off in a boat to die. They'd been allowed to take the corpse of Ann, the Virgin's mother. But they landed safely instead on the far-off Turkish shore. Side. Or Foça. I forget. It might well have been Ephesus. Anyway, that's why they always say where there are three Marys, there's sure to be fine weather. No, that was a wonderful place. Holy. The Virgin died there, you know, or was assumed to heaven. It wasn't godforsaken at all."

"It was a seedy, empty beach. With a filthy tourist-hungry villager boy who had a handy legend."

"There just weren't any monuments! And that boy hadn't asked us for a penny. He was just proud of the history of his place!"

"There were no monuments because nothing of note had ever happened there."

"It was the scene of a miracle, that's all."

"If that were so, your industrious Catholic exploiters would have built some moneymaking fiberglass grotto there, you can be very sure. With statues and plastic holy cards for sale."

"You know, you are such a hypocrite. You love that sort of place if it's Hindu or Buddhist. Anything like that that's geographically and culturally removed from you is poignant and spiritual, but put a Christian anointing on it, and you, with your sophisticated, self-hating, witch-hunting little heart, condemn it. Why do you live in Christian Bavaria anyway, if you hate everything its culture holds sacred? You are detestable."

They mulled this conclusion with furrowed, but not un-happy, brows.

"If you come with me," Claire proposed, "I'll tell you a secret."

"All right."

"On second thought I think I'd better go alone."

"Yes, but now you've got my curiosity up. I'm coming with."

"There will be nothing to see," she warned, then added, "I mean nothing monumental."

"I'll just give Isolde my credit card." Blacky stood. "Then we can take our time."

They found the Marian Münster easily enough, just walked steadily toward its rococo dome. The forester's house was not so easily discovered. No one on the road knew of anything like it. Having Blacky along wasn't such a good idea either. He was hot and thirsty and wanted his beer. Claire was ready to go ring any doorbell, which would have infuriated Claire, when an old man hobbled down the path.

"Yes, yes," he told her in Bavarian so thick it sounded akin to Olde English. He knew the forester's house, but they were on the wrong side of the Marian Münster. They would have to go down and then go up the other side.

"Well, that's it," Blacky proclaimed. "There will be no time now. And you haven't told me a secret, you fraud. You were just trying to entice me."

"You go on back," Claire said. "I've come this far, I really want to see it."

"No! I want my beer. It's hot and I've had enough."

"Yes. It's important to me."

"Isolde will think we've run off."

"Oh, let her be jealous, you old scaredy-cat. She'll like

you more. Come on. It's not as if there were any truth to it."

"No," he insisted, "I won't worry her."

Claire felt a pang of sorrow. "She's a lucky woman," she said, watching him turn to go. He started down the hill. She watched him raise his wrist above his head in jangling farewell.

"And what makes you so sure," she heard him say, "there would be no truth to it?"

The house was brown and winsome, old wood kept up. A whitewashed part had been added on. It was shuttered and window-boxed and adorable. A row of well-tended rosebushes led up to it behind a dark-brown picket fence. There were five different fruit trees, all bearing the starts of their fruit. If you turned, you could look out over the Ammersee. A school had been built on the land next door, but it was set very far back, and there was a boundary of tall pines between them. Real German Hänsel-and-Gretel pines. With wind in the tops. A pebbled walk to the cottage was raked and lined with pansies. Claire opened the latch and walked cautiously up the path. So this was where Iris had lived. She touched the corner of the house. Such a fine house. She could hear the faint laughter of Iris's long-ago mother. But it wasn't Iris's mother. A happy family of intent Bavarians sat comfortably at the table pushed back from the window. They devoured their weekend lunch of *Leberknödelsuppe* and *Sonnenblumenbrot*. They didn't see her, so engrossed and self-secure they were. So safe. It was then she saw the dwarf Japanese maple, gnarled and grown, still there.

A shiver of heartsick despair overwhelmed Claire. There was nothing to do. Openmouthed, she took off, lurching out the well-kept gate. She staggered down the rolling hill, past no one. It was so quiet. All she could hear were her steps and the penetrating drone of invisible bees.

Claire found them boisterously shouting to her from a rowboat. Blacky, imperious at the helm, gave directions to which no one paid any mind. Puffin had the oars but thrust them futilely upward and sideways into the bright air. Isolde lounged, legs up on the sides. She took the sun. She and Puffin were both naked from the waist up. They were all, no doubt, drunk.

Mara, crunched into the corner bench but upright, held on with both hands. She seemed to be trying not to be ill.

"*Da ist sie,*" Isolde hollered. "*Fräulein Soldatenstiefel!,*" Miss Soldierboots.

Claire waved, glad to see them, and took their picture. Blacky pointed her to the beer garden at the water's edge farther on and she nodded agreement, not hearing a word. Mara stood up and stepped, decisively, fully clothed, into the chilly water. This, to everyone's surprise, turned out to be shallow. She stood, woozy but better, her feet sunk ankle-deep in muck. Blacky, delighted, threw her a rope, and they towed her to the shore. Claire took off her own boots and hiked up her skirt and edged out to give her a hand. She moved with squeamish uncertainty. Each step sucked her in. Mara stood waiting for her.

She looked very good, Claire thought, all wet, her perm electrified in stiff, Medusa-like coils, the tips lit by the sun, her mouth relaxed at last by the drama of her resolute flamboyance.

"C'mon, I'll shoot you now, if you don't mind," she said.

"Okay." Mara hummed to herself while Claire carefully adjusted her aperture. The tidy one-masters behind them rocked on the waves from the passing ferry.

Puffin watched them from the boat. He was standing and holding on to his feeble stomach. He never should have had that *Leberkäs* this morning.

"I'm going to get her out of that water," Isolde decided. "She'll catch pneumonia like that." She struggled up out of the boat onto the nearing dock and strode toward them, leisurely reinserting herself into her blouse as she marched.

"I just wish . . ." Claire narrowed her eyes. "Oh, Isolde, good. Could you sort of just, here, just sprinkle water at her, just lightly. No. Yes. Yes, that's it."

Isolde, always happy to be part of the creative effort, took over the special effects and sprinkled just the right amount of droplets onto their movie star. She knew what she was doing. Hadn't she worked with the best photographers when she was young? She could teach Claire a thing or two. She stood humped and alert, ready with her handful of water, set to go at the cry of *"Los!"*

Claire had to admire her. She did, wondering slightly, all the while, why they were still friends. Was she Isolde's audience? Her observer from whose reactions Isolde could read how far she'd come, or how different from her she was? Because Isolde's charm was different. Besides just the obvious money thing. Hers was Magic. Making people feel the moment they were in her presence that they were at a sort of party. That they ought to have a drink. Why not? The gray of everyday skies was no longer just gray, it became, in Isolde's exclusive aura, romantic, meaningful, superbly European. For example, if you were broiling a fish and Isolde came in, she would light up, glow with the opportunity of creativity, elbow you dismissively away with your meager pat of butter. You were assigned the job of shutting off the TV, finding a good tape while she took over. Hauling soy and white wine and garlic from the shelves, she would pull out her sharp silver nail scissors and snip parsley and cilantro from the herb pots. "They'll grow thicker if you use them, *Liebling.*" She would hum, and you would find yourself humming along, no longer tired, alert and alive and as pink-cheeked as she was. So your humble evening of fish and a little white potato on the sofa in front of the news became "Poisson Magnifique," enjoyed at the table with a cloth. Whether you liked it or not.

Isolde never cooked without a phone in her ear, and before you knew it, there were three more people on the way, and you found yourself dispatched to the bistro for another couple bottles of white wine, costly and make sure it's cold.

"Whoops!" Isolde guffawed, and Claire jumped back to the present and away from the spray of water, worried for her lens. She slipped on a stone and almost lost the camera, then righted herself. They all had a good laugh. There was something wrong with Mara's skin anyway. It was all mottled. Then Claire realized Mara was crying. Really crying. Isolde put her arms around her and huddled her out of the water.

"Now you've done it," she scolded Claire. "This is all your fault. You go too far. You don't know when enough is enough. The girl is shivering with cold!"

Mara sniffled in commiseration. They stalked out of the lake, leaving Claire momentarily paralyzed with the fear that she would never be able to pull her sunken feet out of the sucking muck, but she did, then ran-sank-ran-sank-ran-sank with her arms above her head until she got to the other side of the spectrum of discomfort: the sharp vicious white pebbles of agony that stabbed her winter-coddled feet.

Isolde was toweling Mara's hair dry with her unraveled skirt. They ignored her, preferring their intimate basking in each other's attention. Claire removed her own heavy sweater and broke through this ball of privacy as she gave it to Mara. Mara managed a thin smile. They were creating a stir sitting there on the ground until Isolde glared haughtily and long at the dazzled picnickers. So successful was Isolde's mean look that it was the picnickers who got up and moved subserviently away.

Mara and Isolde had their cigarettes.

"Feeling better?" Claire asked.

"No," Mara said, and they all realized at once that they were none of them feeling well. They were tired. This fabulous weather was such a stress. Coming. Going. They huddled together against the impertinent sun, the two puffing an umbrella of smoke around themselves.

"I'm still not over my abortion," Mara confided, plucking at her hair.

"Tch." Isolde smoothed the ground beside her.

"It was such an ordeal. The thing is, I don't think it went very well. I mean, they got it out all right, but then they couldn't stop my bleeding." She threw her arms into the air. "I mean, it wouldn't stop." She leaned closer. "They thought they were going to lose me. Really. The doctor told me. After. They had some time of it, he said. I mean, people still die during operations in this day and age. You would think they wouldn't, but they do. So you never know."

Isolde scratched her cheek. "How far along were you?"

"Four months."

"*Ach.*" Isolde nodded. "That's why."

Claire covered her own belly with her arms and blinked away the sudden assault of sadness. The baby she and Johnny had lost had not been much older than that. They had been battling as usual. Not about the baby, that was something they both wanted. She'd been screaming at Johnny just before she'd begun to bleed. He never did a thing, she'd yelled at him. She hated him, she'd yelled. She'd never said that before. And then she'd started to hemorrhage.

When Claire awoke in the hospital, a doctor had stood beside her bed. She hadn't known this one. His pocket had been full of pens, and her eyes had tried to focus on them. She hadn't been able to understand what it was he'd been saying.

"And what we want to know"—he'd pressed her wrist to reawaken her—"is whether you would be prepared to hand the fetus over for experimental purposes. If you would just sign this release . . ."

She had fallen back into the oblivion of drugged unconsciousness and tuned him out. That was how she'd found out that she'd lost her baby. That had been a good two years ago, and she still couldn't bear to talk about it. She saw herself once again as she walked down the broad sweep of hospital entrance stairs. There was her family waiting there in the car for her, their faces wanting her to be well. To be theirs again. Her empty arms were at her sides.

"You didn't want the baby?" Claire heard Isolde confront Mara.

Mara shrugged. "What could I do? He didn't want it."

'He,' Claire realized, was Temple.

"And," Mara continued, "it wasn't because of that thing I'd had with Puffin, either."

"What thing?" Isolde asked.

"Oh, that little fling. It meant nothing, really. It was over almost before it got started. And the timing was off. So the baby couldn't have been Puffin's."

"You slept with Puffin?" Claire said.

"It was really just a ploy of mine to come between them. I was always jealous of Puffin. They were so close, you see."

"I can't believe you slept with Puffin!" Isolde said.

"Oh, Puffin's all right," Mara said. "He even talked to Temple for me. He told him it was his duty to marry me. Or at least stand by me. But I wouldn't have had to be married. I'm not like that."

"Interesting," Isolde breathed.

Mara went on. "I told him, I said, 'If you didn't want me to get pregnant, you should have opened your mouth instead of your zipper. You should have told me you didn't want a family.' Oh, it was awful. We were staying with his friends on Wienerplatz. It's funny, the things you remember. After I came home from the hospital, the flat was empty. I thought I'd take a bath. A long soak, you know. I must have drifted off. I heard someone let himself into the flat and I—I was startled, like guilty. I jumped from the bath. There was no towel, so I ran to our room. It was Temple. I was relieved until I saw that he was furious. He was so angry. I couldn't understand him at first. He kept talking about how we were guests in this house and how I'd left a great trail of water all over the parquet. The two of us just stood there, in someone else's place. Me naked and him dressed and furious, looking down and down and down at the great puddles of water I'd left on their beautiful waxed floor. Their poor floor."

"You should have had it anyway," Isolde said finally. "He would have come around."

Claire stared at her. What good would that advice do now?

"No." Mara shook her head sadly. "I didn't want him that way. I didn't even want a baby, really, I just wanted him and I thought . . . I thought . . . God. Listen to me! How idiotic I sound. I thought it would make him love me again. And what happened? It wound up making him hate me."

"I'm sure he doesn't hate you," Claire said, hating herself for hoping it was so.

"Oh, he does." Tears ran freely down her cheeks. "He thinks I am the reason for all his troubles. He's as much as said so. And look at my face. Can you blame him? Every time I come out in the sun it gets worse." She pushed her hair away from her skin. A butterfly of dark pigment made a grotesque stain across her features. Now that the makeup was all rubbed off, there was no hiding it.

"The mask of pregnancy," Isolde said. "Some women get it from the pill."

"It looks worse on film," Mara admitted, apprehending Claire's probable waste of film. The makeup doesn't cover it on film. The camera picks it right up. What is it they say? The camera never lies."

"Oh, it will go away," Isolde said, "eventually. I had it too."

"But you have kids to show for it," Mara said bitterly.

"It wasn't those kids." Isolde said. "I had another one, too."

"Oh," she said, very still.

The three of them looked out at the water. The light was fading now. You could see the little bits of filth and advertising, lapping at the shore.

It was dark and chilly when they got back home, but Claire had it in her mind to go up into the tower and inspect the bell. She went to her room, scuttled out of her clothes and into a pair of jeans and her favorite (and only) cashmere sweater from Bendel's After-New-Year's Giant Half-Off Sale. She searched the dresser top for the camera battery she'd left up there. The girl must have mistaken it for *Dreck* and swept it into the trash when she came to reline her trash basket and put the chocolate on her pillow. (Bavarian hospitality required wrapped chocolates on the pillowcase. No matter what else would happen in bed, the dreams must be sweet.) It didn't matter, really; her other battery would still do. At least the girl had left the window open, the way Claire liked it. There was nothing worse for her than some American hotel rooms where they sealed you into a synthetic, suffocating, albeit burglar-proof, gardenia pit.

No one was around, but she decided to take the back stairs anyway. These met the front stairs on the landing just below the bell tower. Up she went, tippy-toeing to a strange sound. What was this, she wondered, rats? People? It was muffled and dry. She opened the creaky door to the attic. The noise stopped. The long, brown, old-fashioned attic, clean as only a German attic could be, silently allowed itself to be inspected in the moonlight. Hell, she thought, as good a place as any to start looking for a cache of World War II diamonds. There were neatly rowed pieces of furniture and rolled-up rugs. Then she saw it. There, on a faded lime-and-maroon-striped silk ottoman, a huge live bird was watching. He regarded her with something between disdain and mild interest. "What's up?" she greeted him with more cool than she felt. He narrowed bird eyes at her.

"Stuck?" she asked him nicely. "Here." She walked cautiously to the window closest to her and heaved it more open. Out the great bird flew. He was white with green and purple markings that fanned out when he flew. Beautiful. She'd seen this fellow before, pecking garden seeds. He must have wandered in, then been unable to take off. She stood at the window and watched him cross the green landscape, watching him arcing smoothly over the pink cherry blossoms and then landing safely on the Roman Bridge, with its lamps. She must go down there. She must look at the Mill from there.

Along the wall were the shelves of neatly packed photograph albums Evangelika had warned her not to touch. She walked over to have a closer look. There were yards of them. She picked up the latest. Recent photographs of Stella and Cosimo, horsing around along the Isar, Cosimo dumping a balloon of water on Stella's laughing head. Pity she didn't want to be a model. She really was photogenic. Well, not a pity. But she was going to be hard not to photograph. Claire trailed her fingers along the shelf of albums, way,

way back to the start, the early, prewar stuff. She pulled a few down and sat, cross-legged, on the rolled-up rug. It took her a couple of albums. She peered closer. It had to be. The same ivory skin and black hair twirled into a fashionable chignon. The same look, only on a young and vibrant woman, flushed by exuberance and . . . what? Love?

Iris was standing, in a hat with a little veil on it, behind a sled. The photograph was supposed to be of the old woman on the sled, but the photographer hadn't been able to stop himself from focusing on the young woman looking at him so unabashedly smitten. So lovely.

There were all sorts of reasons people became what they were in life. Seeing a series of photographs like this, so transportingly beautiful and full of light, Claire was overwhelmed with reassurance and hope. She looked through the albums before and after this one but couldn't find another shot of Iris. Still, it was a marvelous picture and she must show it to Iris. She lifted it from its paper-frame edges and stuck it into her pocket. She also took the one beside it. It was the same striking, snowy view of Saint Hildegard's Mill, but there were no people, only a bird sitting on a fence. The walls around her creaked and groaned. She felt as though she was being observed.

She turned and scoped the trim attic again. No one would have hidden anything here. It was so . . . so occupied. She didn't know why she was so sure, but she was. Did she imagine she had some telepathic connection now with the von Lillienfeld stones? Or was she just tired? She leaned out the window and observed the dark world, shimmering with its newfound frenzied lushness. Yes, she concluded, she did. Somewhere in this mysterious place they waited patiently, cunningly, to be found. And she was the one, by cracky, who would find them.

She left the attic and started up the narrow stairs to the bell tower. Almost there, she thought she heard a noise, a beating or flapping. It was an uncanny sound. She didn't like it. She wished she had a flashlight, for here it was really dark. It was stupid to go up alone to the accident scene on a dark night. So she was a coward. So what? If Hans could lose his footing on that treacherous ledge, then certainly so could she. She turned and started back to her room when she heard Cosimo playing Schuman's "Scenes from Childhood." How deftly he played! The alluring sound pulled her to the closed door. She stood there, rapt, enjoying now the sounds of old creaking beams when they were mixed with music, when someone came up behind her. She jolted.

"Ich bin's. It's me, Fräulein Bibi Wintner." The woman gave her a sour look for being so jumpy. Or for standing outside the family room like a thief. "Bibi," as she now called herself, opened the door after a harsh reprimanding knock, and there, Claire saw, were Stella and Father Metz at the venerable chessboard and Cosimo at the piano. The room was lacquered china red.

She felt idiotic, but Stella smiled and stood and motioned her to come in. It was an exquisite room; there were antique rugs on the tables and jugs of flowers on top of them. *"Bring doch noch eine Tasse."* She bade Bibi to go get another cup. A look passed between them. Fräulein Wintner scowled at Stella as she left. Once more up and down the stairs, Claire could just hear her thinking, and for this cow.

"Really, no," Claire protested, but Stella insisted, and Claire couldn't help thinking what a rude awakening this girl would have had, had she chosen the world. The cloister wasn't going to coddle her either, she was sure, not the way she was used to being coddled. But at least she would be safe. Cosimo went right on playing. He didn't mind strangers so much as he minded noise. Sitting comfortably in a striped Louis XIV wing chair, eating a mixture of dried fruit, nuts, and fresh kiwis imported from Israel, was Temple Fortune.

They held each other's eyes for an unrealistic amount of time. Even as she looked, Claire thought this is ridiculous. And still she looked. The room grew wider and longer, and the lamps on all the tables throbbed peripherally.

"Hi," she finally managed. "I thought you were in London."

"I never left Munich." Temple narrowed his gentle eyes at her. He was so handsome and boyish. His chin went down and his forehead wrinkled into middle-aged familiarity. He was adorable. She could easily climb into his lap and cover him with kisses. She could almost see the strong gust of her desire steam across the room in a white hurling vent that curled up around him like something gossamer, like lunacy, indelible.

"Mr. Temple was detained at the airport," Stella revealed excitedly. She drank, Claire was astonished to see, her mineral water straight from the Überkinger bottle.

Old Father Metz put a soothing hand on her rigid shoulder, stopping her. She was all coiled up, pacing, ready to spring. Father shook his head sadly. "As if there wasn't already enough pain for these children," he said in his heavy accent. "Now the police say that perhaps Hans did not die by falling down but was dead before the fall."

"What?"

"Maybe dead. There's a big difference," Temple said, getting up and padding across the room, each foot touching the floor with wincing squeamishness.

"They are asking no one to leave for the moment," Father Metz qualified, "until they straighten this mess out. Make finished the autopsy. So they stopped Mr. Fortune at the *Passkontrolle*," Father Metz explained.

"And here I am." Temple Fortune put both hands up.

"Surely they don't suspect you." Claire dropped into a fat feather cushion on the rococo *bergère*.

"I'm afraid we're all suspects," Father Metz said, "even

131

me." He barked a laugh that said, "as ludicrous as that sounds."

"Even you." Puffin Hedges, drink in hand, entered the room from the patio and smiled at Claire.

Claire smiled back. A tidy German prison cell for the rest of her life. Very funny. "Well," she said. "I'm sure the German police know what they're doing."

"Only an American would say something like that," Puffin said to Temple Fortune. They shared their chummy look. They must be very close, she thought, picking up a simple piece of raku pottery to admire, appraising it from every angle. It was miraculously plain.

"I hate ceramics." Puffin, watching her, made a face. "My mother had all sorts of those atrocities around the house while I was growing up. Dust catchers. Horrible."

"Ah!" Claire exclaimed. "There's the dog!"

"Yes." Father Metz ruffled the dog's ears and passed him a morsel of *Apfelkuchen* on a party napkin.

"I'm glad to see that." Claire smiled at the old priest. "So you've taken him on, have you?"

"Whoosh! Not me!" the old priest laughed and slapped his hefty thigh, his dandruff shaking down like talcum powder. His old black suit was shiny and worn. You could tell he did his own ironing. His trouser pleats had a many-faceted edge. Claire's heart broke for him. It occurred to her that he was here to see how she liked the car. Did he think she would buy it tonight? Oh my God. He was fidgety and excited, was Father. He held his little plate and transported each crumb carefully onto his waiting tongue, then snapped his keen mouth shut with a surprised, delighted smile to tease the dog. "Na, na, the *Hundi* is young, aren't you, boy? Many years to go yet, eh? *Was?* He'll be needing someone young to take good care of him, won't he? Doesn't need an old master popping off and leaving him in *stich* again, eh? Leaving him alone again. Young

Friedel will take good care of you, won't he? Eh?"

"Is that the gardener?" Claire asked, pale with guilt about the car.

"That's right," Puffin said meaningfully. "You noticed him, did you, mmm?"

"I notice just about everything, Mr. Hedges," Claire said right back. "That's my job, as I see it." The nerve of him! Insinuating she looked at all the boys! For that's what the inference was. And for Temple Fortune's benefit, she was sure. So Puffin liked her well enough, but only for his own amusement. Not, she suspected, because he wanted her to himself, but rather because he wanted Temple Fortune to himself. Never mind. Little boys and their friends. Go figure. She felt her back go up.

"As I *see* it! Get it?" Puffin was bent at the waist and leaning over Father Metz. "Because she's a photographer! Get it?"

"Puff, you're drunk." Temple Fortune, like a permissive parent, shook his head apologetically, but full of love. He turned to Claire. "If he wasn't in charge of our meeting expenses, I'd send him straightaway home." Claire understood. Her own sister Carmela was a never-ending series of embarrassments wherever you took her. She smiled benevolently at Temple.

Bibi Wintner stood at attention beside Claire. "There's a call for you, Fräulein."

"Oh dear," Claire said.

"Use this one, please." Stella Gabriella accommodatively offered her phone.

Bibi Wintner didn't like her using the family phone, Claire noted. She probably was thinking this (paying guests in the family room!) would never be the case if Hans were still alive. Claire probably would have dashed all the way down to the lobby, but it gave her such pleasure to offend this Bibi Wintner who insisted on calling her "Fräulein" when she knew very well she was "Frau." She smiled at them all and picked up the phone. "Hello," she said, expecting Blacky or Isolde. It was Johnny. "Everything all right?" she gasped, imagining Anthony with appendicitis in Disney World.

"Everything's great. You good?"

"Yes. Yes. The kids?"

"I talked to everyone. They're fine. Anthony's spending all his grandma's money, and Dharma is spending all Carmela's."

"That's good." She relaxed. "That's good."

"Hey! You got that job!"

"What job?"

"That Jupiter Dodd thing. The cigarette campaign. He called right after you left. You got it. How about that?"

Claire's heart sank. "Oh. That. I'm afraid I haven't decided whether or not I can take it, Johnny."

"What do you mean? You got it. He told me you did."

"Yes. Well, the thing is, I didn't take that job *yet.*"

"You *what?!*"

The entire room, no longer talking, heard Johnny's incredulous response.

"You see, I'm not exactly sure I can handle that just now." Still calm, she grimaced at them and twirled the telephone cord around her finger.

"What is this, Claire? One of your goddamn moral issues? Is that what this is? Because I got a pile of bills here with your name written all over them."

"Yes, I know, Johnny—"

"I got Macy's, I got A and S, I got American Express, I got—"

"We can talk about this anoth——"

"Or did you forget Christmas, maybe?" he shouted. "All those damn toys the kids *had* to have, couldn't live without? Because I haven't forgotten them, because you

134

know why, Claire? Because I'm standing on top of the whole mess of them right here in the dining room where they left them because nobody the hell wants them anymore, half of them are broken, all right? I got the toys on the floor, I got the bills on the table. I got you over there in la-la land, and after we hang up I got three more bill collectors gonna call and give me their showdown low-down. You got that? So now you tell me how you're too good to contribute to the nicotine addiction of the already washed-up, war-torn European continent, because I know that's what you're gonna say because that's what you always say. You want it both ways, baby. You want the goodies from the high life and the health benefits from a clock-puncher like me. Well, you can't have it both ways. And I'm telling you, if you don't take that cushy effing job, *you* are the one who's being immoral here. You got that? You. Oh. And by the way, I sold the car."

By the change in tone, by the mere civility of this last sentence, Claire's alert antenna went up.

"What car?"

"Your car."

"My car?"

"Yeah, your car, which *I* gave you, which I pay the insurance for, which you don't need, at least that's what you kept telling me; if we moved up to Richmond Hill North, you wouldn't need a car because you could go everywhere on your bicycle. Am I right? Did you tell me that over and over again to get me to move up here or not?"

Claire looked at old Father Metz, uncomfortable in his too-tight visiting pants, and smiled. He had asthma and he could no longer smoke. Only he and Stella did not. The room was full of smoke. They sat in a foggy mushroom of their own making, batting their baby wands of concentrated fire for emphasis. This one coughed. That one coughed. They looked great, though. Svelte.

"I'm still not sure about that job, Johnny. I might not," she said, sure now that she would take it. She could put some kids up on the Roman Bridge, give them some cigarettes, sign them up with releases, and sit back while she pulled in the money. She would buy old Father Metz's car, she mused. She'd have it shipped. Wouldn't that be something?

"I'll kill you, Claire," Johnny said.

Claire trilled a merry laugh. "Do try not to worry about me so much. I'll call you back tomorrow. I'm on someone else's phone." She heard her doorbell ring in Queens. "Who's that?" she asked, curious.

"No one," Johnny said.

"I mean at the door."

"Nobody's here, I told you," he lied.

He couldn't fool her. She knew her opulent doorbell sound. It was so unlike the tinny *bzzz* of her youth, she would recognize it anywhere. It was probably, she decided hotly, the liquor-store delivery boy. If she wasn't mad before, she was now.

"Good-bye," she said.

"Good-bye," he said.

And they both hung up.

"*D*arjeeling or *Pfefferminz?*" Stella held both teapots in the air.

"Oh, *Pfefferminz*," Claire answered absently. She walked across the room to the piano. "That's beautiful," she said to Cosimo. "What's this, now? *Was ist dieses schöne Stück?*"

Stella stood almost immediately beside her, sort of on guard. Her breath was on Claire's cheek. Did prayer and goodness make people smell so sweet? More likely the tea. Stella seemed frightened. What did she think? She was going to hurt Cosimo? Bite him, maybe? Claire was cranky, returned by the phone call to that quarantine family women live in, that isolated spot from where there is no decent way out of, for husbands know that whatever they do or say, their wives will put up with it for the sake of the children, yes, even in this day and age. There was no escape from the life one had chosen for one's self. And there were no tears of frustration and despair to comfort the happily married.

Cosimo turned his grave face to Claire. "It's Schumann's 'Träumerei,' he said in perfect English.

"It's lovely," she said warmly. What a nice fellow. He wasn't crazy at all. "You're an artist," she said, cheered by his existence. There was salvation in the world of art. Anything could happen. Cosimo ducked his head and went on playing. He was as dark as Stella was fair, younger, with great wet South American brown eyes and blue-black hair. Like the grandfather, Claire thought. Like Iris's Adam. Dark and swarthy. Only the long limbs were kin to Stella's. He rewarded her by saying, "Do you like Gershwin?"

"Yes," she said.

He went right into "Rhapsody in Blue."

"And they say America is devoid of culture," Father Metz bellowed.

"Stuff and nonsense!" Puffin clicked his tongue. "They've obviously never seen the 'I Love Lucy' reruns."

"Or listened to jazz," Temple agreed.

"I say, Claire," Puffin Hedges said, "is Breslinsky your husband's name or your family name?"

They all looked at her, interested in her reply.

"My family name. My married name is Benedetto."

"Ah. Now do you spell Breslinsky with *y* or with an *i?*"

"With a *y.*" She took a rough brown sugar cube meant for coffee and dropped it in her delicate and almost-see-through Rosenthal cup. It dissolved to a puddle of amber.

She thought how nice that in the future he would look for her work.

"Hmm. Now the Christian Poles spell 'Breslinski' with an *i*."

She looked up, surprised. "Really?"

"Yes indeed."

"I didn't know that."

"Oh yes. So let's see. So that means your *father's* family would have been Jewish. Your father's father."

"You are only a Jew"—Father Metz swallowed the last of his cake—"if your mother was a Jew."

"Well, yes, but," Stella said, "there are a lot of Jewish people who would say that is not technically so."

"Oh, it is so." Father Metz looked over his specs. He wore them low down on his nose for reading, and there they sat, conveniently out of the way at all times, even when he went looking for them.

"Hang on a minute here." Claire laughed in a labored way. "I'm afraid, as far as I know, I am Irish as the lakes of Killarney, Polish as kielbasa, and both sides as Catholic as Saint Anthony's Lost and Found. I know they shortened the name to Breslin at one time to sound more American. My father changed it back when he was young. Maybe it got misspelled going back and forth." She laughed, a strained laugh. "Knowing my father's spelling, that could well be." No one took much notice of this explanation.

Puffin filled his empty cup. "I suppose it is a bit of a shock. You walk in the room one thing. Then you walk out quite another."

Claire shrugged. "I'm just not so sure you're right." In her mind she was reviewing her father's Polish aunts, lining them up in her mother's chaotic kitchen; those aunts with babka and jars of homegrown fennel and cherries carried in overcoated arms in spring, she thought of their disapproving faces, their high cheekbones and pudgy noses . . .

Naaa . . . Still, she wondered. Wouldn't that be a hoot?

They all scrutinized Claire's until-now Christian face for attic-nook remnants of hidden Judaism.

"You have," Temple Fortune interjected softly, "what I would call a determined face."

He was drinking, Claire noted, not tea but a particular brand of Franconian wine, a *Boxbeutel* from Würzburg. She could do with that herself, she thought, and wondered if anyone would ask.

"Thank you," she said, pleased that he would examine her face at all, "I think."

"Now Stella." Puffin continued on his theme, walking over to her and putting his hand under her chin. "Stella has what everyone would call a beautiful face." Stella flinched and moved his hand away, appalled.

"For a minute I could have sworn you were going to say an Aryan face," Claire said.

"Yes, it is that," Father Metz agreed. They all looked intently into Stella's Aryan face.

"Classical." Temple nodded his head approvingly.

Bibi Wintner, at the sideboard, dropped a china tea ball onto the iron trivet, and it cracked into three pieces.

"Oooh." Cosimo stopping playing, complained out loud. "I liked that one. It had the roosters painted on it."

On second thought, Claire thought, maybe he is off.

Cosimo went over to the sideboard and took the pieces from Bibi Wintner. He cupped them in his hand and held them like a little bird fallen from its nest.

"It was pretty," Stella agreed. "Never mind," she crooned, "perhaps Evangelika can mend it. She's awfully good at mending things." She looked from face to face. "You'd never know they had been broken. In her purse she keeps nails and a hammer."

Fräulein Wintner stood there glaring at the floor. Her mouth was pressed into a tight, dark line. She left the room.

Claire wondered what was going on. She turned and found Temple undressing her with his eyes. Instead of turning away, she narrowed her own and held his gaze. Now he knew that she knew that he knew.

"Who's pretty?" Father Metz's hearing wasn't half as good as it used to be. He struggled into a huffing, corpulent try at a sit-up. "Mara?"

"Nails and a *hammer*," Puffin said crisply. "Not Mara." The way he said it implied there was no question it could be Mara.

"Mara Sauberei," Temple Fortune said loyally, "was the loveliest girl in Munich at one time. She was so brilliant, you could hardly look at her."

Claire doubted, somehow, that Mara would be heartened by this report.

"That the one"—Father Metz tapped his cheek with his palm—"who looks so ill?" All these young women, to him, were becoming a blur.

"She has," Cosimo interjected, "a green and guilty aura."

Temple Fortune became upset. "It's this ghastly place." He got up, walked in a circle, sat down. "It's bloody haunted!"

"Temple brought Mara here to recover, didn't you, Temp?" Puffin said soothingly.

Temple glared at Puffin. "It's this place, I tell you."

"Uh-oh." Puffin went quite meek. "I must have missed something." He got up and trundled across the Oriental. He lit a cigarette. His socks were down around his blue-veined, hairless ankles.

Father Metz, attempting a fresh approach, said smoothly, "Fräulein *Morgen* is one of the great ladies of fashion."

"Well?" Puffin waved his arms like some demented circus ringleader. He had on somebody else's hat. "We have right here an expert on the subject, Claire Breslinsky with a *y*. Photographer of fashion. And that, my dears, will sell."

Claire was beginning to feel fed up. "Yes, but fashion isn't really about selling," she said. "And once it is, it doesn't."

"Sure it does," Father Metz said.

"She means the spring of fashion, doesn't she?" Puffin explained, overly patient. "The source."

"Of course you're right," the priest agreed. He loved this kind of thing. "And if it does, it usually shouldn't."

Claire felt wrong. She shouldn't have said that, she realized. It was the sort of thing Temple Fortune would have liked to have said himself. Her having claimed it as her own left him rather at the opposite end, a place itself accusing him of motive in his art. And not so obscurely at that, especially after his bit about making expenses. Oh well. What was wrong with that? He couldn't be where he was if he were so fragile, would he? Still, she sensed she'd placed herself against him somehow, if only by refusing to allow him to defend his girlfriend around her. Of course he loved her, why shouldn't he?

"My father . . ." Cosimo, who'd gone back to his Schumann after the broken-china incident, stopped playing and folded his music book shut. He certainly had everyone's attention. "My father felt that art was merely a vehicle to riches. He never grasped the joy one could experience creating it. It wasn't his fault, really. His father dead. And Omi—Grandmother—she was plain stupid. So he never had a chance, you see. He never *learned* to love art."

"Never mind," Claire couldn't stop herself from saying, "my husband feels the very same way." Was that Stella administering an Indian burn to Cosimo's wrist? Good Lord.

Of course, Temple Fortune reminded himself, she's happily married.

"It's always the ones who pay the bills who feel that way," Puffin said. "Oops"—he looked from Claire to Cosimo to Stella—"sorry, loveys."

"That's all right," Claire said, wondering suddenly if Iris's diamonds would have fit in Hans's expensive French clock, which sat so charmingly ticking away the years on the mantel. "You're probably right. Or at least half right. I don't know anything anymore. I'm exhausted, tired."

"Not every day one is suspected of murder," Puffin said genially.

"You have more crust than a baker saying something like that, here, now," Temple Fortune said.

"Nevertheless," Cosimo said, "it's true." What did he care what some Brit filmmaker thought.

"I'm leaving," Puffin said.

"Splendid," Temple said.

"And I'm going to bed." Cosimo yawned.

"Coming, Temp?" Puffin Hedges stood waiting at the door for Temple in what he felt was an appropriately haughty pose.

"Go on ahead." Temple didn't look at anyone. He tossed a knight from the chessboard into the air.

Stella went over and gently patted Father Metz's arm. He'd fallen asleep. Abruptly, he woke up and shouted, *"Will sie das Auto?"* Does she want the car?

Stella clucked appropriately calming words and hoisted the old fellow to his feet. The dog got up as well.

"You're going to have to hold the dog," Stella said over her shoulder as she supported him out. "He makes such an awful racket when Father tries to leave."

"I'll get him." Bibi Wintner rushed over and grabbed the dog by the scruff of his neck. The dog yelped in pain.

Shocked, Claire couldn't move. She hadn't even noticed Bibi Wintner had come back in.

Temple Fortune went over and smoothly removed the dog from Bibi's grasp. "You'll be awfully tired after all that's happened. Here. Let me."

"All right." She looked at him gratefully and patted her nice hair. The lace of her slip peeked out from her prim skirt's long-standing tussle with static as she left the room.

Stella rose gracefully and shook hands formally, first with Claire and then with Temple Fortune, before she glided out the door.

The clocks did their rich minuets.

Temple turned and looked at her. "Alone at last." He smiled.

"Yes," she laughed. She felt unsure and got ready to bolt. To make sure she didn't, she took hold of the wooden banister atop the hope chest beside her. She was not going to look back on this moment years down the road and wonder what would have happened had she had the courage to stay and challenge her infernal shyness.

"Wine?" He held the bottle up by the neck.

"I'd love a glass of wine," she said. Thank God. Now that pearly feeling of bliss would loosen her shoulder muscles and she would, if nothing else, sleep well.

Neither of them knew how to begin. Then he said, "Mara told me about your photographs the day we all met. She was very excited. Mara doesn't usually get that way about women, you know. If she feels strongly or is impressed with them at all, it's to despise them. She said she liked your work so much because you did story pictures. I think she meant she enjoys the labyrinthian plot somewhere in the background."

"I beg your pardon! I think she must know what she meant."

"Sorry?"

"I mean I hate it when men explain what it was their girl-friends meant."

They regarded each other carefully.

"There's a nice word." She went to meet him halfway. " 'Labyrinthian.' Not one I would use. An English person's word. Story pictures will do very well for me. But then, I am American."

She was referring to Puffin's comment earlier on, he knew. "I am not British either," he admitted. "I'm Irish."

"Hoo. I knew that."

"Did you." A statement.

"I did. Here's something else that will surprise you. I remember you as Douglas Dougherty, the guitar player for the Salty Dogs."

"No! Oh, God. No one remembers that."

"I do. So now you know my deep secret."

"You mean my secret, don't you?" He sipped his wine.

"Mine too. You were a fantasy of mine. My favorite fantasy, I'm afraid." There.

He blushed. The room grew warm. A mixture of power and tenderness encompassed her.

"I've embarrassed you," she said. Her words came out so slowly and separated. She could hear them still in the airless room. There they were, over the edge.

"I am so glad you have," he said. "I haven't felt this particularly beside myself in a very long time."

"If that is true," she said, "I'm glad."

"You doubt my essence?"

"Only my ability to affect it."

"Well, don't," he said. "Then we might be matched."

"I think we might be," she agreed.

There was nothing courtly or romantic in the way they felt: their eyes held on to each other, the inevitable, lustful recognition of the hunter and the hunted. Which, she only wondered, was which? She had a hard time holding on to her face. It wobbled away from her, her mouth loose and rubbery and uncontrollable.

She turned her back, walked across the room, grabbed hold of her face and squeezed, and put her teacup on the cluttered tray. The clock was in front of her. She would never be able to get that clock open and shut without breaking it. It was too intricate, too sophisticated. Temple came and stood beside her. "Let me help you with that," he said. Their arms were crossed, both holding on to the tray. They stood like that, like ice skaters dancing, looking down at their similar hands, not old or young, long pinkish fingers from the same tribe, scrubbed clean and holding tight. They both wore silver rings with small hunks of turquoise. Hers was from the Himalayas, and his from New Mexico. They watched, spellbound, each other's almost identical adornment. The door opened abruptly and the wind blew in, frightening them both. No one was there. The hall was dark, the light gone out. She pulled away and lifted the tray.

"Leave it," he whispered and she put it down.

"Oh, here you are, oh good." Isolde came galloping in. She wore a peach satin robe, and her long dark hair flew in racy tendrils when she moved her head. Claire wondered if she ever slept. She did, she knew she did, she'd seen her sleeping, but Isolde was one of those people always on their guard, even in sleep, and when she woke it was right up, not groggily and bewildered like herself (needing forty minutes on her own and a potful of coffee). Isolde would open her eyes and start right in on the same conversation she was having when she'd put out the lights.

"I'm going to kill that little housekeeper," Isolde fumed, pacing the room, not noticing the soft dissolve of Claire's and Temple Fortune's passion.

"Where is she?"

"She's gone to bed," Claire murmured.

"She has, has she? That bitch. Wait till I get her. I'll kill her. Do you know what she did? First, and if this isn't bad enough, she accuses me of having an affair with Puffin Hedges! Of all people! And then, when I laughed and told her that wouldn't work, she accused me of murdering Hans. Murdering Hans! She told the police I was up on the second floor with Hans before he died. Can you believe it? She actually incriminated me in a murder investigation!"

Claire was calmed by the news. She hadn't wanted to be the one to tell the police where Isolde had been. She probably never would have. Then again, she might have. This was not just the matter of an unseemly affair but someone's life, never mind that everyone seemed better off that he was dead.

"She always dreaded me," Isolde said, fumbling with the cigarette box.

"What, that wee lass?" Temple said.

"She's the housekeeper," Isolde said. "She ran all Hans's affairs. Wee lass?" she implored Claire. "Men are so innocent! That little bitch! Always sticking her little pig nose in where it doesn't belong. *So eine Drecksau!*" Isolde slammed shut the empty, elaborate china cigarette box. "Who's got one?" she demanded, holding two fingers in the air and standing, other hand on hip. Joan Crawford in a multi-rage.

Where would Claire ever find a friend like this again? She knew well enough not to say a word, though. As no one ran to accommodate Isolde, she glared at them, seeing them finally.

"Aha," she declared. "I've interrupted something."

Temple nimbly picked up the tray and put it out the door on the floor. He shut the door. "I was just going to offer Claire a job shooting stills for our film," he said.

"Is that what you were about to do?" Claire said.

"Claire doesn't handle that line of work." Isolde dismissed the idea with a condescending frown. Then: "I'm going to have that little vixen out of here. Just you wait. She's poured her last little bit of venom on me, that one has!"

"I'd love to shoot the stills," Claire said. "Does it pay actual money?" Maybe she really could afford Father Metz's car. Even without the cigarette campaign.

Isolde regarded Claire with astonished contempt. "Claire"—she practically stomped her foot—"you couldn't be more stupid! Where is your sense of strategy?"

"Not as much as you're used to, I'm sure," Temple continued, troubled. "But I'll talk to Puffin about making it a little more than a regular would get, all right? After all, it's to our benefit. Someone of your talent, aye?"

"Thank you," she said softly.

"You can't go anywhere, can you?" He laughed.

"No," she agreed, "I am yours entirely."

He winced as though he had been struck.

So no sense of strategy was indeed the best strategy. Isolde was furious. Not only didn't they fear her, they didn't even notice her! "Do you know what I'm going to do?" she said, glowering. "I'm going to marry him straightaway. I'll marry him this weekend. I'll fix her cart."

"Wagon," Claire said. "Fix her wagon."

"Yes," Isolde said. She threw back her head and laughed.

"Good a reason as any to wed." Temple's brow crumpled shut. He ought to go, he realized. There was something predatory and unscrupulous about Isolde. He ought to be attracted to her but wasn't, and so she had no use for him. She dismissed him in the strangest way. She simply willed him gone.

He stood up slowly, creaking his medium frame upright. Isolde watched him with lowered eyelids, disdainfully and impatiently.

Claire felt herself flutter with annoyance. He ought to

stand up to Isolde, she couldn't help feeling. Johnny would. Johnny was very good with superior women. But then Johnny was a bully of sorts and reduced flamboyant women with outright disapproval. And Temple was fair and reasonable. She raised her chin rockily in his direction and smiled sweetly at him. He looked at her, bit his lip and shook his head as if to say he was going crazy without her.

"*Gute Nacht,*" Isolde said imperiously. Her upbringing had been exclusive enough that she felt she needn't worry about the likes of him.

"Good night." He bowed stiffly at Isolde, then came back over to Claire and bent down. Claire thought he was about to kiss her forehead. She could feel his breath on her eyes. He picked up her hand and kissed it while he held her eyes with his. "Take care you don't meet the ghost in the hallway," he whispered mockingly. He turned abruptly and left. The door swung shut.

"I'd be careful there if I were you," Isolde said shrewdly.

"You're a fine one to talk." Claire tittered nervously.

"You know I don't mean it from a moral standpoint."

"Well, what then? You can't tell me you feel for Johnny. You've always despised him."

"At least Johnny has a sense of humor about himself. He might be awful, but at least he knows it. I mean, there's nothing you can blame someone for for being a barbarian."

"So what are you doing? Blaming Temple Fortune because he's assumed an attitude of his affluence? Hard-earned affluence?"

"It's just a facade. It came to him too late to make any difference in his character." Isolde got up and threw open the window. She turned and sat on the sill and regarded Claire. "Hot flashes," she said.

"Oh," said Claire, impressed.

"They're not so bad. Actually I rather enjoy them." She

fanned herself. "So sensual, somehow. No, I just mean I can imagine you getting hurt with this Temple. There's something ice-cold about him."

"Really! I—"

"No, I mean it. Why has he got no children? No ex-wives? He's old enough. Successful enough. I'm not sure. Something devious there."

Claire shrugged. "You're just peeved because he's not after you. And I like him."

"Yes, I can see that you like him. You go all pink when he walks up to you. Just be careful."

"All right, mom."

Isolde went to the desk and drove her finger across the calendar. "We can still have it on the seventeenth."

"It has a lovely sound," Claire agreed. "May seventeenth."

"I can't imagine them arresting me on my wedding day, can you?"

"No." Claire leaned forward. "Probably not."

"Oh, come." Isolde stood behind her and unraveled Claire's thick copper braid. With a big-toothed tortoiseshell comb she meandered down the hair, taking long, luxurious, hypnotizing strokes.

"Isolde?" Claire said suddenly.

"Mmmm?"

"Why did you sleep with Hans?"

"You mean why did I betray Blacky, or why did I enjoy sex with Hans?"

"Hans. What was it about him that intrigued you?"

"He was so"—she pushed Claire away and loosened her robe—"delightfully wicked." Then a telltale look of anguish found its way across her face. "You wouldn't think it to know him, but at the moment of truth, he was"—she hesitated—"quite tender."

Then, seeing Claire's unbearable sympathy in the mirror, she narrowed her eyes, grabbed hold of Claire's arms and hurled her against the puffy chair. She then bombarded her with a series of hand-crocheted pillows.

Cosimo, down the hallway, looked up at the sound of their laughter. He listened, then sprang from his messy bed and reassembled the echoing selfsame notes on the rickety upright.

The next day the Mill buzzed with activity. There were the nervous, last-minute scenes for the film *Venus, Cupid, Folly and Time,* and now the added confusion of preparations for the wedding.

Claire didn't know what to shoot first. Every direction held a picture, some alluring scene or angle. There was a softness to the very air. She had just completed what she felt was a brilliant composition of the fruit orchard, what she hoped would be reminiscent of Bonnard's Garden, but in muted gray tones and shadows. She was walking carefully along the muddy path when she found herself near the film crew. They were shooting the scene where the heroine regains her ability to feel, but perhaps only at the expense of all that is precious to her: her loyalty and self-respect.

There Mara was, at the end of a group of young trees. Puffin had explained the script to Claire, but it hadn't really meant anything to her until now. What a brilliant actress Mara was. She had that rare ability to be able to change her accent utterly. It was the scene where she, the staid English-woman, is forced to decide about the love of her life, an inappropriately young German.

"What am I supposed to do?" Mara's character was saying. She held her belly and swayed back and forth. "Oh, life isn't how you think it will be," she moaned. "It doesn't turn out the way you expect, does it? I always thought if I got to a place, a certain place, everything would be settled. I would be there. But there is no place. There is no 'there'! All I ever will remember is my desire." Her head fell to the soft ground. "All I ever will regret. It never was the *boy* I loved, but my desire of him."

The camera was on her, but they were quite far off. The gaffer, spotting Claire, made violent signals toward her to be quiet, but she knew enough and had already stopped. She stayed where she was.

Mara spoke softly, her words garbled at times by the thundering birdsong. She wore silk, bright red in the lush expanse of green. She fluttered like gossamer in the breeze. Temple Fortune stood, his arms bent and in front of him, much like a conductor at a symphony concert. Or, Claire marveled, like a hypnotist, drawing the performance out of a mesmerized Mara.

Mara was so good, Claire forgot everything, even herself, for a moment and was captivated. Then, Temple Fortune's peripheral presence wafted toward Claire like the intrusion of sound waves. The right side of her body, the side toward him, became more alive than the other, or she became more aware of its life. The blood that raced through it did so with an almost wanton obligation and she thought how, how in God's name do people resist such audacious temptation? Why would they even want to? Wasn't its existence justification enough for an affair? "Affair" sounded so shabby compared to the almost spiritual elevation of this drive. She dared not look at him. If simply standing beside him could bring on such shortness of breath, such intense generation of bodily fluids, wasn't one obliged by life itself to meet its fulfillment? Wasn't this something most people spent their entire lives waiting to feel? Wasn't that reason enough to give in? Wasn't one supposed to give in? And if not, wouldn't God forgive any weakness put upon by so magnificent a passion?

Suddenly Mara broke down. "I cannot continue," she

sobbed, "my concentration has been broken!"

"Damn!" Puffin swore. "It was superb."

"Never mind." Temple went gently through the grass to Mara. He smoothed her cheek. "We'll start again in a moment." He patted his assortment of pockets like a kindly grandpa looking for a sweet to placate her.

"My mouth has run dry," she said, full of rage.

"Makeup." Puffin pursed his lips. The sun was moving quickly, and there wasn't much time.

The lighting technician stood behind her and measured the light on her hair. The makeup girl patted her beading face with pats of a rather filthy-looking little sponge.

"Water!" Temple stood behind Mara with the lighting technician and gestured the assistant, who came running.

"Watch the grass, watch the grass!" Puffin yelled. He leaped behind the assistant, smoothing the tall grass with his arm, gently back and forth.

"Not that water." Mara pushed the bottle thrust at her away, and it dropped, spilling, to the ground. "I want my Evian."

"Oh, do take this, Mara," Puffin exclaimed. "The light is changing so fast. We'll miss the shot. German water won't kill you, you know. Überkinger is marvelous stuff." To prove his point, he took a slug.

"I can't do it." Mara began to tremble. "I'm a mess. I don't trust this light. I know I look awful. I can feel it. You know I can feel good and bad light for me, Temple. You know I can."

"Oh, yes." Puffin wagged his head. "We all know quite well that you were a model. We've all heard it before, haven't we?"

"I'm not talking to you." Mara threw the overturned bottle at him, barely missing his ear. "Make him stop, Temple," she cried. But she was looking at Claire. It was Claire who was upsetting her, really.

"Oh, don't cry, for God's sake, she'll have to start all over!" Puffin said.

"I'll run and get some Evian," Claire spoke up.

"Just look at me!" Mara held a mirror at arm's length. "I'm a mess!"

"You're not," Temple soothed her. He looked up and met Claire's eyes. "You're perfect."

Claire turned and fled. Puffin ran up behind her. "Here," he said hurriedly, "take Temple's keys. She's got some water in the trailer. It will be quicker."

Claire moved swiftly through the grass. She didn't stop until she got to the trailer and she let herself in. There was the water on the vanity. She grabbed it and then turned to go. She looked at his keys in her hands. There was a small marbled loop on a chain holding the cluster of keys. His keys. Claire arched her neck, holding the keys between her breasts. The open door of the bathroom allowed the sunlight on the scrubbed white tiles. She lowered her eyes and picked the keys up to her lips. She held them, breathing onto them, drunkenly inhaling their nearness and then she saw herself, accidentally, in the blinding mirror. There was a quick rapping on the trailer door. An assistant had come to relieve her of running back with the water. She lurched and dropped the keys. She let him in and walked, shaken, back to the Mill.

5

———◆•◆•◆———

A *ll the village* showed up for the wedding.
A circle of dirndled Bavarian girls danced gracefully around the maypole surrounded by a larger circle, a
herd of clumping fellows in lederhosen, knee socks, and
starched shirts. They hooted and grabbed the girls around
their waists and twirled them about to the delight of the
more demure guests, not yet drunk enough or carefree
enough in their costumes to be dancing.

No one had asked the villagers directly, but as long as
they wore their *Trachten* they felt they were entitled to
come. It had always been that way when there was a festivity at Saint Hildegard's Mill. Luckily Evangelika knew this
and had a slew of the village women in to help with the
preparations and the serving.

There were tables of rich and unusual foods. An entire
pig, fruit oozing from every orifice, went round and round
on the garden spit. Cosimo and Friedel the gardener had
outdone themselves, having strewn flowers in garlands
from tree to tree. Claire was kept busy shooting everything.
The morning slipped away. All she had to do was turn and
frame and she'd be looking through the lens at yet another
sun-dappled Renoir.

The ceremony itself had been short and sweet. Now the

real, more businesslike, business of celebration was under-
way.

Claire decided to take advantage of the cool dark kitchen
to reload. The sun was too high anyway. She stepped over
the massive beams still used for steps and went in.

Temple Fortune sat in the place of honor, under Evangelika's elbow, at the otherwise unpeopled table. They were
changing scenes, he said. He'd slipped away. The sun was
too high. "I was just thinking that," she said, and they both
smiled, remembering the last time they'd held each other's
eyes.

He was drinking a clear soup. "I have this bloody gastri-
tis and I need something plain," he said.

One thing Evangelika loved was an undernourished
man.

"Will you join me?" he asked Claire.

"Oh no," she said shyly.

"Please," he said.

She lowered herself down across from him, keeping her
spine straight. She must control herself near him.

Evangelika smacked an empty bowl before her, then
eased in some ladlefuls of her magnificent broth. Temple
leaned over the table with a spoon of grated cheese, which
he sprinkled across the top. It melted in. He looked at her
to ask if that was the right amount. But there was much
more to that look.

The noise outside seemed far away. They ate their soup
quietly. He wanted her to take a hunk of the crusty sunflower bread he'd torn off for her and dunk it in the fragrant soup.

Evangelika stood approvingly behind them, waiting,
with her ladle on her hip.

Claire could not remember anything ever tasting better.
He insisted she take a glass of beer. "Full of vitamins." He

smiled. "They don't use preservatives here, you know, it's food after all. And fresh." Then, "I have a lovely kitchen at home," he confided. "I enjoy cooking. It relaxes me."

"Really," Claire said. "I'm afraid I've fallen into the category of hurry up and get it on the table. I never meant to, but I've become that way."

"That's all right. As long as your art stays pure, as they say. I think it's all right if you serve the occasional hamburger."

"Oh you do, eh? I'd better not admit that my son lives on hamburgers and pizza."

"Well. It must be nice at least to have a son."

"I didn't know you were so sulky, Temple."

"Now you do." They held their spoons in midair and regarded each other. "I'm sorry," he said ducking his head "all of a sudden I don't know if the story I'm working on is even the slightest bit interesting."

"Why don't you tell me about it."

"Oh, you know." He leaned back on two legs of his chair looking like an American cowboy with his jeans and his vest. "It started off this wonderfully symbolic story of a woman going through this metamorphosis—this experience—a second chance that goes awry. Ursula Braun wrote the story, you know. I saw it so clearly when I first read it. I loved it. It was so . . ." He held up the palms of his hands. ". . . so simple. Here's a woman who has a second chance at love, at life, but fears she no longer can feel. Worries she has not the heart."

"I'm afraid I don't know the writer." Then, she thought, I do, on the other hand, know the feeling.

"What, really? She's world-famous. The critics' darling. But since you admitted you don't know her, I'll tell you something." He lowered his voice. "I'd never heard of her either."

They grinned at each other.

"I'm afraid I don't keep up with all these literary geniuses. Puffin does. Great reader, Puff. He keeps me abreast. I'm afraid I'm too visual. Good for some things, bad for others." He gazed at her wistfully.

"Puffin turned you on to the story, then?"

"Yaa. I'd be little more than a moron without Puffin. He's too much. Went to all the best schools, did Puff. Knows it all."

Claire's eyes were drawn to the palms of his hands. She wanted to lean over and press her lips to their center.

"And now"—she heard his voice above her imagination—"now it all looks so complicated. So busy." He shook his head. "I don't know if my work is worthy of Ursula Braun's story. You know, the writer took the title from the painting. Bronzino's *Venus, Cupid, Folly and Time.* You know."

"I didn't. I knew the name of your film, but I didn't know the source."

"Oh, it's lovely," Temple said. "Full of angels and screeching supplicants. Sort of lewd."

"Listen," Claire said, "I'm sure once you get back to London and start editing—"

"Now," Temple said worriedly, "I'm not even sure we were wise to shoot it here in Germany. We've lost so much of the spirit of it. The Italian atmosphere. The sharp lines of shadow and light. I was so happy at first. Even Puffin thought it would work."

"It was originally meant for the South?"

"Well, yes, Florence."

"Hmm. Well, all I can comment on is what I've seen you working on this past week. I mean, I shot a lot of your setups. I don't usually like to use someone else's perspectives, but they seemed clear. It seemed . . ." She searched her mind for the word that would soothe him, that would give him back the faith he'd lost in himself. She traced the worry lines across his forehead with her eyes, memorizing them. "Your angle . . . your work in general seemed to have integrity. A mystical integrity."

"Now here's a girl up on all the latest metaphysical jargon," Temple scoffed, but the lines had disappeared. She'd done her job. He slurped his soup, happy again. "You know," he said, "it's funny. Here we are, bugs in a rug, wedding going on, middle of a murder investigation. Life's still a funny old place, isn't it?"

"If they could only decide it *was* murder. I mean, maybe it *was* suicide. I wish it were. They're not sure, are they?"

"Ah. Why would a guy like Hans commit suicide?"

"You knew him, did you?"

"Not well at all. He struck me as content with his lot, though. You know, no-second-thoughts kind of chap. Can't see him kicking it in. I think he fell."

"Maybe," Claire suggested, "he killed himself over Isolde. Getting married to Blacky."

Evangelika smacked the dough she was kneading at the other end of the table. They'd forgotten she was even there. "Not likely," she snorted, and they laughed.

"So what sort of films do you look at in America, Mrs. Benedetto?"

"Ah. You noticed I am married."

"It was the first thing I noticed about you," he said. "Well. The second."

She smiled sadly. "Ah, Mr. Dougherty, ten years ago I went back to America, stayed upstairs in the bed in my mother's house and watched 'Kojak' reruns late at night on a little black-and-white TV. . . . Now I've got a big color set and seventy-eight channels, and I still find myself up in bed late at night watching 'Kojak' reruns."

He didn't laugh. He sat there with his face in his hands, his thoughtful expression filling her with longing.

There was a rustling, hurried change out in the yard. The musicians began their Mozart.

Reluctantly, Temple took his leave. His eyes stayed on her until the door shut with a thud.

Claire decided to go up to the bell tower and get some shots from there. Every time she'd tried to get up there, some forensics person was either scraping stone, or Isolde's twinkle lights were being hung. One thing or another. And to be honest to herself, she had to admit she was apprehensive. She didn't mind going up now, in the daylight, though. It was almost a pleasure, a cleansing. She took the white-washed steps of the tower, laying to rest the awful time she'd come up in the daylight, when she'd seen Hans's body. Never mind. This was a new time, the beginning of a new time for them all. She went up swiftly. There was nothing there. The guardrail was so low, Hans might well have slipped. She leaned over. Christ, it was a long way down.

She got up and felt the bell. She ran her fingers around the inside. There were no niches other than the rim. No little hiding spots she could find. Well, obviously. All those years. Had they been there, someone surely would have found them.

She couldn't get a picture of Hans, couldn't get a handle on his life, his personality. There was something missing. She couldn't hate him. Couldn't like him. And yet Isolde had liked him, cared about him enough to make love to him. There must have been something lovable about him.

She went down the stairs, wanting to see his room. There was no one around. Unable to resist, she poked her head into Cosimo's room. It was a small room, chaotic and churned up with plants and snippings of plants in glasses on the sills. There were birdcages, open. No doubt Cosimo would let out anything caged. There were cookies, *Butter-kekse* and Bahlsen Cookies in wrappers all over the room, just in case of famine, no doubt. It was very much like her own son's room. Busy little molecules of dust churning happily about in tall wedges of sunlight. An upright piano was half buried in handwritten sheet music. Comic books and classics were shoved into overloaded bookcases. She went back out and walked toward Hans's.

She stood outside his room. Open. All the rooms were open and the windows open too. Symbolic, she supposed. What better time, she thought, and went in.

The room was as one would expect: big furniture, very German. Strong, unyielding furniture, crisply clean windows with white starched curtains. She looked around absently, lifting the blotter on his desk. That was where she always stuck her important papers. There was a list. The reason it caught her eye was that it was old, like Iris's scrapbooks, like her own parents' wartime mementos. It was a list of names. Clients. Guests of the Mill, addresses to the side. Third from the bottom—her heart almost stopped at the sight—was written "Iris von Lillienfeld" in old German script, with an English address. Just below it, subsequent addresses had been penciled in, then scratched out. The last read "Richmond Hill." Claire slipped the paper into her waistband.

She went into the family room, closed the door just a bit, and went straight to the clock. With her back to the door, she took our her deluxe eyeglasses repair kit she'd picked up at the supermarket cash register back in Queens. Carefully she turned the clock over. It really was a superb little screwdriver. She got the screws open and the gold plate off in no time at all. She had a vision of herself discovering the diamonds, the brilliant stones trickling out like the sands of time come loose. She got the buckle open. She turned the clock. She looked. Empty. Just the tick-tock back and forth of the ingenious inner workings. Just then, she heard the floorboards behind her creak. She turned halfway and leaped in fright, almost tipping the clock to the floor. She caught it with one hand and stood face-to-face with Fräulein Bibi Wintner. "Ho!" she grasped her chest with the other hand. "You scared the life out of me! I thought it was a ghost!" She laughed.

Fräulein Wintner looked at the clock in Claire's hand.

"Ah," Claire said, her face going red, "I was just admiring the clock. Some clock, eh? I mean the works. They don't make them like that anymore, do they?"

Fräulein Wintner squinted meanly at her. She carried a basket of Stella's hand-embroidered towels. Fresh lavender had been tucked in between every other towel.

Fräulein Wintner was dressed for the wedding, looking, Claire thought, a little more Viennese mother-of-the-bride than German housekeeper, but then, why not? She wore an awfully glittery, if well-cut, suit. There was nothing resembling a *Tracht* about it, which Claire suspected was the very idea. Temple Fortune would have to cut each scene she marched into, wouldn't he?

But why, Claire wondered, would she dislike Temple Fortune? She rested the elegant clock on its side and demonstrated the way she was putting the gold plate neatly back on. She shook her head philosophically as she spoke. "I know this must look sort of silly. Everyone downstairs and me up here poking through this old clock. You wouldn't believe me if I told you what I was looking for." She chuckled ineffectively.

Fräulein Wintner retained her grim demeanor. "I would advise you to say nothing," she finally interrupted Claire's babbling.

"Oh, look, I know this looks awkward but I—"

"You will remain here until I return with the *Polizei*. Now we know for sure who's been doing the stealing."

"Oh, no, you misunderstand." Claire laughed. "What, you thought I was trying to steal the clock? Uh! No! No, you see I was looking at the way it was *made,* see. A friend of mine has a broken one at home and I was just having a look to see how it was ma—"

Fräulein Wintner had turned and left her standing there. As she left, Claire heard her mutter *"Dreckige kleine Jüdin!"* (Dirty little Jew!) So it was true. The first thing that went wrong dredged up the same quick conclusion, did it? Lovely. Then Fräulein Wintner was gone.

Claire heard the heavy door lock click into place. Was it possible? She'd locked her in! Claire's first thought was that Johnny would kill her. Oh, God. This was all she needed. She had to get out. She went and tried the door. Locked nice and tight, all right. What a fix. Oh, boy. She walked around in a frantic circle. She spotted the phone. She picked it up and got an open dial tone. Delighted, she dialed her sister Carmela's number. It was early morning in New York.

"Hello." Carmela had on her Bette Davis voice. This meant she was working and/or smoking.

"It's me."

"Ooh. Innocent abroad. Homesick?"

"No. Yes. How's Dharma?"

"Central Park Zoo with Andrew."

"Good, give her my love. Carmela, could we be Jewish?"

"Why, because our name is Breslinsky with a *y*?"

"I knew you were the one to ask."

"Claire, you know this."

"I do?"

"Don't you remember?"

"No!"

"Tch. Daddy changed it back from Breslin to Breslinsky before he met Mommy. It's supposed to be Breslinski— with an *i*. They'd dropped it to sound more American."

"So he just spelled it wrong?"

"No, he looked in the phone book to make sure he spelled it right. Only he looked in the Kew Gardens phone book. So there were tons of Breslinskys: Abe to Zepheriah—all Jewish. By the time Aunt Kadja yelled at him, he already had his driver's license and insurance and all that with the red tape. He just left it as it was."

"Gotcha. Oh, and listen. One more thing. You know the book, *Venus, Cupid, Folly and Time*?"

"Painting," Carmela said. "Angiolo Bronzino. Sixteenth century. Upsetting."

"Also a book," Claire said. "Recent. Ursula Braun."

"Never heard of it."

"Big critical success, award-winner. Well, anyway. That's the film they're making here. Temple Fortune."

"Mmm. Heard of him! Yummy."

"Gotta go," Claire said.

"See if Mr. Fortune needs any good American scripts."

"Love you."

She hung up the phone and looked around her opulent space. Wait. She remembered there was a balcony. She'd seen Puffin Hedges coming in from it the other night when they'd all been in here. She found it behind the *Spanische Wand,* an elegant old screen like the ones used primarily by saloon girls in Westerns to dress behind. The balcony door behind it was wide open. Relief! She sauntered out onto the balcony and breathed deeply the air of freedom. She even aimed her camera, still around her neck, at the crowd below and zoomed in on them. After a few what she suspected were magnificent shots of Mara Morgen in her fancy aubergine costume (looking for all the world like the character she was supposed to be), Claire raised a distressed hand and waved to the film crew.

Yes, yes, they waved back when they saw her and moved

quickly on to their next shot off in the distance. They didn't have much time to get all this superb atmosphere, and they were making good use of it.

Claire waved to the crowd closer to the Mill, but they were so drunk they didn't even notice her.

She called to Friedel the gardener, standing on the sidelines and dancing with no one; but the small orchestra Blacky had hired was just under her, and she realized that her frantic wavings were not much different from the expressions of the rest of the revelers below, who were dancing and carrying on in their own sort of desperate merrymaking. Claire sighed unhappily. She peered over the side to see if she might climb down. It was a straight drop. Unfortunately, the bougainvillea vines were temporary, springing from great clay pots that could be transported indoors during the cold winters. There was no strength there. The wisteria vines she wouldn't have minded shimmying down, but they were attached to the next balcony, the one next to Cosimo's room. She waved her arms again. Blacky, far off and dancing with Isolde, saw her and, misunderstanding, waved heartily back. He seemed deliriously happy. She would have to wait till the end of the song. Unfortunately, the oompah-pah band in the center of the garden picked up the slack at the last beat of the song and dived right into "The Blue Danube" waltz.

She waved harder. Blacky bowed politely and whisked his Isolde into the air and around and around.

The police! Forget upsetting Johnny. Blacky would never forgive her for bringing the police to his wedding. She thought what to do. She couldn't very well hang over the balcony. At the very best they would say she was drunk, and there she would be, trying to cause havoc at her ex-boyfriend's wedding. She might also fall. She saw Temple Fortune in the distance. He was working on the long shot, with Mara and the festivities of the Mill in the background.

Claire aimed her long lens at him off in the distance. He was too far away to capture in focus, just out of her range, but the figure of him leaning tenderly over Mara's glamorous form gave her a lurch of jealousy. Mara's romantic costume fluttered like a dream in the wind. She put the camera down. Someone was just beneath Claire. She tried to yell at him, but he didn't even hear her. Claire sank to the floor, giving up. Suddenly she was overwhelmed with self-pity. She ought to be more upset by this business with Fräulein Wintner, but seeing Temple Fortune so attentive toward Mara left her weak. You'd think she was a teenager. She knew she ought to be more worried about her husband home alone, but she wasn't. She was glad to be away. She almost hoped he wasn't alone. Lord knew, they had reached the point where instead of greeting each other with joy or even with the searching eyes of the concerned mate, they each performed their solitary little dances of exhaustion at the injustice of routine—their routine. With their eyes glazing over, they'd shake their heads and sigh. "Oh God," they would say. "Oh God"—and look away to the window or wall or the next unavoidable chore that wouldn't be there but for each other. She tried to help, but she couldn't change.

She realized, finally, how much power Temple Fortune was beginning to have over her emotions. She was surprised to notice herself trembling.

There was an open vin d'Alsace on the wrought-iron-and-glass table. It sat respectfully in shards of melting ice. Claire picked it up. Gewürztraminer 1988. From Ribeauvillé. Hmmm. No glass. No need to be fancy. She tipped it into a translucent teacup. Heaven. She had another. Was this Blacky and Isolde's wedding-celebration bottle? She would have liked to share it with Temple Fortune.

She wouldn't let him know, let anyone know, how he made her feel. What good would it possibly do? As far as she knew, he felt nothing with which to compare and justify her ardor. He was hungry to devour her body, of that she was pretty sure. But so, she imagined, would he be hungry for other flesh, all sorts of young and ambitious and available flesh. She would be no end-all for him. She was nobody special. She was no longer young. Only a fool would imagine he would care for her in the grand sense. Only a fool. She put her head down on the sturdy walls of the expensive yellow Scotch broom planter (someone at least had money) and allowed her growing-older, worn-out heart finally to let go by screaming fiercely.

In mid-anguish, she spotted a little boy across on the other balcony. He was a stout little fellow, a bit older than her own Anthony. She knew immediately what he was up to. He was secretly gobbling a great horde of forbidden food. What did he have there? She could just make out his tremendous bowl of *Schlagsahne* and fresh strawberries, no doubt swiped from the kitchen.

She shrugged convivially. He shrugged back. Nothing like a kid to commiserate. Children suffer daily and come unhinged as often. "I'm locked in," she called to him. "*Ich bin eingesperrt.*"

"*Ach,*" he mouthed, having heard her between beats, clucked sympathetically, then resumed eating his whipped cream and strawberries as they continued to regard each other from each other's balconies. She let him have a few more husky bites, then waved him over. He imagined she meant to share her balcony and his strawberries and cream. This idea seemed to appeal to him, misery loving company, and he got off, brushed his lederhosen solidly off, then disappeared.

Claire ran to the locked door. She pressed her ear up to the wood. Nothing. He'd gone away. She looked around her, despairing, when she heard him out there, fiddling with the lock.

"Geht nicht," he announced. "It's locked good."

"You speak English," she said. "What a clever boy."

"I go to the American school," he explained conde-scendingly through the heavy door.

"I see," Claire called back. "You're Dirk, aren't you? Isolde's boy."

"That's right," he said.

Her heart went out to him. She hadn't seen him since he was a baby. He wouldn't remember her. Immediately she understood his craving for comforting food. This couldn't be an easy day for him. "Dirk," she said, "I wonder if you would do me a great favor?"

"Sure," he said to show off his American.

"There will be a lady coming along soon with a ring of keys and maybe a policeman or two. When she comes, I want you to tell her I've escaped. Could you do that? Would you?"

"Natürlich," he said, and sat down on the floor to wait. Before long, Fräulein Wintner came scrambling down the hallway, her elbows out, her tempo up. There were no po-licemen with her, but young Dirk knew who she was. She had the keys, and she smacked of authority.

"Da war jemand drin." He pointed to the door. Some-one was in there.

"Ich weiss," she said. I know. She turned her back on him, dissmissively.

"Ja, sie ist weggelaufen," he said. She ran away.

"Was?" she cried. *"Entwichen?"* She opened the lock with the key and threw open the door. In they went. She looked about. Sure enough, no one was there! Fräulein Wintner looked to the child for affirmation. He stood there, cream on his face, and pointed down the hallway to the stairs. Fräulein Wintner ran out and down the hall, leav-ing the door ajar. Claire ran from behind the screen. "Thanks, Dirk," she said to the boy. They slapped each

other a high five, and Claire ran down the hallway, free.

When she reached the bottom of the stairs and the gaiety of the crowd, she calmed down. And after all, it was Fräulein Wintner's word against her own. Who was Fräulein Wintner, after all, but an employee of the house. Still, Claire had a feeling that here, as in all small villages, the one who'd put more time in was more apt to be believed. She ought, really, to make herself scarce. The reveling dancers made a good cover as they practically swept her away toward the gardens at the side of the house. From there she just picked her way across the field in the direction of the pottery.

The grass was high out here and uncut to allow the strewn wildflowers to flourish. The heat of the day rested heavily now in a low smoggy dew you couldn't feel closer to the Mill, where it was burned off by the tumultuous goings-on. A figure darted away in the distance. It was Temple. No, no, it couldn't be. What would he be doing here, with the film crew around the other end? Her heart called out. (Is that you I see, soft between the fruit trees?) She was a jerk. She laughed at herself. A wind stirred up. Blossoms came down like a perfect snow. She shivered and looked back to see if she was being followed when her foot trod clumsily on someone else's. A bark of fear sprang out of her. It was a man and woman on the ground; they rolled over and he held her with beer-sodden eyes. He was flushed and intent, she was very groggy, but they managed a sporty *"Grüss Gott,"* and a nod as though this were all the casual norm. Claire stumbled politely on. She didn't look back but heard them carry on the concentrated *thud-thud-thud* of their devotions the minute they realized she'd moved off.

*T*he pottery was a dense white cement building partially submerged in the ground. It looked like an ivy-covered, converted bomb shelter in the middle of the orchard. The kiln, in the grass, a steel, drumlike oven, was still warm from an earlier fire. Sawdust was matted to the grass together with fruit-tree blossoms. She thought she would gather her bearings and rest against the pottery door and was surprised when it eased open. There was Stella, turning away at her wheel.

"Hello," Claire said. "Not at the wedding?"

She realized Stella hadn't heard her. She was in an almost trance-like state.

"Hello," she said again, and Stella looked up. She smoothed the folds of the cotton apron across her long lap and gave a wistful smile. The wheel stopped. She was done. She got up and stretched, catlike, comfortable on her own turf.

"No." She shook her head softly as Claire repeated her question. "I wouldn't be at that wedding. Why should I?"

"How do you mean? May I sit down?" She stood awkwardly before a broken stool.

"No, come, sit over here." She pointed to her gathering of great pillows in the colors of stones on the floor. "This is better. May I offer you a cup of tea?"

"I'd love some. There's nothing I'd like more."

"I've green tea. Do you like it?"

"Yes, please."

Claire lowered herself down onto the pillows, feeling a mite stiffer than she had in the days when pillows on the floor were normal for her. "Nice here," she said, hoping she wouldn't go into a sneezing fit from the thick grog dust. "Not so noisy."

"No." Stella stood, her back to her, rinsing her hands with water that had been left cooling near her hot plate. "One needs peace if one is to work."

"I can't stay," Claire assured her. "I mean, I won't trouble you for long. I've got to get back to work, too. I'm working for Temple Fortune now." Did she sound as smug as she heard herself? Was she that desperate to hear any word about him?

"I'm only glad," Stella said, "it's not me."

"Not you what?"

"Not me being married. To Blacky."

"Oh, you mean glad not to be married at all or just not married to Blacky?"

"My father wanted me to marry him. For a while he was terribly insistent, so much so that I had to go away. It was last year at this time. I went to Japan. On a pilgrimage to Kasama, for the pottery fair." She smiled at Claire. "Another potters' town. It was *fantastisch!* I was to be apprenticed to a Master Potter." Her face shone, then it dropped. "My father needed me home, though. At least he said he did. Well, you must know why my father wanted me to marry Doktor von Osterwald. He thought he'd keep me busy. Doktor von Osterwald does have a way of keeping one busy"—here she paused, and they both laughed at the appropriate interval—"and he figured he would look after Cosimo."

"Blacky will do that anyway, won't he?"

"Until the first major dispute, anyway."

"What do you mean?"

"Blacky and Cosimo don't see eye to eye on issues concerning day-to-day living."

"But surely Blacky will make an exception for someone as extraordinary as Cosimo."

"We'll see, won't we?"

"Your pottery is exquisite." Claire looked around, happy to have the opportunity to be with Stella. She was so unusual. "It's so simple and plain," she exclaimed, "yet there's something about it. I can't explain. It's like you."

All the unfinished biscuit-colored pots sat about on

shelves and on the floor. Stella was just doing a teapot. "That one's beautiful," Claire said.

Stella smiled at her with that smile Claire was beginning to recognize as her superior smile. The aren't-you-nonsensical-but-sweet smile. It was almost chilling.

"No, really . . ." Claire refused to be dismissed for valuing what she knew was good.

"Yes, I can see they give you pleasure," Stella relented. "I am glad. So many people find them too plain. Too simple. Like me, as you say." Bright tears shone in her eyes. "Perhaps you are a kindred spirit."

Claire's heart went the other way. "Yes," she said, wishing that she, too, could cry, "I hope I am."

"Isn't it strange," Stella said, "how the enormity of death and birth puts everyone on an equal footing, if only for a little while. Perfect strangers exchange private matters and"—she laughed, her teeth big and white—"other strangers."

"What were you saying about Blacky?"

"Oh, Doktor von Osterwald. As I said, just that I'm glad I didn't have to marry him."

"You make it sound like prison."

"Yes, well, for me it would be. I wouldn't be a good wife. I wouldn't want to be. Not everyone is called to the married state, as I'm sure you know. Not that Doktor von Osterwald wouldn't be a wonderful husband if one wanted a husband."

Was she feeling her out? "Not to change the subject, but do you happen to know that bird? The one with the white body and the black head, with indigo and green on the tail and the wings. Do you know it?"

Stella shrugged. "I can't bear those filthy things. Always coming into the house. *Diebische Elster!*" She shuddered. "It's my brother who knows all that."

"Is he pleased about Blacky and Isolde keeping him on?"

"Pleased? I wouldn't say pleased. Why should he be? Imagine if it were you . . ."

"Yes, I see what you mean. Still . . . things could . . . be worse."

"Oh, things could always be worse." Two vertical lines troubled the space between Stella's gray eyes. "I'm afraid I like everything to be calm and simple. I don't like unnecessary agitation. I don't even like necessary agitation."

"Is that why you chose raku as an art form?"

Stella's eyes sparkled immediately with interest. "Yes, you're right. Although it is, in fact, extremely sophisticated. The word 'raku' originally meant 'pleasure' or 'enjoyment.' Do you know, in the traditional Zen tea ceremony, or cha-no-yu, the wares are made of this pottery. They are kept in special padded boxes." She pulled a plain but exquisitely made wood box from the shelf. "My brother made this box for me," she said proudly. She removed one bowl. The dappled light from the window played across its lustrous finish. Stella held it carefully, lovingly. "The Tea Master selects which bowls are to be used. This is based on subtle aesthetic consideration and, of course, tradition. Westerners most usually have a hard time comprehending the subtle aesthetic considerations of it." She moved the bowl across her cheek. "Raku started in Kyoto, Japan." She spoke as she went about her preparations, taking great care with each movement. "It was first done by an immigrant Korean potter about 1525, and then continued by her son. It's a quite unpredictable firing process, at about one thousand degrees Celsius." She held up one smoky black, lopsided piece. "After I take it from my kiln, I reduce it in sawdust. The glazed pieces frequently have a crackle to the luster. You never know exactly what you are going to get." She got up and trod swiftly about the place, searching for a particular piece to show Claire, then held one up: a simple curved plate dripping matted shades of green.

"Oh, I love it," Claire exclaimed. "It reminds me of blades of young grass."

"Yes, that is the beauty of raku. Every piece is open to interpretation. It's very exciting to watch. The firing method is swift. Sometimes they are unglazed, those are the rich black and smoky grays, and these"—she held one up—"are the glazed. Very often they are crackled. I love the crackle," she said intently, the way a young girl would have confided she loved a man.

"I do too," Claire said.

"As you see, my typical work turns a creamy and jade-like green blush. This is because of the copper-carbonate element in the earth nearby. Wooden tools, handmade wooden tools, are often used by raku potters. I use my fingers. Only my hands. I like this. The hands have a sympathy for the clay that instruments do not."

"Hm," said Claire. She touched the rim of a drying pot and Stella flinched. "I'm sorry," Claire said.

"It's just that they're not dry yet, not set . . ."

"Stella. Did your father ever talk to you about his father, Adam von Grünwald?"

"No."

"Oh."

"My father never spoke to me about anything. He didn't really *know* how to communicate. My mother did, though."

"Did she?"

"Yes, she told me stories about how when they were young and the war was on, they had to live on tulip bulbs and sugar beets and berries. It must have been awful. You had to be sure to boil the tulip bulbs a certain way, else you got poisoned."

"Did your mother ever tell you stories about Adam

173

before he married your grandmother? Kunigunde?"

Stella stopped pouring the water over the cups and watched Claire carefully. "No. Never. Why?"

"Nothing really. I just thought perhaps . . ."

"There was one thing."

"Yes?"

"One thing that might interest you . . . Evangelika used to talk about a Jewish woman who enchanted my grandfather before he married."

"Evangelika told you about this?"

"Yes. Often. I never knew my grandfather, Adam. Cosimo looks like him. Dark. Oh, he was famous around these parts. The local people loved him, they say. Kept a woman in the attic. He died before I was born. And my grandmother, she used to laugh about it, but, you know, even as a small child, you pick things up, you intuit the pain in someone's eyes as they speak. Well, I remember my grandmother saying he was more loyal to the promise he'd made a dead Jew than a living wife."

Claire instantly sat up.

Stella said, "You know those creaking noises you hear at night in the Mill?"

"I'm glad you hear them, too."

"Evangelika always says it is Kunigunde. She says she can't settle in until the treasure finds its way out of hiding."

It occurred to Claire that Evangelika might well have been at the Mill when Iris was.

"My grandmother was a simple woman," Stella continued. "She came from the village and never left it. She . . . well . . . the fact that she was simple did not stop her from being powerful. All those prayers she said from morning to night. She was quite a formidable force, you see."

"Did your grandmother ever tell you what that promise was?"

"No." Stella sadly turned and touched her dry mouth with her fingers. "No, she never did. Sometimes I wish she had. I think it would have helped me. The mystery of things is what children have trouble with. I think they can deal with anything that is forthright and explained to them. Even death. Especially death." She wrung her hands with pathetic agitation. Remembering, Claire imagined, Hans's miserable end.

"Stella," she said gently, "I have a story to tell you. It began long ago, in the village of Diessen. There was a young and beautiful girl. Her name was Iris von Lillienfeld . . ."

The wind outside grew stronger and the light more dim as Claire told her tale. By the time she finished, she realized they'd both been lost on her journey.

Stella had stopped the preparations of her tea ceremony. Politely, she sat back on her slender, young girl's heels, intrigued by the idea of the grandfather she'd never known but heard so much about. His love story. But by the time she finished, Claire realized Stella was not going to be aghast at what had happened long ago. She'd listened politely enough for a while, with appropriate cluckings of commiseration, but soon she went back to preparing their tea. Her main focus was still obviously on what she was doing. This was not the reaction Claire had expected. Stella didn't deny having heard tales of treasure at the Mill; she simply shrugged and said she'd always taken them for legend.

There were three jade-like bowls on the wiped-clean board Stella used as a table. "Do you know what we have here?" she said, placing her fingertips together and getting on with what interested her, as though everything Claire had just said had nothing to do with her. It was as though she'd been impatient for the story to be done so she could get on with hers. "Now," Stella said pointedly at the first opportunity, "this is your choice. The symbol for delving into the universe."

"So, what do you mean?" Claire asked. "A riddle in three parts?"

"You must choose your own bowl." Stella knelt before her and crossed her arms on her knees.

"May I?"

"Ah, you may."

"I feel like 'Simon says.' Okay. So. Let's see. I'll probably choose this one. In the middle. The one with the glaze looking like a crane taking off. Would you like to know why?"

"No."

"No? Don't you care?" she joked.

"Do you want me to dissuade you from your choice?"

"Perhaps," Claire said, imagining how pretty it would look on the baker's rack in her own kitchen.

"Remember, your reasons are the mixture of subtle traditions and aesthetic considerations which are peculiar only to you," Stella reminded her.

"Well, I thought the middle way would appeal to you. Avoiding extremes. As in Buddhistic thought. And, I suppose, I'd like to please you. But then you are a fervent Catholic and have no use perhaps for Buddhistic thought?"

"I see no conflict in Christian dogma and Buddhistic teachings. Buddhism is a way of life. A practice, not a religion. Truth, after all, is truth. And you, after all, are the Master."

Claire didn't know what she meant. She found herself sitting in a suddenly antagonistic atmosphere. Which she herself might be producing. She was waiting for a response to her story of Iris, and she was getting symbols. She could see now what Blacky had meant about Stella making you cuckoo.

"So, I am the Master. You mean me as in 'me,' or me as in 'one'?"

"Oh, you as in 'you.' Of course. You are the master of your destiny, aren't you?"

"Well, sure. But that didn't sound like what you meant. You mean, like the choice is mine?"

Stella wagged her head back and forth, setting Claire to wonder again if it was she who was the insane one and not her brother. But then, Stella usually didn't talk much. She used instead her gift of intent listening. "Help me out here," Claire finally said.

"Choose the goblet," Stella urged, "from which only the poor can drink."

"Don't you mean only the pure?"

"It is the same."

"Oh." Her mind went immediately to the decision of whether or not to shoot cigarette advertisements. She looked again at the middle bowl. The other two bowls swam evocatively on each side. One said "mortgage" and the other "private school tuition." If she didn't shoot the ads, someone else would just come along and do it. Surely once your motives were no longer pure, that was it. They were not going to turn around and become pure because you wanted them to. You couldn't change what already happened. Or did we remake ourselves? Could we? Was that what life was all about? Reinventing ourselves?

"Why do you hesitate?" Stella watched her from a remote place. There were dabbles of the last gold light on her face. She looked like a leopard.

"I feel like I'm throwing my changes," Claire said. "You know, I Ching."

"No, I'm sorry. I don't know."

"It's sort of like reading your fortune."

"You don't need hocus-pocus to choose your fortune."

"No," Claire admitted. "I suppose you don't. Tell me, what are *you* thinking?"

"I was just remembering. In *The Red Shoes*, where the fellow says, 'It is much more disheartening to have to steal . . . than to be stolen from.' "

Outside, the wind stopped running to the west and the sounds of the party drew near.

Claire chose the middle bowl.

By the time she left the pottery and walked back toward the Mill, it was too late for Claire to get any shots. She wouldn't use artificial light. She didn't like to and she almost never did.

She picked her way across the tall grass. The wind stopped suddenly, and the evening was low and purple and still. Any minute it was going to rain. She hurried, shivering, wanting her sweater, going the long way around the meadow to the Mill, past the little chapel, and ran upstairs to her room. Her sweater was in the closet, neatly hung, not left crumpled on the bed where she'd left it. German orderliness was so reassuring. She went down the stairs. The oompah-pah band outside was in full swing. She crossed her arms in front of her and listened for a minute. Everyone was outside. She might just sit in the dining room for a while. Just sit and do nothing. She leaned over and peeked in. There were a few locals in there, enjoying the fire. A woman at the booth table, a man on each side. Both men, intent, had a hand up the front of her blouse. The woman met Claire's eyes. She smiled. It was a brutish, feral smile. "Be careful," Iris's words came back and alerted her. "Something festers there."

Claire turned and fled.

*   *   *

A great ruckus rose from the front of the Mill. Claire joined the throng. The lads of the village had stolen the wood carving at the tip of the next village's maypole and were putting it up on theirs. There was a tremendous seething rivalry about maypole *Spitzen,* or tips, these being a wood cutting of a local theme or nursery rhyme the villagers had grown up with and come to think of as their own. They stole each other's as a matter of course, and the captured *Spitze* was guarded at the top of the pole with their own until the guard was let down and the connivery would begin again. This was a perfect moment to slip into the house, with everyone's attention on the cavorting around the maypole.

There was that bird, she saw as she checked out each window for the lurking Fräulein Wintner. Was he at her window? Yes, it was hers. The bird's beak glinted, as though it had a silver tooth. She watched him as he took off, glided across the lawn and landed softly on the Roman Bridge. A magpie! That was it.

She would go to see old Father Metz. She wanted to give him her traveler's checks anyway, might as well be now. Make it a done deal. But first she should probably show her face at the festivities. She'd shot plenty of film, too much, probably, but it might be construed as deliberately sullen if she didn't show up at all as a celebrant.

Puffin Hedges stood on the other side of the *Kastanianbaum,* the great chestnut tree, where Claire was warily avoiding Fräulein Wintner and any bevy of *Polizei* she'd convinced that Claire was guilty.

Puffin offered her a cigarette in greeting, then lit his own with a shrug when she declined. "Quite a show," he said. "Good for us, though, we got all the background we need. And all at the happy couple's expense."

"Yeah, I wish them luck."

"Luck"—Puffin winked—"is something that comes

179

and goes. Like the tide. The trick is," he added, "to make one's move when the luck is there."

"Yeah, well. I wish them movement when the luck is there, then."

He struck an angler's pose. "I mean, good luck has more to do with restraint than action, don't you think? Holding back and waiting for the right moment."

"There's no denying that," she said, restraining herself from asking where Temple Fortune was. Instinct told her sidekicks spent too much time giving account of where their major partner was. Everyone liked to be enjoyed for themselves, after all. And Puffin was in a philosophical mood. Instead she asked for Cosimo. "I haven't seen him anywhere. Have you? I thought he was going to play during the ceremony. I was looking forward to it."

"As I know Cosimo, he does what he wants to do and when he wants to do it. He is not restricted by the confines of social behavior, is he?"

"No."

"Got the best of both worlds, if you ask me. Everyone thinks he's crackers, don't they? But he's got it made. He can do whatever he likes."

"Yes, still, it can't be easy, being so sensitive. And don't forget, he's just lost his father."

"Pfh. If anything, that would please him. The old keeper of the Mill kept a tight ship, he did. Died just in time, if you ask me."

His bitterness surprised her. "It's very still," she remarked.

"Rain any minute," Puffin agreed.

"So where will you be off to next?" she asked.

"What, us? Well, let's see. Home, for the editing—London. The San Sebastian Film Festival opens in Spain in September." He chewed his poor thumbnail. "Of course we can't make Cannes. That's on now, and we can't wait till next spring again. It's too long."

"Can't you do both?"

"No. You can't have both. If we enter San Sebastian, we are ineligible for Cannes"—his eyes twitched—"and we are married to this film. For better or for worse."

And so she knew, all at once, that Temple Fortune must be frightened, maybe terrified. It was everything on the line here. All or nothing. Now or never.

"How come you never married, Puffin?" she changed the subject.

"Me?" He laughed with fond self-derision, then had a sneezing fit. "I can't take the spring," he wheezed.

"Oh, I know," she sympathized. "My season's the fall. I can't go out at all."

He found his handkerchief and finally mopped his bright red nose to a stop.

"Ah," he sighed, glad to get back to the grand subject of himself. "No, not me. I never did. Had plenty of pets, Lord knows." He shrugged. "No one ever really fit the bill, know what I mean? I guess it was Mum stopped me more often than not."

Claire smiled obligingly, appreciating his cockney bit, then realized he wasn't "doing" the cockney accent but, rather, falling back into it. It had never occurred to her that Puffin wasn't the high-born fellow he pretended to be. Ah, well, where was the harm?

"It was a laugh, you know," he talked away, hardly noticing her response anyway, "every time I brought some little girl home, Mum always would say just the right thing to put me off. It was like she would come and go and me ma would say, 'Wasn't she lovely,' and 'Such a nice young lady,' and then she'd top it off with, 'Isn't it a shame about that mole on the tip of her nose? That'll get nice and big now, the older she gets, you see if it doesn't. Nice girl, though, isn't she? Lovely. Why don't you take *her* out more often?' And you know, whenever I would look at that girl again, what was it I would see? Not a lovely girl as I had brought home to tea, but the mole at the tip of her nose. Heh. It was always the same, this one had 'an awfully small head' and that one had 'such a nice pair of hands, wasn't it a pity they were too big for her fine body.' Funny, that."

"Yes. Yes, it is."

"Don't go feeling sorry for me now." He nicked her with his elbow.

"Good heavens! I wouldn't think of it," she lied. "You've clearly got one of the more desirous lives, haven't you. I mean, look at you, making films, enjoying the good life. Going about the world, playing tennis and backgammon."

"Yeah, that's it," he agreed with her, squinting suavely into the boisterous crowd. "Taking in the high life in Bavaria."

"You know," she said, "I have a feeling you're a little bit like me. More an observer than a participant. We're both in the visual-arts end, aren't we?"

"Well, I'm a writer myself," Puffin admitted.

"Are you now? Now, see, I never would have known that if you hadn't told me. I thought you were assistant directing as well as producing."

"Really?"

"Yes, you know, the way you set everything up. Well, I don't know. I just thought . . ."

"My, no." He laughed. "We'll leave all that to the experts now, won't we. No, no, I deal in publicity, then a little of this and a little of that. I write a column, you know, when I feel like it."

"I didn't know!"

"Oh, yeah, sure. When I have the time. Not your everyday stuff. More thoughtful pieces. Not like a gossip column or anything. I despise that sort of thing."

So Claire knew that he never did write. She had so many friends who "could" write if they had the time. Her sister, Carmela, who was always busy, produced an unbelievably consistent supply of work. Poor Puffin. He was so brilliant, so shrewd and perceptive, she could imagine he despised himself most of all. He looked urgently at his magnificent watch as though that were the issue here, this time business. "I hope Temple gets back to see this."

Claire turned to see Blacky smashing his fist into someone's face. Someone else who'd gone, she supposed, too far with Isolde at last, and this time Blacky felt justified sticking it to him.

Blacky was a compact man. The other was the smaller, but Blacky was that much drunker, so it evened out fine. They were each giving the other a run for the money, swinging away. Claire couldn't help worrying about Blacky's fine caps. She remembered when he had them put in, with the new dentist on Prinzregentenplatz. Of course, they might have been replaced a few times since then. Blacky loved a good brawl, no hard feelings once it was over. As a matter of fact, he became quite good friends with everyone he'd ever had a go at, as far as she could recall.

The crowd let up in delighted horror as the other fellow landed a crasher in Blacky's gut.

"Where on earth is Isolde?" Claire scanned the party with no luck. She ought to be here. She could stop this nonsense.

Blacky took a great sock in the jaw and went sprawling past Claire. The crowd on the side of the Mill sent up a cheer.

She stepped back into the shadow of the chestnut tree. "Well," she said, "I hope everything works out. For you and Temple."

"Temple will always make out." He took a sip from his *Birnenschnapps* and perched the glass on a stump. He rocked back and forth on his very big feet. "Even as we speak . . ."

"I'm sorry?"

Puffin looked to the front room of the Mill, to the upstairs suite assigned to Temple. The curtains were shut. All the others around the second floor were open, as she had found them and left them.

Puffin smirked. "They often finish up a day of business with a friendly 'chat.' "

She'd walked right past their room. "How good of you to share that with me," she said, stung.

He bowed. "Didn't know you cared."

"Oh, you knew very well."

Puffin wobbled his head with lighthearted smugness.

"Just tell me one thing." She steadied herself on the dipping branches. "Why did you make me think he hates her?"

"He does, love. He does." He cocked one wispy eyebrow up. "Sometimes that makes it all the more exciting, eh? Hold on! What's this? The coppers!"

Sure enough, two uniformed policemen shouldered their way through the throng.

Claire slipped urgently away. Puffin was still talking to her when she disappeared, retracing her steps across the meadow, where she felt the first drops of rain. She put her camera in her vest. This time she would go to the Rectory. No one would find her there. She could leave her traveler's checks for Father Metz in his box. Sanctuary, that was what she needed. Damn, she would have thought knowing Temple and Mara were still intimate would throw a bucket of water on her feelings for him. They ought to have. She was too grown up for this sort of hysteria, these devastating paralyzations of emotion. It was too much. She ought to be glad for Temple that his relationship was in functioning order. Yet all it did was dismay her. Some perverse longing in her for him refused to believe he didn't want her the same way, that they weren't physically meant for each other. She wasn't used to being a dreamer about men. This was a pipe dream. She would be better off getting away from this place entirely. For the first time in a long time she wanted a cigarette herself. Always, before, romantic love had been the beginning, but this, this left her wanting to drag the man into the bushes and tear his quiet subtlety violently off. It was so violent an attraction. And after all, even if it was fulfilled, it would only end in the gloomy pyre of self-retribution.

There was a pay phone on the road. She asked the operator to put in a collect call to Iris von Lillienfeld and told her the number in New York.

Iris picked up right away and accepted the charges.

"Iris, it's Claire."

"Claire! I've tried to reach you all yesterday afternoon!"

"Iris, there's a time change. They don't answer the phone here after eleven. It's not that sort of place. They just shut the phone off."

"I know the kind of place that is!" Iris said angrily, always upset at any indication of frailty on her part. "Let me talk!"

"I found a photograph of you, Iris. Here. When you were young." Claire fumbled around in her bag to find the photograph.

"Ah, yes. Believe it or not, even I was young once. How did I look? Good?"

"Gorgeous!"

"Huh! You don't have to tell me that. That's one thing you don't forget!"

"I thought I put it in my purse. One second. Damn. I'm so unorganized. Hang on. Ah, here it is. Saint Hildegard's

Mill is covered in snow. It's all lit up with snow and sunshine. When I saw it, my first thought was that I should have come in winter, that's how beautiful it makes everything look. Like a big vanilla cream cake. You know, the way it looks just after it's snowed for days and then the sun comes out and it absolutely blazes with light. The photographer must have been as taken with the scene as well because there were two pages of the Mill in that snow scene. So anyway, there I am enjoying the Mill in days gone by and all of a sudden my eyes zoom in on who do you think?"

"Me?"

"Yes. I'm sure it's you." Not only had it looked like Iris, Claire had a feeling she'd even seen that hat Iris had had on. It was black and had a veil. She stood behind a woman on a sled, an old-fashioned, basket-like sled with swirled front runners.

Claire pressed against the telephone and held the photograph out into the weakening light. Against, in fact, the same view of the Mill today. Yes, it had to be Iris. The woman in the photograph was on the other side of the life spectrum, but those fierce eyebrows against white skin and delicate mouth were so peculiar to her.

And Iris, an old and lonely woman in a tattered velvet chair in New York, was suddenly transported to the exact moment Claire described so many years ago.

It was one of those storms that had gone on for days and days. Adam's mother, ill for so long (ever since Iris herself had gotten well), finally felt strong enough to allow them to take her outdoors.

Iris felt doubly responsible for the old woman's illness. She'd brought the influenza with her when she'd arrived at Saint Hildegard's. Or perhaps she'd caught it there herself, she, so exhausted and devastated by what had happened to her family. Still, she had felt responsible at least for weakening the old woman with the strain of having a Jew under her roof. She'd heard Adam and the old woman arguing about her even as the old woman had lain ill. Iris had come with the bedpan but hesitated to enter with so personal an item, and then she was stuck because she heard it was she they were arguing about. Adam wouldn't hear of Iris's being sent away.

"Let her go to Paris," the mother said. "They're still giving the Jews visas to Paris. At least she will be safe there."

"They let them go to Paris just to see how much money they're trying to take out of the country, and then they arrest them," Adam insisted. "And if she *would* get to Paris undeterred, they'd make her come back as soon as her visa was up. You know they would. And it's just too dangerous to cross the border. *Mutti.* How good she has been to you since you have been ill! All through your fever she nursed you. No one will object to her staying on as your nurse."

"Yes, they will, and they do." Frau von Grünwald had banged her cane on the floor. "Just today I overheard the servants muttering about Iris taking work from the local girls. They called her an outsider, a stranger from another village, but all it takes is underlying animosity these days, Adam. You know what can happen. These are jealous and ignorant people. You must not forget that. I know that you love the villagers and you believe they love you because they have watched you grow and have been here your whole life, but you mark my words, they will betray you the moment it becomes advantageous to them. They don't like her for her soft hands and cultivated accent. If they knew she was a Jew! *Mein Gott!*"

"*Mutti*, I'm not going to send her away. I shall go with her if you force me."

"What? You say such a thing to me? You would let this girl drive a wedge between us, you and me?"

Iris had heard no more. Adam had certainly run and

hushed his mother with one of his all-encompassing, affectionate hugs. He couldn't bear to inflict pain on those he loved. And he loved his mother.

Saint Hildegard's Mill stood hushed and still. Only the chimneys poked through. The voice of Adam, young and jubilant, crossed the years and the black-and-white picture as he adjusted the aperture of his 1913 Zeiss-Ikon camera.

Iris had wheeled his mother out of doors and put her on the sled. This was the first time she had been outside since she'd gotten ill. They blinked and pulled their hats down over their eyes in the blazing light. They'd been indoors so long, it was almost unbearably bright. So many things had been going on in Munich, unspeakable things; no one had wanted to go out. But this storm had stopped the world, somehow, and placed it in a time unrelated to the terrible present. After Adam's crisp young voice, there was no sound. Only the clear white, untrod snow in every direction. A magpie on the fence was the only sharp dark place. There was a row of trees. The branches were so weighed down with snow, they arched and brushed the drifts along the ground. Frau von Grünwald smiled, coughed, smiled again. "Stop!" She waved at Adam with her mittened fist. "Wait until I'm at least ready!"

But Adam hardly heard. All he saw was the sweet face of Iris, who was standing alongside, patiently waiting for him to focus, patiently waiting for the moment he would look into her knowing eyes. It was difficult for both of them not to smile.

How beautiful she is, was all he could think.

How beautiful I feel when he looks at me, she thought, feeling the glistening moment so intently, she knew even then she would never forget it.

She lurched back to Claire and the present. "Claire, what's going on? I got a copy of the *Süddeutsche* over in Ridgewood. It says Hans von Grünwald of Saint Hildegard's Mill is dead! From a fall, it said."

"Yes, it's true, Iris. Just after I arrived. I didn't want to upset you, but—"

"Listen to me, Claire. Don't do that. Don't protect me. Do you understand? I do not need protection from you, all right?" She was totally agitated. "I am worried for you . . ."

"All right, all right. Anyway, the reason I called . . . to be honest, I just don't know where to start looking for the diamonds. I . . . I thought it would be easier. I don't know, I thought I'd have some sort of clue, you know, make some sense out of the past once I got here, but it's so confounding!"

It began to drizzle. She tried to fit herself under the telephone awning, but part of her stuck out. "The truth is, I'm afraid I'll never find the darn treasure."

"I know, dear." Iris spoke more gently. "I know. That's because there is none. At least not yet."

"Iris, what are you talking about? What not yet?"

"I mean I will let you know what the treasure really is when you find it for yourself."

"What the hell is this? What are you playing at?"

"There is no treasure, dear. At least not the kind you thought it would be."

"Iris, I am standing here in the damp. It's going to pour any minute. I've left my family to fend for themselves—"

"It's about time they fended for themselves a bit, too. The way you spoil them! It's offensive. I thought you were a suffragette!"

"You mean a feminist!" Claire shouted.

"Feminist," Iris agreed.

"I am," Claire choked. "I think I'm going to cry," she whined, knowing that even now she couldn't. She didn't have it in her. If only she could.

"Oh, don't cry. It's fun. Aren't you having fun?"

189

"I was until I found out I'm being duped. You mean you sent me all this way under false pretenses?"

"Certainly . . ." The line went fuzzy. Then Iris's harsh, laryngitic voice tuned back in with a blast of clarity. ". . . till I got rid of this *verdammte* arthritis. Such a terrible thing, to be cursed with arthritis. You cannot know because you are young. I don't complain about it, but believe you me, I could. Plenty of days I can just about barely make it out from the bed. Young people don't understand. That's why I always say, Claire, enjoy your life while you still can."

Claire waited impatiently while Iris went on for a while about her arthritis. Then she said, "Iris, I'm hanging up now. I just want to tell you I'm furious with you and your tricks. I can't believe you would do this to me. I can't believe it. Are you serious? Do you mean to tell me there never was a treasure? There never were diamonds?"

"Well, that was years ago. Sometimes we old folks forget the way things really were, you know."

"I'm hanging up," she said, and did. She stood there getting wetter and wetter. She had the strangest feeling that Iris hadn't lied before, but that she was lying now.

Her bag, wedged between the phone and the post, fell with a thud, and the contents spewed all over the wet ground. "Shit," she said and bent down to collect the lot. The photograph of the snowy Mill, propped up against the outdoor phone, melted and shimmered in the spring rain. Claire ran off, crablike, without looking back, almost knowing, as she did, she had forgotten something.

6

*C*laire *found the* curved wooden gates in the fine
stone house of the Rectory locked. She knocked.
Birds called wildly in the trees behind her in the rain. It was
twilight now. Lilac bushes on each side of the gates were
filled with heady drooping blossoms. She gave the rusted
bell a good push, then again another. She turned and
watched the path. An oboe-like sweetness drenched the
very green and empty pasture with glistening rain. After a
while she could hear footsteps down a staircase within. The
door. There was old Father Metz himself just as the rain let
go and came down cats and dogs.

"Hi!" she cried.

"Ja so was!" He took her hand in his fat one and shook it
heartily. *"Komm! Kommen Sie 'rein!"* He invited her in,
practically pulling her across the threshold. They went together up the curving wrought-iron stairway to his cham-
bers. "I am so happy to see you," he told her again and
again. *"Kaffee oder Tee?"*

"Hmmm," Claire deliberated. In the last few days she
had consumed more caffeine and alcohol than she would
normally in months. Never mind. She'd been through the
mill, ha-ha, she'd have yet another coffee.

Father rang a little communion bell. He had been busy,
she noticed, cutting out Christmas-card fronts for book-

marks. A stout, aproned lady with water in her legs and a furry mole on her cheek appeared at the door and was told to prepare *"einen schönen Kaffee und etwas kleines Süsses, bitte schön."* She was gone and they were left alone. It was a nice big room. Too big, probably, when winter came and you had to heat it. Tall ceilings and too loosely lead-paned glass diamonds. Charming but drafty.

"Did you know," he chatted as he straightened the room, looking for papers she would need, "the car was made after the war, but from prewar materials? That's why the running boards. It was the Bishop's car. I inherited it from his chauffeur. So you know the car's lineage," he said.

"Did you come from Munich, Father?"

"Me? *Ach, nein.* I come from Warteweil. *Ja, ja. Das schöne Warteweil.* It's quite near Aidenried." He peered at her over his glasses. "You've been to Aidenried, I hear."

She shivered. He put another log on the fire and it blazed cheerfully up.

Father had a nice lumpy sofa and an even lumpier easy chair. There was a good bronze standing lamp beside it and a table overflowing with books and missals and parish information. There was a worn leather hassock with a pouchy groove for his slippered feet. He'd been listening to Mendelssohn. He turned it off.

"I'm glad to find you home," she said. "I was afraid I might have missed you in the crowd at the wedding."

"That I couldn't do, *nein.*" He sucked in his breath. "I wish them very well, but until the new Frau von Osterwald gets an annulment from her first marriage, I cannot sanction the union, *na?*"

"That's right." Claire remembered. "Isolde's first marriage was Catholic, wasn't it."

A gargantuan television was placed dead in front of his space, and a hefty volume of *Lives of the Saints* had its place in the crook of the arm of the chair. There was a pastel, hand-crocheted shawl cast discreetly behind the chair but sticking out by its few giveaway tassels.

"*Also denn.*" He snuggled into his spot. Claire sat on the sofa. "For what can I do you?" he asked politely, looking to see if she had brought her purse. It took Father a while to get into the gear of speaking English. Once he got going he did very well, but the getting there was a bumpy road.

"I've come to give you your money." She smiled.

Father Metz was so delighted with this news, she had a sudden realistic doubt as to what she'd done, but at last she remembered the dashboard and was happy again.

After they completed their paperwork, they exchanged pleasantries for a while until the housekeeper came and went, leaving them with roasted coffee and a *Bienenstich,* a sticky conglomeration of honey-toasted almond clusters atop a custard-filled, sliced yellow layer cake.

"I couldn't," she vowed.

"*Ach, komm!*" Father Metz became so childishly deflated at the prospect of having to wait till she left to enjoy it, she let herself be coerced.

"Oh, all right," she said.

They sat dividing their sweets.

Claire cleared her throat. "You know," she said, "I feel a little guilty."

Father stopped his eating, fork midair. He was used to this and good at it. He waited.

"I found, well, stole would be the more appropriate word here, something from Hans's room."

"Is this, as you Americans say, 'off from the record'?"

"You mean am I asking you to hear my confession?"

"*Ja.*"

"Okay. If we can do this like this. In here. I mean I haven't been to confession for a while."

"Just say what is in your heart, my child."

"Well, here I was, snooping around Hans von Grünwald's room, and I came across this." She handed the priest the old list of names and addresses.

Father took it from her. He readjusted his glasses and read it carefully. *"Tya,"* he said. "I'm afraid I don't—"

"I think it's a list of old clients from the Mill. People who used to stay there years ago. I believe someone, Hans probably, hid this, well, stuck it under his desk blotter; and when I came across it, I found something someone, maybe the murderer, was looking for."

"Nana, na, na, na!" Father held up his hand to put a stop to this. "First let us get one very thing straightened! Hans did *not* was murdered! For heaven's sake. No wonder you are all upset. This all happening just when you first arrived! *Mein Gott! Alles auf einmal!* Everything at once. Everyone upset at one time! Cosimo and Stella Gabriella don't know what to do about the Mill! There are bills. Fräulein Wintner complaining why all the bills? Money going out to England, to the Church, for fuel to heat. What does she think, the Mill owes no money to the Church? A tenth of the income should go automatically to the Church! This is something every civilized person knows. The minute a person starts tithing his income with the poor, his luck will change. This is known fact. The most successful people in the world will tell you this. You have to give to get!" He was out of breath. He sat back with a whoosh. He remembered Claire. "And you, poor little *Amerikanerin,* coming into the middle of this. Of course you are feeling upset! No wonder!"

And so she told him briefly about Iris and the diamonds story in New York, and then her abrupt denial they'd ever existed.

"First, I don't know of any treasure." This almost burst out of him, as though he couldn't wait to get that off his chest. "You know," he then said more kindly, "lots of people come back here to Germany. It is not only because what

194

they lived through here was so terrible but because it was so intense. People have, how can I put this, people have a hard time *feeling* anything as they go along in life. That is the terrible thing. Oh, I'm not talking about people who have grave, painful illnesses. That is different, of course. No, I mean, sometimes, when people have lived through a war, nothing else in their life can compare with its intensity, and they spend great amounts of time reliving that. Going over and over the terrible and wonderful moments. When, perhaps, they should be moving on. You know, getting on and enjoying what it is, what is happening now. You get what I mean?"

Claire moved in her chair. "Yeah, well, I don't know. I just don't know. I just can't come to terms with what the Germans did to all those Jews, you know? I mean, I lived here ten years, and I never met anyone who admitted to being a Nazi."

"Well, what did you think? Someone would come and tell you, exactly you, what it was happened to them back then? I mean you think it was only the Jews went through the hell? Lost their whole families? *Nein, nein.* Everybody lost their families, my Fräulein. It was easier to watch it happen to the Jews, perhaps, because the Jews had so much before the trouble started. It's easier to see someone destroyed if they have everything you want and cannot get your hands on. For example, if you wanted to have a university career before the war, it was hardly possible if you weren't a Jew. So people resented that they could not become a doctor in their own country when the Jews could. Never mind that the Jews might have been more clever and earned that privilege and were Germans since hundreds of years. What I am meaning to say is that people *let* terrible things happen to people they are jealous of more easily."

"I appreciate what you're saying, Father. I just wasn't really talking about that, I mean, we could go on and on about this for days. I was thinking of the treasure."

"All this talk of treasure. I, myself, was in Italy during the war. But of course, over the years, I too have heard the stories, the dreams of finding a treasure at the Mill. But it all always comes to nothing. Nothing but frust."

"Frustration."

"Yes, frustration." He laughed at his faulty English.

"But there are stories," Claire went on. "I mean, everyone believes them. Or part of them. And what about the haunting? Some people say the Mill is haunted because of the treasure. Stella Gabriella says her grandmother, Kunigunde, won't rest until the treasure goes where it belongs. She says she's the ghost."

"*Was? Nein.* That comes from the child that was killed."

"Child? What child?"

"Well." Father snuggled into his chair. "I will tell you what I know." The rain continued to beat down outside. "There *was* a woman kept secretly at the Mill. She was a Jew. She was the mistress of old Adam von Grünwald." He noticed the sudden flush on Claire's pale cheeks. "Oh yes, it's true. Enough people knew about her after she was discovered. But for a long while, she was kept secretly in the attic over there. She became pregnant. But because the woman was a Jew, it was said that Adam's mother gave her something, made her so sick that the baby died. It was something a woman could take to abort. Only the fetus was almost full term."

"What! You mean the woman who was Adam von Grünwald's mistress years ago almost had his child?"

"That is the story." Father Metz shook his head sadly. Human nature could do very little to shock this old fellow.

Claire clapped one hand over her mouth. She was stunned. So Iris had lost a child! How horrible. And she had never told her! Never told anyone, probably. That explained so much. People her age didn't go about telling stories of their lost children the way they did nowadays. She would have held on to that grief all these years. She closed her eyes in silent mourning for Iris's grief. No wonder she drank. Poor thing. Everyone she'd loved around her killed. Murdered. All except for Adam. And she'd lost him as well. No wonder she had never returned. After his mother had murdered her child! And he continued to live with the mother. That must have been the most unforgivable part.

Claire shivered. Temple was right. This was a horrible place. With the ghosts of children murdered.

"You know, Father," she said, "I really am beginning to wonder if Hans was murdered. I am. I can't prove it and I don't even know who to suspect, but I believe he could have been murdered."

Father shook his head sadly. "If he was murdered," he whispered, "it could have been almost anyone who did it."

"You're right. It seems everyone had a reason, didn't they?"

"He was not an easy man." Father Metz removed his spectacles and rubbed his tired eyes. He remembered his own feelings of dislike for von Grünwald. He was a man devoid of faith. But more than that, he'd despised those who had it. Father Metz wished, at times, the world would leave the past alone.

"I was wondering if you knew of some private greed that would make someone hate him enough to kill him," Claire pursued.

"No." Father shook his head. "Not greed. No, it must have been love. Love is far more treacherous than greed, farther-reaching."

Claire watched him, her mouth open. She realized he was right. "There's something else I'd sort of like to talk to you about, if you have another minute."

"Of course, of course." He knew this was what was really on her mind.

Claire took a deep breath. "Well. I'm married. I'm a married woman. And there's this man, this man I see—" The room went white with sudden lightning.

"You have been intimate with this man?" Father got right to the point.

"No. Not yet. I mean, no. I'm not going to be intimate with him, either. It's just that I feel . . . my feelings for him are so strong, so real." She got up and walked across to the window. Rain poured down. "I'm almost afraid," she said, laughing, "of myself. My weakness. I almost know that, given the chance, I would do anything, anything with him." They both jumped at the clap of thunder.

"That is not a given." Father came over and put a hefty hand on her shoulder. "If that were so, you would not be telling me all this now. Is that not right?"

Claire shook her head, not knowing anything right now.

"Fräulein Claire." He called her "Fräulein" as he would a child, not out of disrespect. He clasped her hands in his. "Do not be so hard to judge yourself before you've done the deed. Your strength and goodness might surprise you."

"But if I have sinned already in my heart, I have already sinned," she said. "Isn't that the way it goes?"

"The way it goes is that that is the way the world gets by, living from one harmless imagined episode to the next." He shrugged. "So long as nothing happens."

But it wasn't so. He was wrong, she knew. Ideas and imaginings were real, existing forever in some underlying dimension, permanent, changing everything. How had he forgotten? He couldn't have become a priest and not known it once. It was getting dark. She wanted to get back to the Mill.

"Father"—she collected her camera from the floor and shook hands—"thank you so much for everything. Will I see you in the morning? May I pick up the car then?"

"And I will have the papers ready for you," he promised. Come anytime, *ja?*"

"Okay." She stood before him while he gave her his blessing. She started to leave.

"Oh, and Fräulein," he called her back. "It wasn't 'they' that crucified Him. It was us. And if He could forgive us; so"—he extended his hands as if to say *Voilà!*—"then why can't we?"

"Why"—she looked into his knowing eyes—"indeed."

A*s she began* her descent on the curving wrought-iron stairway, she was attacked by a dog. With no regard for its own safety on the stairs, the small dog herded her with snaps and snarls until she was forced back up.

"Hier! Komm!" Father Metz stood behind her, doing no good whatsoever, blocking her ascent and not being able to get his hands on the dog. It was, Claire saw, Hans's old dog. She took her mesh bag of films from her vest pocket and smacked the animal lightly on the nose with it. He got the message all right and hightailed it down the rest of the staircase, yelping dramatically. By the time he got to the kitchen, Claire could hear his barks had regained their pepper.

"I thought you were going to let someone else take that dog." She grinned.

Father shrugged. "Some things," he admitted sheepishly, "Nature decides for us. It's not forever, I know, but how long is forever anyway? Eh? *Was?*"

The rain had stopped. Claire crossed the meadow. She hadn't even mentioned Johnny to the priest. She hadn't even thought of him, if she were honest, since she'd landed in Germany, except as a sort of necessary encumbrance. The muddy ground was rutted, and she was far from the path. She turned her ankle twice and was grateful when she saw a car coming toward her to light her way. To her surprise, Otto von Auto came rolling along. Whoever's driving will surely give me a ride, she thought, and then realized they well might, as it was her own car. And something else occurred to her. If the dog always hacked a bark at anyone who left, and he hadn't barked at the time of the murder, then the murderer had never left the Mill.

She tried to peer behind the windshield. It was Cosimo. She had such a concentrated image of him at the Mill that it was almost a shock to see him like this behind the wheel, tooling about the countryside willy-nilly on his fine day out. He opened the door to her by leaning over and stretching his long self across the passenger seat. She had a moment of stark warning and then, looking into the liquid eyes beneath ferocious brows, this evaporated and she felt quite safe. She climbed irrevocably in.

He drove a little way before either of them said anything. She felt the car slide graciously back onto the road and said, "Thank you. I was turning my ankle left and right out there."

"Hedgehog," he explained. "Bad gullies."

"It's so dark so quickly," she marveled. "It never gets really dark in Queens. Between the lights from the city and the airports."

The car still smelled of Father Metz. Incense and dandruff and leathery age. The Saint Christopher medal, worn but still recognizable, remained on the glove box. She touched it fondly.

"Watch," Cosimo said, and turned the headlights off by pulling out the ivory knob on the dash. He was still heading in the direction he'd been driving when he'd picked her up, away from the Mill.

They left the Rectory and Saint Hildegard's off to their right. There was nothing here, only fields and rolling hills with dark orchards. The stars were fierce and close. She felt the car axle bump down onto the field again. He'd taken it off the road. "What are you doing?" she cried. "We're going the wrong way! The tires!"

"Look!" His eyes glittered. She forced herself to look away from him and into the night. It was clean with the rain and puddles everywhere. The clouds, moving swiftly, pulled apart. A hauntingly beautiful full moon rose up before them.

"The moon to plant," Cosimo said. He stopped the car.

They looked together at the suddenly luminous pitch of the world.

"You're not afraid of me, are you." He said it as a fact, not a question.

"No," she said, surprised at the truth of it. "I'm not."

"Almost everyone is, you know. The whole village of Saint Hildegard's. They even cross themselves when I walk by. They call me a changeling. Left by fairies."

"What nonsense," Claire said. "Your mother was one of them."

"Oh, she was the one who started that rumor."

Claire tilted her head at him curiously. Was he putting her on? Well, if he was, he was still a frightened and disturbed boy to confide such thoughts to a relative stranger like herself. "You know what you are?" She smiled gently. "One of those rare persons, sensitive to every vibration. The world is just more cruel and unevolved than the likes of you, Cosimo."

"You don't think I killed my father, do you?"

"I must admit, the thought did occur to me, but I dismissed the idea just as quickly."

He narrowed his eyes at her. "Why that?"

She sighed and dropped her head back on the worn gray-brown upholstery. "Instinct, I guess. I can't imagine it. Don't forget, I was there when you saw your father . . .

there. It didn't seem to me as though you were acting."

They remembered, together, that terrible sight. Whoever had done that, she realized, was capable of anything. She shuddered. "It must be awful for you," she said. "All this. Just awful."

"It's not as if we were orphans," he said with childlike optimism. "Fräulein Wintner always takes care of us. She looks after all our finances, so we need not be troubled by that." He said this with relief. Whew. Not having to pay the bills. Claire almost laughed.

"I quite like Fräulein Wintner," Cosimo said, defending her from Claire's obvious skepticism. "She's different from other girls."

"Really?"

"Mmm. Sometimes she lets me—" He looked shrewdly at Claire. "We won't bother about that, though."

"No," Claire agreed, imagining all the same what Fräulein Wintner let him do.

"You know, she had a rough time of it, as a child. Have you ever seen her thumb? No? It's like a ball. A globe. She sucked it into a ball when she was a little girl. She used to worry so. Her parents would fight terribly. She would suck it with great force." Cosimo stuck his thumb into his mouth and gobbled it with such rigorous noises, Claire was taken aback. They both laughed.

"And of course, there's Evangelika." Cosimo stopped laughing. "She won't leave. She raised us, after all. She'll stay and always give me my meals. That's sure. She's been here forever. Well. Since the war. And she does the wash when the girl doesn't come. She doesn't mind too much. Well, she yells a bit."

"Really. And Fräulein Wintner too? She won't leave either?"

"Stella says she won't want to now. Now Father's gone and she's had a setback of her plans and will have to regroup. Like in a game of chess, when it's 'Check!' "

"Plans?"

"You didn't know? Wanting to marry Father."

"I'm shocked. Your father wanted to marry Bibi Wintner?"

"Let's put it this way, he let her believe he did. Stella says Father thought he could use everyone."

"What do you think?"

"I think it's an illusion to imagine ourselves in charge." He raised his chin to the magnificent moon. "I mean, in charge of what? Confusion?" They were silent for a bit, transfixed by the Bavarian stars and the black Alps in the south. Then he said, "Bibi—Fräulein Wintner—she's always trying to drum up business so Father would want to sell. She wants to live where it is warm. Where there are palm trees and wild beasts. Heard too many of my father's adventure tales, I think, from trips to Kenya and Thailand and all. Oh, she is a keen little thing. You have to give her that. Wait!" He reached his long fingers across the dash. With the other hand he fiddled with the radio.

"What is it?" Claire cried, concerned.

"It's Beethoven's 'Appassionata.' " He shushed her.

"Oh," she said, "I thought something must have happened."

He managed to get the station in tune. It was no chore to sit and listen. It really was splendid. They sat religiously and heard it the rest of the way through.

"Perhaps, before I leave, you will play the whole thing through for me," Claire said.

He hung his beautiful head. "I'm afraid I never could. It was the piece I played always for my mother, you see. I could never play it for anyone else. Never."

"What a pity."

He turned on her, startling her. "What do you mean?" He loomed, hostilely, above her.

"All that beauty bottled up and put away on a shelf for no one to enjoy. Just that you are fortunate, Cosimo, to have access to such beauty. And I am sorry for whoever won't hear you play it."

"Oy. Beauty, beauty, beauty." He made a goony face. "You're like Stella. Loving things just because they're beautiful."

"I love beauty for beauty's sake, yes," she defended herself, stung.

"You love it for its meaning. Everything with you has to *mean* something. Be so profound."

"Yes," Claire said. "Otherwise I might as well be a piece of fluff spinning in the wind, being everywhere but never knowing it. So in that sense I suppose you're right."

"Ach! You need not be so arbitrary. At least not with me. You see, I know your secret."

"Do you really? So, you're good at other people's business, eh? And I had you pegged for being oblivious."

He opened the car door, the hinges squeaking, and he pulled up a handful of green.

"What secret do you know?" She smiled carefully.

He held the stuff up to his nose and sniffed it like a dog at a bush. *"Engelwurz,"* he pronounced, ignoring her question and handing it over for her to inspect with her nose. *"Angelica archangelica.* Used to expel evil and disease. Contaminated air won't infect you if you have it in your mouth."

"Hmmm. Sounds good."

"The Archangel drove the Devil from Paradise with its help."

"No fooling."

"Good for toothaches, poisoning, and rabies bite as well."

"Wow."

"The birds go wild for it. That's what spreads the seeds. Usually it's happier in shady spots."

"Cosimo, what about these birds around the Mill? The magpie. You know. What's the name?"

Cosimo looked at her suspiciously. *"Elster. Raubvogel."*

"That's it. Magpie is 'robber bird.' I found one in the attic."

"You didn't hurt it?"

"I let him out."

Cosimo smiled. "He just comes back because when he was young, he had some trouble with his wing, and I kept him up there till he could fly again. I used to feed him *Bauernschinken.* You know, meat. He loved it so." His face relaxed as he remembered and he looked really beautiful, his long black eyelashes sweeping his cheek.

How tragic, all that had happened to these two beautiful children.

"Does that bird you took care of ever, sort of, I don't know, take things?"

"Only shiny little things. You know, soda-tin tops. Pop tops. Like that. Harmless things." He looked, worried, at Claire. "He's mad for shiny things."

"Cosimo, is there a treasure at the Mill?"

His face changed to one of elaborate scorn. "If there was, my father used it up."

"No, I don't mean like a fountain of youth or a grotto of faith or anything like that. I mean something tangible." She knitted her brows and tried to peer more closely into his face. "Something, perhaps, your mother might have told you about?"

A large, great teardrop traveled down his cheek. "My mother *was* the treasure," he said. He turned and grabbed hold of Claire's shoulders. He shook them back and forth.

"You can't imagine what it's like if your mother shouts at you. If she shouts she doesn't understand you, could never understand you! Ooh! I hate so much that we must die," he cried. "I hate it so!" He shook her again and again.

Claire held on to the edge of her seat, trying not to scream. No one would hear them here. Then suddenly he stopped. He let her go and he slumped back into his seat. "We'd better go back," he said, waking up. "Stella won't like it."

"Shall I drive, Cosimo?"

"That's a good idea." He shrugged. "I stole the car."

Temple Fortune was the first person she saw when they drove up the gravel path. Their eyes locked and the feeling of dizzy levitation she was beginning to recognize as what accompanied his being near took over. Then he noticed Cosimo. Disappointment flashed across his face. She had an urge to push Cosimo from the car. Fortunately, presence of mind prevailed, and she managed to sit still and let him leave. Nothing seemed to have calmed down since she'd left. If anything, the decibel level had been revved up. The strolling musicians had been let go or had cleared out at the first drops of rain, and rock music from tapes was blaring. Claire looked around for the police and saw none. Cosimo skulked away into the house, as was his way. She could hear Evangelika squawking at him, furious about the mud on his Sunday shoes. She noticed Mara sidle up to Temple Fortune and push up against him in her devotional and sultry way. Claire slammed the car door, feeling it shut with her own possessive finality. Try as she might, though, there was no comfort there. At least she hadn't made a fool of herself. He didn't know, he would never know the extent of her feelings. She would stay right here and watch him with his Mara. She would swallow the truth whole, let it sink in so she could grieve and get over it.

She locked the car door with her own set of keys. And just let Fräulein Bibi Wintner try to have her arrested! She would make such a stink they would hear her in Toledo. Or at least in Queens. She reminded herself, if doubtfully, that she was, by gum, an American citizen.

The girls in their yellow organza gowns danced in swirls around her. She held her breath until they passed, knowing she looked neither graceful nor lovely. Her hair was frizzed, her boots muddy, her forehead shiny. Blacky waved to her from across the garden. He had a great bandage across his nose. At least he was enjoying his wedding. Isolde was nowhere to be seen, and Claire decided, this once, to stay away. She looked for Puffin but couldn't find him either for the throng. Discouragement overtook her. She sat down on the nearest bench. Puffin appeared, wizard-like, and handed her a stein of Spaten beer. She took a grateful, huge draft. She was going to go home with no cache of diamonds as she had imagined. She might as well admit it.

"What's up?" He joined her on the bench.

"Oh, you know, nothing. I was just feeling a little low."

"Weddings," Puffin sympathized.

"No, not that. Well, maybe partly that. Also, I guess it bothers me that someone is probably going to get away with murder." She didn't give a hoot who got away with murder till now, but as she heard herself say it, she did care.

Puffin made a face. "If there *was* a murder. Personally, I'm beginning to think we've got a couple of overactive imaginations here. And after the first twenty-four hours, if no one is arrested, the chances are slim anyone will ever be."

"I don't know where you heard that." Claire frowned. "My sister is a detective on the New York City Police Department, and she says ninety-five percent of all murder cases are solved." And, she did not add, her sister also said it was most often someone in the victim's own family who'd done it.

"Well, if someone did kill him, love, I say let's run him for office."

"No." Claire had another delicious slurp. "There I can't agree with you, Puffin. Nobody has a right to kill another human being. No matter what he's done."

"So they shouldn't have stopped Hitler in Munich before he got started. That's what you mean?"

"You've got me there."

Mara Morgen was dancing with Blacky. Her eyes flashed, and she pressed provocatively against him. Blacky twirled her romantically into a dip and leaned, apache-like, above her.

Temple Fortune sat down on the bench beside Puffin. "Shall I remove her for you, darling?" Puffin asked him sweetly.

Temple sighed good-naturedly. "Let her be. She hasn't had the easiest time of it."

They sat there watching the party, watching Mara, really, for Isolde was nowhere to be seen. They watched her do her belle-of-the-ball until it became uncomfortable. She was a mite overdoing the sultry vamp, Claire decided, feeling Temple's self-consciousness, feeling sorry for him.

"Mara looks great," Claire remarked.

"She doesn't, really," Puffin said. "She just never took her film makeup off. She'll be broken out tomorrow. I told her to take it off but she would insist on running to see an old friend in Schwabing. She wanted to do it intact."

"That's all right," Temple said, tapping his foot, listening with one ear higher than the other. He's probably a little deaf in that ear, Claire thought indulgently. That's why the right side of his forehead wrinkles like that. "I got the last close-ups today," Temple added. "Let her have fun.

Whoever you got to do her face today was brilliant."

"Yes, brilliant," Puffin nodded, pleased.

They watched Mara from their professional, sophisticated stances, but even then there was something a little sordid about a grown woman acting so silly about a man just married. Even if it was just for the benefit of Temple Fortune, it had the ring of desperation about it for a woman who, Puffin had been so quick to point out, had just been satisfied. Perhaps Mara and Temple hadn't been together after all. But then where had they been?

"What's that you're eating, Claire?" Puffin leaned over and picked from her plate.

"*Radi,*" she said and handed him the dish of sweltering, salted radish, long and fat and white.

"Mmmm. Delicious." He licked his fingers.

"Keep it. Keep it," she insisted. She didn't want it now.

Mara came tottering over, just in time, too, because Isolde was making her way back on the scene, heading for Blacky, rolling her broad runway shoulders. Mara was flushed and excited. Her flimsy dress outlined her flesh. She didn't look quite so good up close. It didn't matter now. The night was almost over.

"Enjoying yourself, Mara?" Puffin inquired.

"Oh, oh, oh. That sounds like a reprimand! I am neglecting my sweetie, aren't I?" She pressed Temple's ears into his head. "Jealous, darling?" Her words came out too loud and slurred. He flinched. She jackknifed her body over and pulled up her stockings in three different places. People turned to look. Claire could almost feel Temple's dismay. "Come." Mara yanked Temple to his feet.

"I don't want to dance with you," he told her firmly. Then, more politely, "Thank you."

"Then dance with our poor Claire." She jostled him away as though she'd meant this from the start. "She has nobody, do you, Claire? Come on, up with both of you.

No more sticking in the mud!" She practically shoved them together. She wasn't worried about competition from Claire. Claire was older and heavier than she was. And from what Isolde had told her, poor as a church mouse. So what was to worry?

It took Claire and Temple a few clumsy steps to get into position. Then the music stopped, and they had to wait foolishly for a new song to start up. Mara winked at Puffin. He went to get her a fresh glass of champagne, but when he came back, she was already passed out, dead drunk, on two chairs. He'd have to call Friedel the gardener to help carry her to bed.

The song started up. It was Elvis singing "Are You Lonesome Tonight?"

"You see that?" Puffin said to a woozy Friedel. "Not one of you can speak a word of English. But just put on old Elvis and you all know the words. Go figure." It was true. The entire German festivity had turned into a quite hearty Elvis sing-along. Entire tables of guests swayed back and forth. "You can really just imagine the war," he remarked to Friedel. "All this sentimental, euphoric camaraderie."

Friedel slapped his thigh with buffoon-like glee.

Puffin looked worriedly at Temple and Claire out on the dance floor. Temple had one hand on the small of Claire's back and the other wrapped lightly around her fingers. They stayed in one spot and rocked very slightly back and forth. Claire could hardly breathe. She wouldn't look at him. He wouldn't look at her. They were both so happy that what they suspected was true: they fit. They moved in sync. When the music came to the hook, he put his cheek a little closer to hers and pressed her lower back in toward him. Here's where I pass out, she thought, but she didn't. He carried her through it, lifting her with his intoxicating scent. And then it was over, the longest and the shortest dance she'd ever done. She blinked as though she'd been dreaming. He cupped her elbow with his hand in the old-fashioned way and escorted her back to the bench. He sat her down, bowed almost imperceptibly, then took his spot up on the other side of Puffin.

"Well," Puffin sniffed. "I'm glad that's over. You had me worried there for a minute, dears." He fanned his face with one of those cardboard beer-stein coasters. "The whole yard was warming up. Well, well, I suppose it was bound to happen. Still, I'm glad it's over now. No harm done, what? Sounds like the American hour, doesn't it? First the Viennese hour and then a little limber-them-up with the Yanks. Let them think they know how to dance by putting in a couple of black-and-blues."

"*Out of the night the light is shining, it's twilight time.*" The song filled the garden. Claire and Temple sat like book-ends, trembling, as Puffin chatted gaily on.

Claire, oblivious to Puffin, was thinking. Temple made her realize she was more given to wondering than other people, maybe, but it was okay, he wanted her that way. She even, if she wasn't mistaken, cheered him up.

Temple thought, she likes me because I am Irish, something no one ever did. Her I could handle, he thought. This one I could persuade to the point of not minding a thing.

So they sat, Puffin between them, unsure, waiting for a chance, fearing what would happen only a little more than what wouldn't. Finally, Claire thought, this is silly. I'm a married woman. She didn't think about Johnny, just that she was married to him. She stood up abruptly, and Temple stood at the same time.

Propriety! she berated herself as she walked away with finality. Oh, you fool. You'll never have the chance again. You fool!

Halfway across the dance floor, Fräulein Bibi Wintner in her snazzy glamour jacket harrumphed onto the scene. "Uh-oh," Claire said and turned and bumped into the very arms she would have gone upstairs to dream about.

"You won't get away this time." His lips touched her ear.

"Okay," she said, and he danced her away.

7

———————◆•◆•◆—————————

*H*e led her by the hand away from the lights and the
Mill. They scarcely made it into the cover of trees
by the stream before he turned and kissed her. He seized
her by the waist, lifting her toward him. Her arms went
down, out and open. Then she took his beautiful face in her
hands and pulled it in to her, drawing his lips in and in.
They fell to the soft, damp ground in a swirl of mystical
vertigo. He raised himself up, his small teeth glinting in the
moonlight. He lifted her wall of hair and attached his face
to the back of her neck. Her mouth opened, the small flowers in the grass, their petals, closed for the night, touched
her tongue. She closed her lips and broke them off; Angelica Arch Angelica. *"It brings back a night,"* came the
song from the crackling speakers, *"of tropical splendor. It
brings back a memory evergreen. . . ."*

The clouds moved, and a trail of stars swept the sky.

They picked each other up. "There's a wee chapel up
ahead," he whispered. She took the hand he held behind
him and followed the sure black step of his boots.

The chapel stood open. They blessed themselves and
hurried in. He turned and put his arms at last around her. A
sniffling sound came from the dark blue of the corner.
"Who's there?" they cried out together, holding on.

213

Another low, unhappy sniveling sound while they strained to adjust their eyes.

"*Ich bin's*," came a small voice. "It's me, Dirk."

"Dirk!" she cried.

"Aw, Christ," Temple swore.

"It's all right," Claire told the little boy, moving toward him, trembling still. "You poor kid." She felt his shoulders in the dark, imagined if it were her own son, Anthony, all alone with strangers. "What are you doing here? What's wrong? You ought to be at the party."

"No one missed me," he said, his fist against his dripping nose.

"All right, all right." She helped him up. "And no one will. We'll get you back before the *Kindermädchen* knows you're gone."

"I don't care," he said.

Thank God, Claire thought, they'd noticed him now instead of later.

Temple crouched down next to him. "Ya know," he spoke softly, "I hated being a kid."

Dirk said nothing.

"Yah. I really did. I thought, you know, if it doesn't get better, I'll go to America. It was that or jump off the cliff, you know what I mean? So I thought, here, I'll just wait till I get a bit bigger, get myself a passport and skip off. And I did, you know. I did just that," Temple chatted as they left the chapel and escorted the boy firmly to the Mill. As they neared the dwindling, but still raucous, party scene, Temple stopped Claire with one hand. "Look," he whispered, "if you go back in there, something will happen, and we'll never get to be alone."

"Well, I can't very well not deliver the boy to the au pair now, can I?" She brushed a lock of his hair from his forehead. "And anyway, what could happen?"

He hesitated. "I'll just go attend to something, then."

214

He released her. "I'll meet you back here in half an hour, all right?"

"You don't have to be so mysterious." She smiled lopsidedly at him. He's going to find me a gift, she thought. Or, oh my God, protection.

"One hour." He changed their meeting time.

"Fine." She shrugged, disappointed. She went in and turned Dirk over to an inappropriately tipsy, but appropriately frantic, au pair girl.

She went outside and started for the trees where she'd left Temple, then decided to sit instead near them but at the edge of the party. She wanted a cup of something hot to clear her mind. He would find her if he wanted her. She sat with Friedel the gardener. He was so drunk he was beyond making conversation, let alone a pass, and he was big enough so she could position herself behind him should Fräulein Wintner or her policemen come looking. Everyone, in fact, appeared to be drunk. Even the waiter, when she finally got him, staggered away in a dignified decks-awash. One lubricated throng wove a reeling conga line in front of and behind her. There was no sense in appearing civil toward them, they were that shellacked.

Claire was just finishing her coffee, wondering if she ought to give up on Temple, when she felt him watching her through the forest of woozy people.

"Well, I'd like to thank you for your charming company," she said to Friedel, who stared unblinking into his own beery world as they left.

"It was good of you," Claire said to Temple as they fell into step, "the way you talked to Dirk. You were so good."

"Ah, he's only as big as a minute, poor thing. I hope Blacky will know how to treat him."

"He will, he will," she assured him. They spoke like strangers now, the spell quite broken.

"What now?" he said.

"Let's walk," she said. "It's almost light anyway."

"It breaks your heart it is so green," he said. He put his arm around her, and they stood together looking at the sweep of the lightening hill.

"Let's watch from the Roman Bridge," she suggested. "I want to see if there's a way to climb up underneath it."

"And just what is it you hope to find?"

"Treasure." She grinned.

"Oh. In that case."

"I'm serious. I'll need you to hoist me up," she said.

They trudged up the dell and made their way under the bridge's lip, sinking into the pebbly, groggy soil. The magpie spotted them and took off. She watched the ledge he came from and counted the stones she'd have to pass to reach it.

"It's a good thing you're here," she called above the water as he hoisted her heels up with his hands. "I'd never get up here on my own."

"Not that far! Don't go up that far! Come on down! Let me go up," he shouted, pissed.

"You won't fit."

"Just be careful!"

She reached the ledge and wedged her foot in one of the worn parts between the stones to steady herself.

"What do you see?" Temple called from the ground.

She had known how old the bridge was before she'd gone up, but she hadn't felt it. Now here she was. She looked up, and the crazed stillness of a cave, unexplored except for amphibious hoveling, sent a chill right through her. It must be the wrong stopping place she'd seen the magpie come out of, though, because there was nothing, no droppings, just cold rock, and, below, the slimy clean green of the Isar in a hurry.

"Don't fall," he called, and she almost did, her hand

grabbing on the chink in a stone that let loose when she held it.

And then there it was. A ransom of shiny things: bottle caps, nails, an earring; a recent acquisition—her camera battery—pay dirt! She put her fingers through it, riddling the private estate of nature's pirate, feeling like a pirate herself, an interloper. A brooch was on top. No, wait, it was a medal. Some sort of religious medal. Oh dear, yes. A miraculous medal. She put it in her pocket. She swept the lot of dust-covered glittery things into her scarf, knotted it, and folded it into her belt, stopping to hear what Temple was shouting, but just as she was about to turn, the bird came home. With an almost comic show of surprise, he reared up and screamed.

She screamed at just the same moment, and the two of them tumbled. The bird recovered halfway down and took off. Claire lurched in a series of free falls and rolling hits along the side of the bridge's leg. "I'm all right, I'm all right," she said over and over. "My camera's all right. It's okay."

"The hell with the camera." He was on top of her, testing her for broken bones, searching her eyes for unfocused concussion.

She was practically in tears. "I dropped the treasure," she cried. "I can't believe I did that. Where did it fall?"

They looked together at the churned-up stream. "Great." She shook her head and rubbed her arm. She must have banged it hard. It started to ache horribly. "Where are you going?" she called to his back.

"I'm going on top of the bridge. Maybe I can see where it's headed."

"I'll tell you where it's headed," she grumbled, "it's headed downstream." Her arm throbbing, her hip hot with pain, she hobbled after him, knowing, even as she did, that the diamonds weren't in that lot. She would have seen them through the dust, felt them with the tips of her hungry fingers.

They leaned across the rail of the bridge and traced the curving trail of it.

"No luck," he sighed.

"There," she cried, pointing. The sun, just rising, spangled like a bevy of stars across the water under a leaning willow.

They ran, falling over each other, down the banks to the other side of the water. He was faster, and she shuffled behind him while he made his way out of the tangled part in his black boots. The berry bushes riddled the path, sticking to them both. He stopped suddenly, and she almost ran into him. "What is it?" she asked.

He leaned toward the raging stream. "It's a stick, a fine one, stopped by the reeds. It's Hans's." Temple pulled back, shocked, recognizing the carved magpie head. "It's his walking stick."

He clung to her ankle as she leaned way over the rushing water. "Let me lower," she said. She wouldn't want to fall in. The Isar was deep and icy and swift. Many a good swimmer told tales of its treachery. "Don't let me go," she called above its whooshing clarity. She got hold of it and he pulled her back.

"It's cocobolo," she said. Then, "My father works in wood. It must be hollowed out to let it float like that. Cocobolo doesn't float unless it is. It's too dense. It's beautiful, isn't it? It's too expensive to make anything but ornaments from it. Or pharmaceutical mortars and pestles."

Temple fondled the dripping cane thoughtfully. "We'll bring it back for Cosimo. Now, about letting you go," he started to say, but the bells from Saint Hildegard's pealed out. "Ah," he said. "The King is dead. Long live the King."

"Probably Blacky showing off his new manor."

"More likely Isolde."

He drew her to him. "No, wait," she said, "let me still see if we can get the bird's hoard first." He let her go and pulled the rattling cane handle. The beginning of a glinting sword came out. He shivered and tightened it back in.

Claire ran the rest of the way to the willow, excited. Here she had been sure there were no diamonds, and if she hurried—

She stopped as though slugged.

"Are they sunk?" he called from behind. "It's so clear we might still find them if they are." He came up beside her. They looked at Fräulein Bibi Wintner sitting upright under the cold clear water in a place of tangled willow bark and reeds. Her eyes were opaque. It was her glittering party jacket that had sparkled so. Her one hand was up, as though she were on the phone. She looked at them, as if surprised. Little fish darted through her undulating hair.

The bells from Saint Hildegard's chimed up and down the cool, still-sleeping valley.

8

There's a dreadful lot of press outside." Stella peered through the curtains in the family room.

"Isn't it lovely," Puffin exclaimed. "Marvelous for the film. All this advance publicity."

"Puffin, you are a sick puppy," Temple said, looking apologetically from face to face.

"Could go the other way, you know," Puffin reminded him. "Such and such a film, doomed from the start. Happens all the time."

"Oop. There goes the ambulance. They've taken the body away in the ambulance."

Father Metz puffed on his beloved, strongly forbidden meerschaum pipe. "It is hard to believe Frau Doktor von Osterwald is arrested. It is not possible. Not possible."

Claire sat huddled in the red wing chair, her feet pulled up under her skirt. She shivered as she turned the pages Cosimo had given her. *Seymour's Garten Brevier.* She couldn't even see the print. Isolde being questioned for murder! Of course it wasn't so. It was a mistake. Isolde couldn't kill anyone. On second thought, she admitted to herself, Isolde very well could. But not these people. Not Hans. And now Fräulein Wintner. Not when Isolde had so much going for her, she wouldn't. Isolde was full of surprises, but even those usually made sense. At least to her they did, and Claire could usually piece the logic together. This was absurd. Isolde would never care for either of them enough to kill them. Even if they had been blackmailing her—which seemed farfetched enough, considering Isolde was about as notorious as a body could be and still be in Bavarian society—Isolde would have certainly found a more clever way to do it than this! This was so weird.

"Where's Doktor von Osterwald?" Stella pushed the rattan dessert cart to and fro, peeling the ends and poking the splinters into a doll's fence around the potted orange tree.

"He'll be right back, my dear," Father Metz soothed her.

Claire blurted out, "Stella, what did you mean when you said, '*Es war Cosimo!* It was Cosimo.' What did you mean?"

"Oh, he told me to cut my hair. He said, 'Go ahead. Just do it.' "

Puffin said, "Temple, don't sit there looking like you were hit with the bloody porridge dish. Your mouth is open. You'll catch the odd bug."

Temple stirred. He'd been off in another world. He looked to Claire.

"Nice," Claire said, "the way you talk to people, Puffin."

"*Moi?*" Puffin splayed his fingers across his silk shirt.

"Don't mind him," Temple said wearily. "He's got more songs than the radio."

I can't take another minute of this, Claire thought. She got up and went outside. She hardly felt anything but shock. The car was standing on the pebble drive out back. It was a perfect afternoon. She took the grand key out and opened the door. There was a rich, well-oiled feel to an old Mercedes. When you shut yourself in, there was a silent, raised-up sense of privilege that set you away from everything and everyone. And that was just what she needed, to be away from all of them. To think. The idea that Isolde might be a murderer was boggling.

Of course, the idea that it was somebody else of them was equally horrifying. Temple Fortune hadn't been with her when Fräulein Wintner was killed. He'd been off on his own for a good hour. And there was something else. When she'd first come to Saint Hildegard's, Temple had referred to "sixty blue-white diamonds" as the treasure. No one else she'd heard had known the treasure was *of* diamonds, let alone sixty. How would he know there were sixty? Good Lord, she berated herself, she was becoming paranoid. Temple Fortune had had nothing to do with Saint Hildegard's Mill years ago. She really must relax! Anyone might have been told tales of the Mill treasure. People talked about it all the time. She sucked a loud breath of air through her nostrils and held it in. She closed her eyes. She blew out her mouth and took another loud, lifting breath in her nostrils. And out. At last she breathed deeply. The passenger door opened and she heard herself scream.

"Lord." Temple climbed in and shut the door behind himself. "Don't *do* that! There are reporters all over the front yard. They'll all come running."

"My nerves must be shot."

"No rest for the weary," he said.

"Yes." She smiled, remembering last night. A reporter burst from the big hydrangea bush. They ducked below the dashboard. The reporter scurried off. Still sunk down, Claire said, "May I ask you something? Why do you let Puffin speak to you the way he does?"

"Oh, that. I don't mind, really. He doesn't mean it."

"He does too. And even if he doesn't, either way it's demeaning."

"You don't understand."

"I understand no one has a right to say things the way he does. No matter what you've done—"

"It's not what I've done. It's what I haven't done. And, by the way, I wouldn't be anywhere without Puff's connections."

"Oh, please."

"It's true. You of all people should understand how important it is to know the right people. Doesn't matter how good you are for a minute if no one sees your work. You know that. Puffin hooked me up. I'll never be able to thank him for that."

"I can't believe you're saying this. He should thank *you* for letting him tag along on your talented shirttails."

"It doesn't work like that. In this business—"

"In any business. You should hear yourself, you sound like a battered wife." They sat very still. "Oh, look," she said, "let's not argue. Please. I have no right." She took his hand. "I am so happy. Even through all this, everything that's happened, I . . . I can't help being happy."

A yearning sadness came over his blue-green eyes. She felt it like a tug on her heart. There were some people like that in your life. You could feel with them as if there were a line stretched between you, even when they didn't speak. "I don't even have the excuse of a failed marriage," she said. "My husband is a decent man. A good father."

"That can't be true. If you were happy in your marriage, you never would have seen me, felt me."

"You talk like someone never married, Mr. Fortune."

"Call me Douglas now," he said. He put both hands around her waist. "Just once."

"Douglas," she whispered.

They shared a fervent kiss. He looked into her eyes. "I'm sorry I am such a coward," he said.

She started to protest, but he touched her lips with his

fingers and sighed. "I am. I know I am. Look. I know how you feel about me. I feel it. Just the way I feel it for you. But if I left Mara, the next thing would be you'd have me leaving Puffin."

"I never would think to ask you to leave Mara," she protested. "I think we're getting a little ahead of ourselves here." His words had stung her into aloofness.

"No, wait. Let me finish. You think you're terribly sophisticated and European, but you're not. You're hopelessly American, with your idealism and your belief that right must prevail. I don't say you're wrong. For God's sake, I love you for it. I do. I love you." His voice caught with emotion. "But it's too late for me. I am a maelstrom of vice. Don't laugh. I am. You don't know what it was like for me before I had my bit of success. It wasn't charming and cozy where I'm from in Ireland. It was cold and dirty and damp. Where I grew up there were so many babies, the house smelled of diapers. And if not diapers, then cabbage. Boiling bloody cabbage. Every time I smell the stuff I can see my mother. Her broad back at the stove. You never saw the front of the woman because she was always busy off doing something. There was nothing. No jobs. My father sodden from year after year of the drink. No hope. He'd sort of bumble out of his stupor long enough to rabbit my mother yet another time, she too old for any of it. Never complaining. Just doin'. Doin' and doin'.

"I swore I'd get out. Brendan Timmons, this kid, moved to Belfast to marry a Protestant, and his mother threw his guitar in the rubbish bin. I snatched it right out. I was, like, fourteen. I learned all the songs. There was a lot going on back then. You remember. Out of Liverpool and all. Well, I didn't have any other records to play but a pile of old rhythm-and-blues things from the Rectory. So when I saw an ad in a London paper for a lead guitar player with experience in rhythm and blues, I swiped my mother's savings out of her extra teapot and I ran. I never looked back. I sent the money. I did that. I went back once. And again for her funeral. And again for his. The kids were spread all over. It was bad." His eyes glazed over in the memory. Then he snapped out of it. "Anyway," he said, "that's when I met Puffin. Harry, then. Harry Almut Brown. He was managing another group. We hit it off straightaway. Used to get high together like a couple of fiends. I got stuck. That was when me mum died. He gave me the money for the flight, Puffin did. Said not to worry about payin' it back. Just like that. He said his father was a bigwig and he had plenty of cash, so not to worry. I found out he didn't, though. Didn't even have a father, truth be told, just a mum. Very grand. A lady. Kept to herself in London. But he meant the bit about not bothering to pay back. I'll never forget that. I won't. Then, after the group thing went bad—all of a sudden there were six thousand groups coming from out of nowhere, everybody was a musician. And I wasn't terrific, you know, just going along with the flow, carried by the times. But I'd bought myself one of those little film cameras, and I would record all our adventures. They had us flying all over the States, y'know? It was just a blur of hotels and stadiums and that. But I filmed it all. Musicians throwing electric guitars out hotel windows into swimming pools; their faces afterward. You know, I'd keep the camera on the faces after the main action. It was lovely, really. Little girls coming up to the door. Teenyboppers. Puffin would chat them up, and they would say the most amazing things. Family secrets. Offers of sex. Anything. It was wild. And the film was very good. I had a knack. Well, I stood still. King of the close-ups, me. Everybody used to come over and get high. We smoked a lot of hashish back then. We used to laugh. Yeah. A lot of laughs. But then Puffin got me to enter one of my films in the Berlin Film Festival, and don't you know, it won. I didn't mind leaving the music world. The rock world, anyway. I was always more of a Coleman-Hawkins, Nina Simone–type, rather than rock. I used their music in my next film, by the way. I swear I think that's why it won. So we got some backing, thanks to Puffin's contacts up at school, and I made this other one, a serious one, and took a first at Cannes.

"Sure, I couldn't do anything wrong. Then I met Mara. At Cannes. I was the up-and-coming filmmaker, and she was the model-turned-actress who was really going to make it. She had that film out about the Polish girl who fell in love with the border-patrol guard that was such a hit. Everybody wanted her. Hollywood. Everybody. But she fell passionately in love with me. I loved who she was, what she was. You know, a star. I told her. I admitted it. But the more I'd try to make her understand the way it was with me, the more she fell in love with me. She wouldn't leave me. She would even come with me to the dentist's office, she was that afraid I'd fall in love with someone on the street. But I never did. I never fell in love with a soul."

"You don't have to tell me this," Claire interrupted, still holding on to his words from some few moments ago. Her tone was cool.

He grabbed hold of her wrist and pulled her toward him with brutal force. "Yes, I must. You must let me tell you every bit of it. Everything." He released his grip and pressed his mouth into her wrist, holding her with his eyes.

Obediently she let him finish.

"We got along okay, except for her jealousy. But it was all right. Up until a year or so ago. She started wanting a baby, and I told her I wouldn't. It wasn't right. I didn't want one. God. The whole idea horrified me. And on top of that, the last two films didn't make a farthing. Nothing. Now she decides if we have a baby, everything will turn around and be all right. Yeah, I would say, and what shall I do to support it, shoot kiddy birthday parties for the folks in Essex? And what does she do? She goes and lets herself get pregnant anyhow. I tell you I almost hit her. I could have. If I ever hated anyone, I hated her then. I used to wish she would die. Just fall away and die. She knew what I felt. How things were. And she went and took herself off the pill anyway. Claire, I never wanted it to be like that. I swear to God. She didn't tell me until she was too far gone to do anything about it. And then I reacted so negatively that she went and had the abortion—after it was too late. Four months. Four months! Do you know what a baby looks like at four months? Christ! She went and had it out. It's so damn easy to get one, you know. You hardly have to think about it. It's only later, when you see what a ruin your life becomes, you bother to think of the consequences. It almost killed her, too. I'm telling you. She doesn't really look the way she's looking now. She's really very beautiful. Was. But nobody could go through what she went through and not come up looking bad. And we had this film to do. I don't know. I don't know anymore if this film is any good. I trust Puffin, though. He's got all the book knowledge. He loves this story. I don't know."

Claire didn't know either. *Venus, Cupid, Folly and Time* was beginning to look more like her own story more than anyone else's.

Together they sat watching the house. The bird, the magpie, flew down and pecked at some seed in the vegetable garden.

"Wooh. There he is! He's down and out now, too," Temple sympathized, "now you've gone and stolen his treasure."

Claire tried to laugh and couldn't.

Evangelika came out the back door and threw a pan of dishwater at the magpie. *"Weg!"* she cried. *"Geh weg!"*

The large bird reared up, fluttered a couple of times for show and then settled impudently down right where he was before.

Evangelika, enraged, threw the heavy enamel dishpan at him. She missed him, but just barely grazed his left wing. "*Scheissvogel!*" she croaked.

"Christ!" Claire said.

"Here now," Temple said, "she's a hot-cross bun." He pulled an apple from his vest and stroked it with his supple thumb.

Several men turned the corner of the house. One of them, no longer in *Tracht* but wearing a suit and tie, was the fellow Claire had seen on several occasions on the hill. "The Whistler!" she cried. "Temple, that's the man. The one I told you about."

"That the chap? He's a copper. Can't you tell? He's the one questioned me at the airport. Detective Sergeant Martin Engel. He'll be interviewing you next, you know."

"No! I didn't even think of that. I half thought he was the murderer!" Her throat felt stretched and tense. "I hoped he was."

"Why hoped?"

"Because if he isn't, then one of us has got to be."

Temple slipped his hand under her hair and held the curve of her neck. "I know it couldn't be you," he said.

"You don't even know what I'm like," she muttered, pulling away.

"I think I know exactly how you are," he said, cutting a slice of the apple with a Swiss Army knife identical to hers. Uncomfortably, she watched the juice of the apple leak from the slit as he ran the point down the skin. "Let me describe. You listen to listener-sponsored radio . . ."

"That's true," she laughed.

"You pick violets and put them on the table or in the window. On a doily, like."

"When I can find them, yeah. What else?"

"You like this, don't you, when we discuss the ways of you?"

"Yes," she allowed, "who doesn't? Go on."

"You like it regular. No tricks or fancy effects. Oh, come on, don't go red on me. I'm only teasing."

There was a startling rap on the side window. It was Puffin, gasping and out of breath. Temple opened the back lock and he climbed in.

"I have such a thirst!" he complained, loosening his necktie. "Saw you both in here, out of harm's way. I didn't think you'd mind," he said.

"Heavens!" Claire cried. "Why would we mind!"

"Where is everyone?" Temple said.

"Blacky went with Isolde. He'll be back soon, though. She didn't bring anything with her."

"What?" Claire worried. "Do you think they'll keep her?"

"At least overnight. She'll need her things. Her toothbrush, her makeup."

"Can't Blacky put up bail?" she said.

"Don't they have to post it first or something? I don't know how it works, do you?"

"No," Temple said.

"Well, have they arrested her or just taken her in for questioning?" Claire wanted to know.

Both men looked at her and shrugged. She couldn't help thinking how unlike her husband they both were. He would have flown from the car, strode up to the detectives, spoken with them in professional, hushed tones. Knowing just what to do. He would protect her. That wasn't true, she corrected herself carefully. He wasn't like that at all. Why was she romanticizing her husband? It wasn't as if he in any way were kind to her, wanted to spend even an hour of his time with her. He'd be upstairs in bed for the day, sleeping off the night's beer.

Temple sat quietly, his mouth in his hand. Her heart went out to him. He didn't understand this business any more than she did.

If they kept Isolde, she would have to go visit her. Maybe she'd just better go now. See if there was anything she could do. She started up the car. It didn't go. She tried it again.

"What are you doing?" Temple said worriedly.

"I'm trying to start the car."

"May I ask where we are off to? If we're off?" Temple said. "It's not going."

"Smart," Puffin said.

"I am smart," Temple said jauntily, for Claire's benefit.

"If you're so smart, why ain't you rich?" Claire turned the key again.

"He is rich," Puffin said easily. "So am I."

"If you're so rich, why ain't you smart?" Claire said.

"It's probably the generator." Puffin sat with one ear cocked.

"I can't imagine it's the generator." Claire frowned.

"Oh, generators go whether anyone wonders about them or not," Temple said.

"Come on, Otto von Auto," Claire pleaded, "turn over."

"Only understands *Deutsch*," Temple reminded her.

"*Mach mal!*" she crooned and petted the dash. "*Tu es doch für mich.*"

The car started right up. They jolted forward, then tooled down the drive and out onto the road.

"How about that," they all cried and smacked one another's shoulders.

It suddenly occurred to Claire that Fräulein Wintner might have spoken to the police about her just before she was killed. Wouldn't that be a kick in the head. And why wouldn't she have? She'd said she would. No one had asked her about it, but maybe they were being cute. She suddenly lost her taste for the police station.

Her hand rested on something in her pocket that pricked. The miraculous medal. The one she'd grabbed hold of as she'd fallen down the bridge. She must show someone. Evangelika would know whose it was. Holding on to it, Claire felt suddenly sure Evangelika would certainly know, and had known Iris as well. She was old enough. It was feasible. How could she have been so stupid not to have put her and Iris together? She knew how. She looked over at Temple's handsome profile. She'd been blind for the stars in her eyes.

She pulled over to the side of the road.

"Don't turn it off," both men cried.

"No, I won't. I've got to go back. You go on ahead."

"Hey, wait. I'm not sure I fancy the police station without any sleep," Temple protested, "and without you."

"Right." She smirked sarcastically. "I thought you just decided you're far better off without me."

As though pained, he lowered the lids of his seductive eyes. "I cannot sleep for the wanting of you," he said. "What am I to do? What? Leave the ones who love me so that the minute you're sure you've *got* me, you'll turn around and go back to your husband?"

Puffin sat huddled in the backseat. Strangely, it was his eyes she saw before she rose in protest. He was looking so cornered and woeful, sunk into his collar. He was cold, his hands in his pockets. Did even this have to be in front of him?

"And if you wouldn't leave me for your husband"— Temple shook his head knowingly—"you would leave me for your family. You can't deny that."

Just then Blacky pulled up, coming from the other direction. He bounded out of the car and crossed the road over to them.

"How is she?" Claire said to Blacky, guiltily. Here she was discussing her love life, and his wife was being accused of murder.

"How do you bloody think she is!" he shouted at her.

"Who's in the car?" Puffin bobbed his head up and down, craning to see.

"Oh, it's Dirk," Claire said. "Isolde's son."

"I've got to drop him at his old *Kindermädchen's*," Blacky said. "She's to take him back to his school. The other one is half dead with *Katzenjammer*, hangover."

"I'll take him," Temple volunteered. "I don't want to go to the station house." He glared at Claire.

Blacky waved Dirk over. The boy was happy to come and ride in the old-timer.

"Tell Isolde I'll bring her things this afternoon," Claire told Blacky. "Then you won't have to waste time at the Mill."

"Let me out, old boy," Puffin said to Temple. "I'll stay with Claire."

Blacky gave Temple the address, and he sped back to Isolde. Temple took Dirk, and Claire and Puffin headed back to the Mill on foot.

Two police cars drove past, cutting Blacky off, headed back to town, followed by some reporters in Audis and timeworn Mercedes. On, she supposed, to the station house to question Isolde. Puffin was all wound up. One thing he loved was a catastrophe.

Claire walked slowly, trying to get her brain to clear. She kept feeling she was missing something. Puffin's excited chatter was distracting, and she was relieved when he saw Friedel the gardener out back and went off to talk to him.

The yard was strewn with rice and broken glass. Wires

from the twinkle lights hung, disconnected, from the branches. The kitchen door stood open. Evangelika was in there preparing a leg of lamb for the oven. She stabbed it full of garlic slices, surrounded it with wild rice and carrots and fresh rosemary branches.

"No Temple Fortune?" she greeted Claire meaningfully.

Claire's eyes adjusted to the dark. "He's gone back to take Frau von Osterwald's son to the *Kindermädchen*. Doktor von Osterwald went back to the station house. They're going up to see Isolde."

"I thought you were keeping him away from the house so he wouldn't be arrested."

"Why should he be arrested?" Claire felt something coming. The kind of feeling you get at the start of a toothache.

Evangelika spit in the oven to test if it was hot enough, then slid the tray in. The serving girl came in with a pile of dishes, then left. Evangelika wiped her sinewy hands on the parchment-like apron. "Wasn't her. That's sure."

"Wasn't who?"

"Frau von Osterwald."

"Wait a minute. You know it wasn't Isolde who killed Fräulein Wintner? Why didn't you tell the police?"

Evangelika shrugged. "I'll wait till she knows what it feels like behind bars. Let her be good and grateful to me when I tell them. Thinks she'll get rid of me, does she!"

"You can't do that!"

"She did it. She did that very thing. She was up there with Hans before he died. She could have told the *Polizei* she'd been with him. Maybe she saw someone. Who knows?"

"You do! You know, don't you!" Claire leaned up against her. Evangelika sat, *flump,* down on one of the chairs. Claire realized she was bullying an old woman; she sat down too. Evangelika was older than her mother. As old as Iris. She thought again of Iris's wartime story. She'd been out with friends the night her family had been arrested. Claire remembered Iris's description of that night on Ammersee. A girl had kept her out later than her curfew. A flighty girl. Effi. Effi?

"You're Effi!" she cried.

Evangelika smiled. "Long time no one called me that."

"You knew Iris von Lillienfeld, didn't you?"

"Took you long enough." Evangelika got up and hauled the bundles of white asparagus from the pantry. She sat across from Claire. She handed her a knife. "Long as you are sitting doing nothing, you can peel. You know the way?"

"Isolde taught me," Claire said. "Not too much and not too little."

"That's right. I have eighteen bunches for tonight. You want to get busy. So. She told you about Effi, did she? Probably mentioned what a good-lookin' hoofer I was, eh?"

Claire didn't say no. They sat across from each other and peeled. "You're Effi," Claire said again. "The girl who kept Iris von Lillienfeld from going home the night her family was arrested."

"*Ja, ja.* I was Effi then. Those were different times," Evangelika said. "You wouldn't believe what it was like then. How naive people like Iris von Lillienfeld were. Her whole family. None of them could believe the Germans would hurt them. They believed themselves to be Germans. Their families had lived in Berlin for more than a hundred years. You couldn't blame them. I was different. I grew up on a farm outside Diessen. You learn quick on a farm. You know who is capable of what." The words came tumbling out. It was as though she'd been waiting a long time to be rid of them.

234

"The von Lillienfelds were like children," she said. "They thought the people who worked for them liked them. Loved them. They thought animals were for petting. For pets. Not survival. Iris had a cat. Muschi. She used to sit and talk to that cat like it was a person. Oooh, she loved that cat. When I came to Saint Hildegard's, I brought it with me, for her." Here she lit a cigarette, an H-B. She blew the smoke out rigorously as if to demonstrate how ridiculous this idea had been. She put her cigarette in the ashtray and let it fume as she continued to work. She smelled of garlic and the raw, uncooked lamb.

"You see, Iris wrote to me while she was at Saint Hildegard's. She knew I had connections, men. She knew I knew some men in the SS. She thought I could help her find her parents. Thought it was my doing that she hadn't been arrested. That was accidental, but I didn't tell her that. She said she had 'means' and could pay. I couldn't help. Who could help? They'd stick you in the camps if you even sympathized; you couldn't even greet them on the street. They'd take you down to the *Zollfahndungsstelle* for questioning if you had anything to do with them. But then all the men left the farms. It was only women doing the work. Diessen was hard hit. Not as bad as later on. This was still early; this was in '38. Later it got worse, of course. Then they had to break up the tar from the streets to boil up. For heat, you know. This was just the start of the bad times. All the elderly men were dying. Not the women. All the old men you saw had a stick, and at the end of the stick was a nail on the bottom for to pick up the cigarette butts. But the young people still had fun. I didn't smoke, but if we were in a club and a soldier would offer me a cigarette, I always took it. Slipped it into my bra. I would give it to my father later. I used to carry a little bottle, like a jar. I would tip the drinks I got into the bottle when no one was looking. Put a little whisky in for my mother. But what I mean to say is they weren't all bad, those days. We were young. We had a lot of fun. You know. It got worse. But in '38 it was still all right.

"I know what you're thinking. How could we enjoy ourselves with what was going on with the Jews? But ask yourself, isn't it the same now? Aren't you having fun while the world is suffering?"

"It's not the same."

"Isn't it? You only know a small part. And yet you know so much more. With television. The world is smaller now."

Sadly, they both shook their heads.

"My father had a kiln," Evangelika continued. "You know, to bake the pottery. I don't know what happened. He used some other fuel because he couldn't get the normal stuff, and it blew up. Burned down the whole house. The barn. All the buildings. It wouldn't have been so bad, but it was November tenth. All the fire brigades were lined up by the synagogues. That was the day the synagogues were burned, and the firemen had orders to stand guard in case the fires spread to Aryan buildings. Well. We were out in the countryside. No one would leave their posts. We burned to the ground. November tenth. *Kristallnacht.* There was nowhere left, so I wrote to Iris in care of Adam. I lied. I told her I might be able to help. She sent me a stone."

"A diamond."

"*Ja, ja, ein Brilliant.* A diamond. I got to Saint Hildegard's. Iris was away. They told me she was away, in Paris. Looking for her parents. Adam was such a handsome, big man. What did he care for a farm girl from Diessen, like me, looking for work? Everyone was looking for work.

"But I had that letter from Iris promising me a place to stay. And I had Iris's cat, Muschi. I thought I was smart. He, Adam, thought I was her friend. He was so good to me because of that. His mother honored Iris's promise. She

236

gave me a home. Work. Later, I had my parents here.

"I'd brought this girl with me, Ursula. She was in trouble. Something wrong with her. One heard stories in Diessen about her father and her, you know. But no one ever knew for sure. I remember her very well, too well. She was witty, funny. She made me laugh. She made a mess of things for me, though."

"How was that?"

"She was man-crazy. There was no one here but Adam. No young men but him. Had her go with Adam von Grünwald, she did. Then tried to tell him she was pregnant with his child. That was all lies. Adam was truly in love with Iris. Only reason he slept with his wife was to get an heir for the Mill." Evangelika looked furtively left and right. "Once they had Hans, he never slept with Kunigunde again."

"How can you be so sure?"

"She told me. Kunigunde told me. Shame. She was a sweet woman. Swine dumb. But sweet. She didn't deserve that life."

"She had her grandchildren, though," Claire reminded her.

Evangelika snorted. "I had her grandchildren. They were more mine than hers. She wasn't capable. You wouldn't notice, though, because I took care of everything. Did everything. Amazing how normal you can make someone look when nothing is expected of them. She was good at her roses. Used to sit out there with Stella Gabriella. It was Imogene, the mother, who filled Stella's head with nonsense. She's the one we can thank for Stella's 'vocation.' Nothing wrong with that one's brain, though. That child. She's bright as a shiny new *Pfennig*. I used to take her home with me to Diessen when she was just a very little girl. She used to love to go to the tin market and the pottery fair each May. That's how she started out. Was me who got her started up, nobody else. Nothing really wrong with

Cosimo either. It's more nerves with him. Not stupidity. He just can't cope with the world. The way it is. He can't take pressure. And it's no wonder. His mother, Imogene, always belittled him, used to say he was her punishment. He was so dark, you see. So foreign to her. She hated that. He was a regular rough-and-tumble little boy. She used to make him kneel with her and say the rosary. Over and over. Poor child."

"But back to Adam for a moment, please. I'm confused. If Adam was so in love with Iris, why would he sleep with another woman?"

"Oh, that's about the easiest answer. Same reason as everyone else. Drinking. Lonely. Despair. You know, I still remember Ursula dressing up one night in a black hat when Iris was gone. I thought it was so strange, you know, I remember I was frightened. I thought it was Iris von Lillienfeld come back. That upstart Ursula tried everything to get Adam. Nothing worked. He really loved her. He really loved his Iris."

Claire hung her head. She thought of Iris, old and all alone. No children. "But why didn't Adam look for Iris? Why didn't they get together after the war? Why did he marry this . . . Kunigunde? And I thought Iris went to Paris. Why would she have come back when it was so dangerous?"

"That's just it, you see. Iris never really went to Paris to look for her parents."

Claire was shocked. "Well, where was she?"

Evangelika snorted. "That was a funny thing. You know, when we first came to Saint Hildegard's, Ursula and I, we were both astonished how happily the cat, Muschi, took to the place. She just raced up the stairs behind the kitchen. It was like she fit right in. We laughed. It hadn't been easy transporting a surly large cat all that way from the country in nothing more than a covered basket. It was

238

Ursula's idea to bring it. 'It's our ticket,' she told me, so I did it. Frau von Grünwald, Adam's mother, didn't want her at all. They didn't have surplus to feed another animal, she told us. Oh, she was a grand, haughty woman. If Iris were still here, she told us, it would be different. But now, with her in Paris, why should they take her cat?

"Ursula, she was a quick thinker, Ursula was. Said off the top of her hat that the cat was a great mouser. 'An excellent mouser,' she said. Well, that was all Frau Grünwald had to hear. There had been strange noises in the night, she said. Banging and twisting sounds from the attic. She was sure there were rats in the house. All right, then, she said, the cat could stay. You'd have thought the cat understood. She jumped from my basket and ran up the back stairs to the attic. Oh, we laughed. We would not have laughed if we had known what was to come.

"One morning, months after I'd first come to live at Saint Hildegard's, I was shelling the last of the peas in the garden. Right out there on that very bench. It was peaceful, and I had been there so long, making no sound. I guess I was invisible. It was still winter. Snow was everywhere. But in the sun it was hot. Really hot, the way it can get. So I was outside. I heard muffled laughter. Noises. Up in the attic. I thought, look at this, someone is up there. No one was supposed to be at home at all, everyone off to the *Viktualienmarkt* because it was a Wednesday. I should have gone too, but at the last minute I came back. I have these sinuses. They were acting up. Well, I went carefully up the steps. I brought an iron saucepan with me. You could have knocked me down with a dandelion fluff when I saw what it was! There I was with my pan held high in the air, and when I threw open the door, it was Iris von Lillienfeld and Adam von Grünwald, locked fast in a grip. He was loving her! And she—well, you never get used to some things, growing up on a farm or not—but she was pregnant. And not just a little. I was very shocked, I tell you."

"My God! What happened?"

"Well, they calmed me down and got tidy and then they took me into their confidence. There was nothing else they could do. At that point, even old Frau von Grünwald didn't know. She was sickly. Always had been. It wasn't hard to pull the wool over her eyes."

"I can't believe this."

"Oh, it's true."

"What happened then?"

"Nothing happened right away. Things went on as they were. Only now, everything was different for me, see. I was in league with them. I didn't want to be. You see, I had fallen in love with Adam myself."

Claire watched the stringy old woman remember. She found it difficult to imagine her young, but she could see how her heart's dream had been shattered in that moment. "So what did you do?"

"What could I do? I helped them. They were so . . . beautiful. When they came together, they would both sort of light up, you know. Despite all that was going on, they had each other up there." She nicked her chin in the direction of the stairway to the attic. "They kept each other. She was like his treasure. His obsession. He couldn't bear to hear of her leaving. Something had to be done, though. Even if they were not thinking straight, I was. I knew when a baby came there would be no more hiding either of them. The child was not far off. I had to find a way to get them away from Munich. It was terrible to think of what would happen to them. And I had another problem. Ursula. She was, as I said, strange. And she was beginning to suspect something. I could feel her watching me. Whenever I would turn a corner, she would be there. She didn't like Adam talking to me. Whispering. Oh, she didn't like that at all."

Evangelika took a deep breath. "Ursula had ingratiated

herself with the old woman, Adam's mother. She brought her her tea. Washed her hair. That sort of thing. Made herself useful. One night I heard the two of them talking. I was coming down the back stairs from the attic. I wore no shoes, just my old *Pantoffeln,* so no sound I should make. That's why they didn't hear me. Ursula was telling Frau von Grünwald how they got rid of rats on the farm. How they would put poison down. Wrap it in the *Konfitüre,* the marmalade. Oh, they loved it. They were dead before they knew it. I remember Frau von Grünwald's enthusiasm. Good Lord, I thought. I hope she doesn't go putting poison down around here! That's all we need with Iris's cat about. Well, not two days later, Iris took sick. Real sick. Vomiting. Loud, horrible retches you could hear throughout the house. She was dying. *Ja.* Really dying. Poisoned. By accident? I didn't believe that, not for one moment! Not even then. I know what really happened. Adam's mother. Frau von Grünwald. Thought she was above the law. She figured one Jew more or less—well, no one was going to imagine it wasn't suicide. Adam would get over it. She was not going to see her dear son destroyed by a Jew. Oh no. A love affair was one thing. A family quite another. That's what I think drove her to murder. But killing someone isn't easy. People don't just tip over and go to sleep. They agonize. Iris wouldn't die peacefully. She wouldn't cooperate, you see.

"Now, it was past caring if she was discovered. The whole house could hear what was going on. Now, Adam only cared that she should live. And of course it didn't look like it. Adam wanted the doctor. His mother refused. She acted as if this was the first she knew of Iris in the attic. But of course she must have known. It was she who did the poisoning. Otherwise she wouldn't have kept refusing to send for the doctor. She said they would arrest the whole house if they knew we were hiding a Jew. She was right, of course. We were all petrified. No one wanted to be sent to the camps. Ursula said get her out of here. Away from the house. That way, if she dies or not, they cannot say we hid her here. 'Take her to the chapel,' Ursula said. The mother said if Adam would do that, she would send for the doctor. Adam agreed. He carried her himself, out the Mill and up to the chapel. That little one, you know. Up on the hill."

Claire listened, holding on to every word.

"So the doctor came. I don't know if it was he who saved her or her own strength and will to live. But, live she did. Barely, at first. The child didn't make it. He died."

"He?"

"The doctor told her later it had been a boy. She never saw it."

Claire felt awful. Iris had had a son and never held it. Oh, the poor, poor thing.

"So then," Evangelika went on, "things happened very rapidly. The village began to talk. You couldn't hold back an entire village from knowing what they knew. We were all frightened. Iris was so sick. She was a liability. Finally, Frau von Grünwald persuaded Adam to get rid of her, or we would all be arrested. I remember it like it was yesterday. Here was this old woman who could barely walk. Adam's mother. And she came running up the front staircase. Flying, she was. Adam wouldn't believe old Frau von Grünwald had poisoned his Iris. His mother could do no wrong in his eyes. The mother suggested they pay someone to take her away. Far away. To London. Well. That was not an easy thing. Especially as she was so ill. She would have to be smuggled over land. It would take a lot of money. So. Adam knew a man in Schwenningen, in the Black Forest. It was near the French border. It was a man he could trust. A schoolteacher. It was impossible to trust anyone in the village. Adam had told them Iris was already gone, off to Paris to search for her parents, and now here she was, half dead.

242

"The next night, very late, a car pulled up to the Mill. A truck. Like a bakery truck. I watched from the window upstairs. The main guest room, now. There was an argument. Adam did not want Iris to be taken that way, he kept shouting. Frau von Grünwald told him if she didn't go this way, there was no hope for her. Already there was talk. She would be arrested and sent to the camp if she lived. So Adam let her go the way the schoolteacher planned. They carried her out in the old grandfather clock."

Claire swallowed but said nothing. The faucet dripped in the deep porcelain sink.

"*Ja.* It was the only way they could think of to get her safely away. They took her out, Adam and the schoolteacher. I put the blankets down in the truck. They put the clock on top. I saw her through the glass. Her eyes. I said, 'Auf Wiedersehen.' "

"It's horrible." Claire shuddered.

"Maybe so. But she lived, didn't she? There were others. Many, many others not so lucky. Somehow, she made her way to England. She had *Geld.* Money."

"But why, then, did Adam marry this Kunigunde? Why didn't Iris come back after the war?"

Evangelika stood up. She walked around the kitchen in a circle and then sat back down. "That's my doing. I wrote to her."

"But why? How could you do that?"

"I will explain." She lit another cigarette. Then she went to the cupboard and poured herself a glass of schnapps. She sat back down. "Adam was arrested. The Nazis wanted the Mill for their own use. It was rumored that Adam was associating with a Jewess. So it was very easy for them to get rid of him. I went to the *Zollfahndungsstelle.* They let me see him. He was frightened. Not for himself. For his mother. They had arrested her, too. They wanted to make a

243

case against them for harboring Jews. Jews guilty of illegally taking money out of the country. Then they could confiscate the Mill.

"Somebody had given them details of Iris von Lillienfeld. They knew everything about her. I always thought it was Ursula, my girlfriend, the upstart, who betrayed her. She and I were both in love with Adam. I knew I had no chance with him. Anyone could see how he loved Iris. He carried her picture with him all the time. It was enough for me that I was in his confidence. Well, it wasn't enough, but it had to be. I had no choice. And it was better than nothing. I was part of his life. A big part. But Ursula, Ursula had these crazy ideas. She was convinced Adam would love her if there was no hope for him and Iris. Later, when he rejected her, threw her out, she couldn't accept it. Wanted to pay him back. I never could prove it, but I had my suspicions." Evangelika shook her head sadly. "Ursula had such high and mighty notions of herself. And such fears! She was such a mix of majesty and fear! Well. To make a long story short, Adam needed money. A lot of money, and I didn't have it. Nobody did. There was a family living in the village. In Saint Hildegard's proper. Very wealthy. Their name was Asam. A nice family. They had a daughter, Kunigunden. She was sweet and fair and pretty. There was one problem: she was pregnant. And a bit of a fool, people might say. A little bit 'touched.' But just a little. Well, it was time for Kunigunde to marry, and the father must have been dead. Anyway, he was nowhere to be found. A lot of the men were gone. Adam, of course, had to stay because someone had to run the Mill. His mother wasn't well enough to handle the whole Mill. Saint Hildegard's has always been a self-sufficient, working mill. The water mill powers the mill grinder for the grain. Bread was as important as weapons. Adam had to stay.

"Well. Herr Asam was pleased by the idea of the marriage for Kunigunde. It wouldn't hurt for her to marry an *Adliger*. A noble. They had the money, the Asams, but no aristocracy. Old Herr Asam was a self-made man. He started as a stone mason. I knew he would love for his daughter to marry into the aristocracy. Adam's family would consider the union a horrible step down. Despite the money. But never mind. They were desperate.

"I made up a story. I told the *Polizei* that it was all lies about Adam and his mother knowingly hiding a Jew. Adam was engaged to Kunigunde Asam. I told them. They had been in love for months but had to be secretive about anyone finding out before they told his mother, Adam's mother. She had been ill.

" '*Da hat sie schon recht,*'—There she's right—the one *Polizist*, the policeman, told the other, 'Frau von Grünwald was never a healthy woman.'

"Yes, I said, she would be devastated if she heard it from someone else. But now—here I pretended to be embarrassed—'now Kunigunde is *schwanger,* pregnant,' I told them. They would have to marry.

" '*Ja, ja, ja,*' the *Polizei* agreed, 'they would have to marry!' Every villager knows the shame unmarried people would live with. Things were not like they are today. You wouldn't believe what it was like. You see old World War Two films on the television, and you think you know, but you can't. Nowadays, there's no such thing as scandal. Everything's out in the open. Back then . . . Well, anyhow, it was known in the village that Kunigunde was reclusive. So it all seemed to fit. I made it sound as though they were pulling the story from me. I could see them giving each other meaningful looks, those two policemen. They knew Herr Asam had friends in high places. It was not a good idea to arrest the wrong people. It could cost you your career. The policemen finally let me see Adam. I told him my plan. He was agreeable, but only to save his mother. All he cared about was that I should write to Iris, get in touch with her in England and make sure she was all right. He knew she was staying at a small hotel in Hampstead. It was a respectable place. She was still very sick, but she was alive. There was a fine man there, he was a professor. His name was Dr. Opal. Young. He gave the Jewish refugees lessons in English for free. So that's where she was staying, and I should write to her there. Well. I wrote to her. But I did something else. I told her what had happened, too. I explained about the Asam girl, Kunigunde, and how it was the only chance for Adam. They were to be married that week. There was no other way. I explained that they would send Adam's mother to a camp if she was in any way associated with Jews. Iris knew Adam loved Saint Hildegard's. She knew what it meant to him. I said if she really loved him, she would not write to him. If she loved him, she would never come back. Then I went to see Herr Asam."

Claire's mind reeled. "So it was you. You were the reason Iris von Lillienfeld and Adam von Grünwald never got together."

"I told Iris that she had to let Adam go, yes. Kunigunde could marry him then, and the Mill would be saved."

"The Mill. All this for the Mill."

"Not the Mill. What the Mill represented. I almost didn't save it. Ursula, the girl I had with me, *she* accused Adam of making *her* pregnant. Well, he was in prison, still. But she told me. She said as soon as he got out of prison, she would make him marry her. She confided in me. She also told me that he would pay for what he had done. Well. I knew she was lying. Just trying to be like Iris. I don't believe Adam ever slept with Ursula. I didn't believe it then, and I still don't believe it now. She had a loose way with her, as I said. Adam might have been the only young man in the village, but there were still plenty of old ones at that time. Oh, she knew which side her bread was buttered on, that one did. She was good enough to blame Adam for another man's shame. She knew where to go for the money, all right. So. I knew what I was dealing with here. I told her good. I explained to her that I knew what she was up to and if she interfered, I would swear that it was all lies. I would go to the *Polizei* and swear that she had told me she just wanted money from him and that had been her plan all along. You should have seen her. I thought she was going to kill me. I was frightened. Really frightened. But then something clicked in her, and she changed. She remembered I had the diamond Iris von Lillienfeld had sent me. She knew I still had it. She said if I gave it to her, she would leave. She would go away and never come back."

Claire had stopped peeling the asparagus. She leaned forward. "But why didn't Adam use the diamonds? Iris had sixty valuable diamonds. And why didn't he use them to get out of jail?"

"Ah. That was it. The diamonds were to be their future. When they went to look for them, they were gone."

"Wow."

"Someone had stolen them."

"So the diamonds were never found."

"Never found. That's why people talk still of the treasure at the Mill."

"Where were they supposed to have been?" Claire asked.

Evangelika shrugged. "Adam could never find them. Kunigunde used to say, 'Oh, they're safe. The good Lord watches over them,' she'd say. God knows where they are."

Claire wondered if Iris had thought Adam had stolen the diamonds. Just put them to the side. No. Iris had been vehement in her belief that Adam would keep them here for her. Claire was sure that Iris had never doubted this promise. "So then what happened?"

Evangelika folded her hands. "That's exactly what Ursula did. She left. And she left for good. I suspected that she was pregnant, but I was highly doubtful that it was from Adam. I was taking a chance, threatening her with the *Polizei*. But people were afraid of any dealings with the *Polizei*. They would send you off for the littlest thing. Ursula was terrified of being locked up. She had been locked up when she was little. You see, Ursula lived in such fear as a child. I knew she was despicable, but I also knew why.

"Her family had a farm, very small and rather broken down, but a farm, just at the edge of Diessen. Her mother would come and do work for my mother. She wasn't very efficient, and we didn't have much ourselves, but my mother had pity for her because she had such a difficult husband. He beat her. The whole village knew. He was a terrible man. Filthy. Unshaven. A frustrated man. Always blaming everyone else for his troubles. He even blamed my father. Especially he blamed the von Lillienfelds. Said they had taken the villagers' chances for success, buying up land that belonged to the locals at a cheap price. Called Iris's father a big Jew, of course. The usual. Anyway, the mother would come sometimes to the back door, looking for work. My mother was soft-hearted and knew she had the little girl, Ursula. You could see the woman was worn out. She would give her little odd jobs to do. I guess everyone did because the husband did nothing to earn, but the poor woman could never get ahead. Everyone thought, oh, you know, he's just another good-for-nothing done in by the drink, but it wasn't just that. There was something else wrong with him. Not everyone knew about that. Or they knew and they didn't talk about it. In those times you didn't talk about everything. You know. The way people do now. He was somehow perverted.

"Ursula was terrified of her father. And with good reason. He kept her tied up, in a stall off the house. She would cry out when we would pass her father's broken-down farm. Everybody heard her. But, you see, times were different then. If a parent punished, beat a child, no one thought it was their business to interfere. Everyone knew if you heard little Ursula yelling. 'Uh-oh,' you would say, 'Ursula's gone and got herself punished again.' Once, I heard that child yelling, and I started to weep myself. I pulled on my mother in our cart. We were passing on the way to Diessen to market, and my mother wouldn't hear of it. It was their business, she said. But I knew she didn't like it either. I knew she was shocked because I heard her telling my father about it. 'The child was crying out in fear of her own father,' I heard my mother tell my father. 'That's nonsense,' said my father. He wouldn't believe her. And I, who had been listening beside the *Kachelofen,* the tiled stove, ran out. 'Yes,' I agreed, 'I saw him come out from the outhouse where he kept her when he heard our cart. He must have beat her,' I told them. My mother was angry I had been listening. 'It wasn't an outhouse,' she shushed me. 'Yes, it was,' I insisted. 'Her father, Herr Braun, had his trousers down and unfastened when he came outside.' "

Evangelika looked meaningfully at Claire and sighed. "My parents went to see Herr Braun after that. They took some small crockery and went over there one Sunday. Pretending to bring a small neighborly gift of my father's 'Topferei,' his ceramics. Only nothing came of it. I heard my mother tell our other neighbor that they didn't even get to see Herr Braun. Only Frau Braun came out and took the crockery and thanked them and they went away. That was the end of that. My father said that would be the end of him scaring that child because he knew we were on to him. But it didn't stop him, I think. I think they knew it, too.

"The thing was, I always felt I had this bond, a sort of bond with Ursula. From guilt. Not mine. I was just a child. But my parents. I felt bound to her by the guilt of my parents. Maybe they could have done more. Ursula was just a few years younger than me. I thought if I gave her the diamond, she could go and start over, start a new life away from everything. Away from Deutschland. Away from her terrible past. So I gave her the diamond, and she went away."

Evangelika sniffed. "So you can figure her story was all lies. But I was glad when she left. I was relieved. It was like a dark cloud was lifted from the Mill. Her presence was so . . . so oppressive. It was worth the diamond to me to be rid of her." Evangelika shuddered. "There was something very wrong about her. The day after she left, I went up the hill, walking. I went to the Isar banks. I saw something, a purple sack, tied to the old mill wheel. It was tangled and hard to drag up, but I pulled it out. You know what it was? It was Muschi, Iris's favorite old cat, drowned to death."

Claire sucked in her breath.

"*Ja, ja.*" Evangelika nodded her head. "For spite. Ursula had drowned the thing Iris had loved so much. There should be nothing left of her. Nothing left."

"Evangelika, did you write to Iris and tell her to come here?"

"I . . ." She hesitated. "That was Fräulein Wintner. I let her find Iris's address with all Adam's papers and she sent a brochure. Hans found her address some months before he died. He kept it on his desk. Like everyone else, she got a brochure. I was afraid she would come. When you came, I was relieved. And then you called her. I listened on the extension. Oooh! It was terrible for me! I felt like my teeth were coming out all at once." To demonstrate this emotion, she shocked Claire by reaching into her mouth and pulling out her false teeth. She put them on the table with an emphatic *clack.* Her cheeks were sunk in and she looked a hundred years old.

Claire gripped her chest.

Evangelika put her teeth back in and had another schnapps. "And as bad as that was," Evangelika went on, "I was almost disappointed. I was, in a strange way, looking forward to seeing Iris, who Adam had so loved. This reserved young girl who had changed so many lives. I wasn't really frightened of her. Just the changes she would start up. I was only afraid Fräulein Wintner would convince Hans to sell the Mill. I couldn't let Hans sell the Mill. What would happen to Cosimo? Where would he go?" She sniffed. "Fräulein Wintner. She was saving her nest egg. She was going to make a business in the Seychelles with Hans one day, she thought. A hotel, but first she would make Saint Hildegard's Mill making money again, real money. She had it all planned. She was writing to all the guests of the Mill. All the people who ever stayed here got a brochure. She thought she could do whatever she wanted. Step on everybody's toes. She thought Hans would just go off and leave the children. She was completely stupid, as clever as she was. That was the one thing he would never do, desert his children. He would have taken them with him."

"You mean, wait a minute. It wasn't you who killed Hans?"

"*Ich?* Me? Why would I kill Hans? I loved him like my own. Fräulein Wintner killed Hans because he wouldn't keep to her. He humiliated her with Isolde. That's why she killed herself."

"Drowned herself? Bibi Wintner? I can't believe it. Go off on her own and start over, maybe. But kill herself? No."

"That's the way it was, though." Evangelika sat down and brusquely resumed peeling her fat asparagus. This was her story. She should know. Why was Claire embroidering on it? If anyone knew the truth, she did.

Claire took out the miraculous medal and laid it on the table. Evangelika snatched it up. "Where did you get this?"

"I found it. The magpie had it in its nest."

"It belonged to Imogene, Cosimo and Stella's mother." She pressed it to her lips.

"Thank you, Evangelika," Claire said. "Thank you for telling me all this."

Claire pushed her chair off, scraping it along the floor, and walked out into the sunshine. Otto von Auto was just coming down the drive, Temple at the wheel. "Here you are." He smiled happily. "I got rid of Dirk. Left him with the au pair's sister, actually. The au pair wasn't there, so she said he'd stay with her until she got back from Mass."

Was it Sunday then? Claire held her head.

"What's the matter?" He came to her. "You look a sight. Here. C'mere. Sit down."

"Temple, why did you come to Saint Hildegard's Mill?"

"To shoot *Venus, Cupid, Folly and Time*, Claire. You know that."

"Yes, but why here? Was there some reason you particularly came here?"

"We thought it would be perfect for the film. And, well, you know why else. We thought it would be good for Mara to recover here."

"But who suggested coming to the Mill? Who knew of it?"

"Why, Puffin. He'd come here as a child. Don't you know all this?"

"But wasn't the story *Venus, Cupid, Folly and Time* supposed to be set in Italy? I mean, why come to Munich to shoot an Italian story when it certainly would have been warmer and healthier to go to Italy for Mara to recover?"

"Well, Puffin explained that the story was originally written for Germany and then changed because the author couldn't get a buyer. The author rightly thought it would sell if it played near Florence. What is this all about?"

Claire remembered when she'd phoned her sister Carmela about the spelling of their name. She'd mentioned the award-winning book to her and had been surprised when

Carmela had never heard of it. Carmela was a bookaholic and read before she ate. It had struck Claire as odd then. Now it made sense.

"Temple, could it be possible that Puffin wrote the script of *Venus, Cupid, Folly and Time?* Could that have been?"

Temple looked incredulously at her. Then, slowly, she watched the scoffing expression in his eyes turn to skepticism, then doubt, then maybe, then, yes, yes, it might make sense after all.

"But why would he lie about that?" Temple shook his head.

"Why not? If it failed, it wouldn't be his failure, but yours and the author's. If it succeeded, he could surprise you with the happy news. A hero."

"Yes." Temple looked both sheepish and stunned. "It would be just the sort of thing he would do."

"So let's just think about this a minute now." Claire got up and wandered, distracted, in a circle. Two people were dead. The real question was, what connected them? If she knew that, she would know why they'd been killed.

They were lovers, that was the obvious thing. Who else had been a lover of one of them? Isolde. However she juggled it, she always came back to Isolde. And yet something kept telling her that her old friend had not done it. There was something unconnected to the past, to the time when Iris had been at Saint Hildegard's herself. It was all too coincidental otherwise. Had someone summoned her to Saint Hildegard's Mill? Who else knew Iris back then? Was Evangelika capable of murder? Or was there someone, somewhere, who tied the ends together? Someone from long ago. What was it Father Metz had said? Something he had said had irked her and then she'd forgotten, lost it before she could turn it over in her mind. Something about Fräulein Wintner. She was upset because so much money had gone to England. Claire remembered the ledger of the Mill's finances. And Puffin, laughing, scoffing at his own pretentious name.

The wedding tent rustled, unshackled, in the wind. It sounded like a flight of birds taking off.

"Did you ever meet Puffin's mom, Temple?"

"No, never." Temple blushed. "Puffin always said she was delicate. Didn't take company."

"Was she German?"

"No, she was British. Puffin always talked about how posh she was. 'The shabby gentile' he always called her, because she was too tight to buy new bedroom slippers. 'Mrs. Brown and her worn-out Bee-Bops.' " He shrugged. "I always figured I was too, well, shanty, to be introduced."

"But could she have been German? Lower-class German? I mean, didn't you ever talk to her on the phone? In all those years?"

"No. No, I never did. You mean the housekeeper. I only ever met the housekeeper. Many a cup of tea I had with her. Puffin didn't want anyone to bother his mum. Wait. Once I did call her. I couldn't get hold of him, and we had to leave for Cannes. But, no, she wasn't there. Only her housekeeper was there."

"Was she German? The housekeeper?"

He looked at her. "Yeah. A strange old bird. Makeup, feathers. Uri. What's going on?"

"That's it." Claire sank down onto the car bumper beside Temple. "That wasn't the housekeeper. That was Puffin's mother, Ursula Brown, née Ursula Braun. So that's it. Jesus, I'm a total idiot."

"Wait. Ursula Braun wrote *Venus, Cupid, Folly and Time.*"

"No. Puffin did. He just used his mother's real name."

"Hold on now. What do you mean? Do you mean like for poetic justice? Oh, come."

254

"Yes, I do mean that. Temple, what happens at the end of the story? What's the last scene of *Venus, Cupid, Folly and Time?*"

"It's where the main character gets justice. It's during the war. Venus and Folly are pierced by Cupid's arrow. It's all symbolic. Time teaches them. In the words of the book, 'Venus and Folly knelt, embracing. Though madness shrieked for watching them, they would remain serene. They had no choice, those two, the children of sin. Time held out the forgiving cloak of eternal blue sky with which to cover them. And I, at last, would be fathered and free. Free as the pealing of bells.' "

Claire stood up. "I wonder where Stella and Cosimo are?"

"I know where they are. Puffin just went off to meet them. He said it was only right that he show them the beginning of the story. He took the cane to give Cosimo."

"Why did you give it to him?"

"Because he asked me to."

"I wish I didn't have such a bad feeling." She couldn't sit still. She walked around, then came back and stood in front of him. "Temple," she said, "I don't suppose Puffin could be insane."

"What?"

"I mean, did it ever occur to you that he might be . . . insane?"

Temple looked at her. He didn't answer her, they just kept looking at each other, all the while Temple's mind going a mile a minute. Finally, he said, "It can't be. Why would he?"

"I don't know. I'm as confused as you are. I only am sure of one thing: Puffin Hedges did write that story. He did. He had to have. And his mother is Ursula Braun, who lived here at Saint Hildegard's Mill in 1938."

"But why would he never tell me?"

"Temple, anyone whose mother convinced them they were the rightful heir to half the Mill would have a whole bevy of secrets."

"What heir to what mill? This mill?"

"I don't know. I'm just thinking it through. Could it be that Puffin believes himself to be the rightful heir?"

"You mean like in the script?"

"Is that what happens in the story?"

"Yes."

Temple wrenched her shoulder and made her look at him. "What are you thinking?"

"I think it was Puffin. I think he killed Hans. And then Bibi Wintner because she suspected."

"You're mad!" Now he turned away.

Claire touched him from behind. "But it could be. It had to be."

"Puffin has been kinder to me than my entire family. Of all the people I've ever known, he's the only one who ever—"

"That's why there were checks going out to England every month. Maybe Ursula Brown was blackmailing Hans. Just the way she'd blackmailed the father, Adam. Maybe Bibi Wintner found out."

"But why would she blackmail him? What could he have done to her?"

"Ursula must have convinced Hans that Puffin was Adam's son, too. Adam certainly believed it. Otherwise, why would he have sent money all those years? Someone was sending money to England all those years. He must have paid for his schooling. Anything to keep her away. I know Adam despised Ursula. Evangelika told me. Adam would have paid just to keep her and her bastard away from the Mill. Away from his adopted son, whom he loved. Kunigunde's son. Later, Hans must have known, must have found out after Adam died and he took over the Mill. He wouldn't want Puffin to come and take his share. Only maybe he got the idea that Puffin wasn't really the rightful son of Adam. Maybe something made him doubt it. Or some*one*. What if he'd suggested a paternity blood test, something like that, something they wouldn't have had years ago. Why should he keep on paying, he probably figured, if there was no reason to!"

"I can't . . . I can't imagine. Mrs. Brown is a lady. A great lady . . ."

Claire turned and faced him squarely. "No. She is Ursula Braun. She's a common blackmailer, gussied up. Evangelika gave her a diamond years ago, if only she would never come back. Oh, the rage! Imagine Ursula Braun's rage! Imagine how she must have hated them and raised her son Almut to hate them. Her precious son, Harry Almut Brown. Hans's second name was Almut, too. Remember? The list of names from Adam's files had his full name on it, Adam Almut von Grünwald. I knew I'd seen or heard that name Almut before, but I couldn't put them together. Only now it all falls into place. Ursula told her son his father was keeper of the Mill. Told herself, probably. How much nicer it was to believe."

"It can't be the same . . ."

"Oh, Temple, really! It has to be!"

Temple flared at her. "You are so pleased that it is so!"

"What should I be? Pleased they're holding my friend Isolde in prison for two murders she didn't commit? No, I've got to tell you what I know. However much it hurts you. Puffin believes himself to be the rightful heir, and whether it's true or not doesn't matter anymore to him. He's out of his mind."

"He's not!" he cried, knowing, already, that he must be.

"Don't you see he planned all this?"

"Claire, you've got to be wrong." Temple kept shaking his head. "Puffin never would have killed Bibi Wintner."

"He had to have," Claire insisted. "Bibi had an argument with Isolde. Isolde told me she, Bibi Wintner, accused her of having an affair with Puffin. Maybe she only thought that because she *saw* Puffin in the stairwell near Isolde's room at the time of the murder. And she knew where the money was being sent to London every month. She found the accounts. She was in charge of them since Hans was killed. She figured it had to be Isolde or Puffin. And Puffin was the one from England. Bibi must have confronted Puffin just the way she confronted me. She was the kind of woman who wasn't used to being crossed. She had no experience with someone more desperate than herself. Desperate enough to kill. She never would have believed there was no reasoning with Puffin. She couldn't know just how demoralized he must have been."

Claire saw the anguish wrench Temple's face. She watched it fall, and she knew there could be no happiness for them now. It was the end of both their illusions. He would never forgive her for bearing such a truth.

"We'd better find Cosimo and Stella," Temple said.

A car pulled up the drive. It was full of Müncheners.

Evangelika stood in the doorway. She knocked on the woodwork to get their attention. "What is it about Cosimo and Stella Gabriella?" Her face had turned to ashes.

The carload of customers opened the great Mercedes doors. Loud music and laughter barreled out.

"Where are they?" Temple called to Evangelika. "Where did they go?"

"*Was?*" She cupped one ear. "*Wie?*"

"Where are they?" Temple called again.

Evangelika lurched out the door. The rollicking customers cruised toward them. They were between Evangelika and Temple and Claire when Evangelika slumped against the side of the house and slid to the ground. She sat upright, her open palm kept tapping her cheek. None of the merrymakers stopped; they kept on walking. They hadn't noticed her go down. Claire and Temple ran across to her and helped her up from both sides.

Claire said, "Temple, what was the line again? The line at the end of *Venus, Cupid, Folly and Time*?"

" 'And I, at last, would be fathered and free.' "

"No, the line right before that."

" 'Time held out the forgiving cloak of eternal blue sky with which to cover them.' "

Claire gnawed at a cuticle. She looked up. Temple looked up, too. Their eyes both went to the same place, the bell tower.

"Herr Ober!" the customer from the grand Mercedes, dripping with importance and urgency, signaled Temple over. He mistook him for the waiter.

"It wasn't Fräulein Wintner who killed Hans, then," Evangelika said. "It was someone else, wasn't it?"

"Where did they go?" Claire tried to sound normal. All she could think was getting to those kids before something terrible happened.

"Who was it?" Evangelika tried to stand.

"Did they go up to the bell tower, Evangelika? Did they go up there?"

The three of them looked up. There was no flash of movement from the tower. It was still.

"They're dead!" Evangelika cried.

"They're not dead." Claire grabbed hold of Evangelika's chin and looked up at the tower. "The bell hasn't rung. There's still time."

"Evangelika," Claire whispered in a voice that sounded calm, "I want you to go to the telephone. Call the police. What was his name? The detective?"

"Engel." Temple let Evangelika's arm go. He was shocked.

"Martin Engel," Claire said. "Go to the phone and ask

for Detective Sergeant Martin Engel. Tell he must come back to the Mill. All right? Tell him Isolde couldn't have committed the murders because the murderer is here now. Tell him Cosimo and Stella are in danger." She ran through the kitchen to the back stairs. Temple came up behind her.

Evangelika grappled with her legs, then pulled herself along the wall into the house. She moved as in slow motion, but she moved.

"My God," Temple said, "it's just like in the film. My God. He did it, didn't he? He killed Hans." He sat down on the bottom step of the spiral stairs and put his head in his hands.

Claire bounded past him. She took the stairs two and three at a time. By the second floor she thought she might have a heart attack. Still she climbed. The bell was so high up. She reached the third floor and the lighthouse-like steps of the bell tower. Time was indeed on the steps, on and on. Please, she prayed silently, don't let them be dead. She burst through the portico door.

They were sitting, the three of them, with their legs over the sides, swinging, easy as you please. They might have been children entranced with the view.

Claire almost passed out. They looked across at her, astonished.

All around, the countryside was to be seen. The dismal, bright white light pressed against them. Claire reeled with vertigo. Only the bell itself seemed safe, nestled under its roof. Claire wanted to hold on to something. The bell was too far in. She sat down and held on to the frail wrought-iron rim the others had stuck their legs through.

"I've been telling them a story." Puffin stood. His lips were very red, his hair slicked back and cut in a straight blunt line at his crisp linen collar.

"Hey!" the voice of the outraged customer down below reached them. *"Was soll denn das?! Ober!"*

Puffin leaned in and ran his finger along the rim of the bell. "Did you know," he said, "they've used the Mill bell ever since they bombed the church." He might have been a tour guide.

"Right," Claire smiled. "You came here as a child."

"That's right." Puffin's eyes swam with reminiscence. "I was a little boy. Mum thought Hans and I would play together. I was older, but not by much. A couple of months. And Hans was such a big boy." Puffin's eyes clouded over. "He didn't care for me, though. We had nothing in common, really." He held his elbows. "Hans was rough. We even came up here once. He threatened to throw me off. He said I was a *Mädele,* a girl." Puffin heaved a sigh. "He was coarse, you see. He had no mother. 'That's what happens when you have no upbringing,' Mum used to say. Oh, she knew he'd hurt my feelings. We'd put so much into this trip, you see. It meant so much to the both of us. She told me we were going to go back and meet my father, Adam von Grünwald. But he didn't like me either." Puffin's eyes filled with tears. "We were in the upstairs room, Hans's room. The father said, *'Nein.'* He said I didn't bear the slightest resemblance to him . . . He said get that ugly brat away from him. That's what he said! Mum's heart just about broke." Puffin rattled his head. "Mum didn't think I understood, but I did. I understood more German than she thought. Even then.

"Yes, yes." Puffin strode along the rim of the tower. He was balanced with his own bravado, unafraid now of the terrible height. "I was always excellent at German," he muttered. "All languages, really."

There was a scuffle behind Claire. The portico door flew open. It was Temple. The magpie, worried about its nest, flew over him and up into the tower.

Puffin faltered and almost fell. Cosimo instinctively reached out his hand to him. Puffin saw it and stopped. He didn't take it, but it steadied him. He was safe.

"That's just like me." Puffin smirked at Temple. "I mean that bird. You see, I wasn't well-named after all. I was never a Puffin. I was more like the shifty magpie. I was always after shiny things." He pursed his wet lips. His pale eyes went blank. "Robbing other people's shiny things."

Cosimo's dark brows drew together. He sensed something was about to happen. He took Stella's hand.

Puffin sucked in his breath. That he wouldn't have! He leaned down and removed Cosimo's hand from his sister's. "Lucky Cosimo." He raised one eyebrow tartly. "Always the lucky one!"

Claire thought, two more minutes. Just keep talking for two more minutes. Someone will come. The police will be here any minute. They'll know what to do. "It must have been terrible for you," she said.

Evangelika, recharged with purpose, came up behind Temple. She cowered behind him.

Puffin fluffed his hair. "It wasn't so bad for me. It was Mum. She took it so hard. Especially because Hans had been so cruel to me. She felt for me, Mum did. That the father would rather have a filthy Jew boy for a son than a fine Aryan boy like me."

"Don't tell! Don't tell!" Evangelika cried in a horrified voice.

"My father was not Jewish," Stella said from her small place on the rim. She held her rosary in her hand.

"Oh yes," Puffin said, "he was Jewish. That woman Adam von Grünwald married wasn't really Hans's mother. What? Did you really believe she was? She was just a replacement. Handy."

"Don't tell," Evangelika whimpered.

"What do you mean?" Stella whispered.

"I thought everybody knew. You really didn't know?" Puffin glared at Stella and at Cosimo with wicked merriment. "Your father wasn't Adam and Kunigunde's child. That was just a trick. Hans's real mother was a Jew. A dirty Jew. Adam von Grünwald's dirty Jewish whore!" He spat the words. Blue veins stood out on his neck.

He'd shocked the fear from all their faces. They gaped at him.

"My mum told me the whole story," Puffin said, "many times."

"Oh, don't tell, don't tell," Evangelika crooned. She held on to Temple's back.

Puffin eyed her coldly. "That *Jew*ess was ruining everything. She poisoned the Mill with her tricks. With her charms. Playing fancy piano. Having sex with Adam von Grünwald in return for sanctuary."

Claire looked at Cosimo. He looked, she realized at once, like Iris.

"It wasn't like that!" Evangelika shrieked.

"She had Adam von Grünwald captivated," Puffin continued coolly, ignoring her. "He was going to lose the Mill. And it was all because of *her*. And *she*, this Iris von Lillienfeld, this Jew, was just using him."

"*Nein*," Evangelika murmured, "she loved him. And he really, truly loved her."

"Oh, he *thought* he did," Puffin mimicked in a womanish voice. "But she was a vamp. A sneak. Stealing him away from his own *mother!*"

He paced along the catwalk, closer each time he came by.

Claire hooked one foot under the wrought-iron fence. If he would only come that close one more time, she could grab hold of his ankle.

"What does it mean?" Stella asked in a small voice.

Puffin looked at her with disdain. "My mother"—he pulled himself up to his full meager height—". . . my mother poisoned her. She poisoned your grandmother the way you would any rat. They were like rats, you know.

Those people. Deserting the ship. Taking their money out of the country."

"She was my grandmother?" Stella asked wonderingly. "The Jewess was my grandmother?"

"*Liebling*"—Evangelika reached out a useless arm across the void to Stella—"Iris von Lillienfeld was not the way he says she was." Tears were streaming down her cheek from only one eye. The other didn't work.

"But Iris's baby was stillborn," Claire protested. "The baby died when Adam's mother poisoned Iris!"

Evangelika rocked herself. Her voice reverberated in the hollow belfry. "Adam was weeping so! There was no hope there. No sound would come out of it. 'Iris!' Adam kept calling. 'Save Iris!' The doctor said Iris would die too. But she kept living! 'Take it away,' the doctor said to me, 'and bury it. Else who knows what the villagers will do with a Jewish corpse.' I took the baby out, away from the Mill. I thought I would bury it in the Christian cemetery. Oh, it was so blue. So cold. I covered it in my shawl, no one should see it. I went to get something to dig with. I found a stick. I started to dig. I thought I heard something. I thought it was a ghost. I was so frightened. I kept digging, quickly. Then I heard it again. It sounded like a cat. I thought a cat was by the body. I went over to the *kleine* body. I leaned over it . . ." Evangelika clapped her hands and held them together. "It was alive. The boy was alive! I didn't know what to do. I thought Hans's mother had poisoned Iris. I thought if I brought the baby back alive, they would kill it. I was frightened. I thought to bring it to the priest. I wrapped it up in my shawl again and went on my way. By and by, as I walked along, it came to me. I would bring the baby to Kunigunde."

"Hans was Iris's son!" Claire marveled. "And Iris never knew. Never held her son!" She was horrified. All those years Iris believed Adam had stayed on to live with a mother who'd tried to poison her. But it hadn't been Adam's mother who'd done the terrible deed. It had been Ursula. Cruel Ursula.

"Kunigunde loved the baby right away." Evangelika looked over her shoulder as though someone might be following her. "She named him Hans. She thought he was her doll. The villagers really believed he was hers. He was so new, you see. So fair. And Kunigunde was such a recluse. It might well have been that she was pregnant all those long months she was locked away, praying.

"But later she got tired of the poor thing. His leg wasn't right. It never had been right, from lack of oxygen when he was born, you see. That's why he limped. But to Kunigunde he was like a broken doll. If he couldn't be fixed, she didn't want him anymore."

"So you raised him," Claire said.

"That's it. I raised him, *ja.* He was mine. Kunigunde sat in her garden, and I got to raise Hans. My boy. My poor boy." She looked morosely over the side where Hans had fallen.

Stella Gabriella crossed herself. "And we never knew—"

"My mum knew," Puffin hurried to say. He wouldn't have Evangelika taking over now. This was his show here. "My mum knew all along. She figured that out fast enough. She saw Evangelika go into the cemetery with a bundle and she saw her come out. Still with a bundle. She knew something was up. Always dead clever, my mum." His face was drained of color. "I couldn't believe it when the housekeeper called and told me Mum had packed it in. I mustn't fret, Uri said. Uri, that's the housekeeper, she rang up the other day. Oh, she's the fastidious one, Uri is. 'Pills,' she said. 'Nice and neat. Wouldn't want your mum to be locked up. Never want that . . .' It's not Mum's fault she saves things. The flat all filled with rubbish. Just so many years she had to do without, you see. Was it more than a week ago?" He bit his lip. "The day before Hans died, it was. I didn't tell you, Temp? Funny, that. I ought to have told you. She said I mustn't worry. Mum's time was up, and there was nothing we could have done to change that. As the Arab says, it is written . . ." Distraught, he snatched at his hair.

Claire shivered, knowing now that Uri, the housekeeper, was Ursula herself. She had called Puffin as her own housekeeper, to tell him of his mother's suicide. Then committed suicide. It was ghastly.

"That's why," Cosimo spoke. He touched his face, his own hair, his strong, long nose. "That's where I come from. That's why."

"You can't know what it was like," Evangelika said. "It was the war." She looked from face to face. "I had to keep him. It was perfect. You see, no one knew. Only Kunigunde and I. And after a while, she forgot . . ." She felt Claire's eyes on her. "I had nothing else," she pleaded. "Iris had so much. She had a new life. She would never know. She couldn't come back. The Jews would never come back."

Temple said to Puffin, "It was you, then, rang the bells?" Still hardly believing, unable to say, "It was you who killed them." Even now.

"Hans laughed at me," Puffin said to Temple in a quiet voice. "I told him I would tell, and he *laughed* at me. He said, 'Go ahead, tell the children. They're grown now. What harm will it do?' He turned his back on me. I said 'Wait. Just wait.' 'What is it?' he snapped. He was so brusque. 'I only wanted to talk,' I said. 'After all, our destinies have been entwined.' " Puffin held his palms up, empty. "But he saw no romance in our tragedy. He had no romance in him.

"He pushed me out of the way. Right here, it was." Puffin touched the air around his thigh. "He pushed me to the side like a sack of old potatoes. I said then I wanted my share of the treasure. I knew it was still here. My mother knew it would still be here. It was part of my inheritance, whether we were brothers or not. Anyone could see that. I was willing to be reasonable. I told him he could keep the Mill, but he would have to share the treasure with me. He had to share.

"You should have heard him laugh. Oh, I do wish I'd never heard him laugh. One didn't often hear that sound. So big and metallic. It was not his nicest feature. He said Cosimo had searched the whole of Saint Hildegard's Mill for it when he was a little child. If he couldn't find it, nobody could. He said his father, Adam, had given the treasure to his mother, Kunigunde, to hide. His father said that way, someday, the true owner would have to come back for it. He laughèd and laughed. He just kept laughing.

"I pushed him. Once. I shoved him just the way he'd pushed me. I didn't expect him to go over. I didn't think of it. But his foot was caught up in the rope. He fell backward. He looked into my eyes while he was falling . . ." Puffin looked intently at his nails. "I heard his head crack against the side . . ." He raised his eyes to Temple. "I didn't really care about the money. I only ever wanted it for you."

"Why did you never tell me!" Temple cried.

"You? I'd never tell you, dear. I'm the one to protect you. Know what I mean?"

"But look," Claire pleaded, "it's not too late. We could tell the police how it was—"

"It was Fräulein Wintner," Puffin interrupted her. He put his gray gloves on, wedging down each finger with the other hand. "She was cold as ice. I took great pleasure in killing her."

Someone clattered up the stairway.

Nobody moved. The door was violently thrown open. It was Mara. All she saw was whom she expected to see, Temple and Claire. So sure had she been to find them in an embrace, she was taken aback at the sight of the others.

"You!" She aimed her fury at Puffin.

"It's always been me, love," Puffin said, eyelids lowered, mocking her.

Then they heard the disturbing *dee-da-dee-da* of the police siren drawing close.

"That's what you think," Evangelika said in her crusty voice, surprising everyone. "That's what you've always thought. You, you, you! Ursula and you! The only ones with secrets. Well, it wasn't Hans your mother Ursula was blackmailing." She pounded her scrawny fist on Temple's back, "it was me. I was the one who paid all your fancy schools and fancy needs. All those years. Every *Pfennig* I earned. Every last *Pfennig!* I never bought for me. It all went to you. I had to. Else Ursula would have told that Iris was Hans's mother. She knew. She saw me take the baby to Kunigunde. She was hiding in the woods. She would have told. And I would have lost him." She wrung her hands, still leaning on Temple.

"No," Puffin said, not believing.

"Oh, *ja.*" Evangelika nodded her head emphatically. "I am the Keeper of the Mill. *Ich bin's!*" She touched the wall of the belfry. Hers. "Who else kept the secret, never told that it was Kunigunde kept the diamonds? I did. It was me who kept the secrets."

Puffin gazed woefully at Temple. The *Polizei* were coming into the Mill. Puffin stood up.

"Puffin! Don't do it! Don't do it!" Temple cried.

Puffin saw his old friend's eyes swimming in tears across the way. "It's done," he said. "Already done." Puffin smiled. He bowed. He picked up Hans's cane from where it was wedged between Cosimo and the white wall behind him.

"Don't hurt them," Claire called across the well of space. "Just let them go."

"Promise me"—Puffin winked at Temple—"you'll ring the bell."

Temple, his face wet with tears, nodded.

"Say it." Puffin pointed a finger at Temple.

"I'll ring the bell," Temple said.

There was a moment of timeless grace. The belfry beheld Puffin Hedges. Like a magician in slow motion, he picked up Hans's cane. Absently, he stroked the bird's carved head. He unsheathed the short sword. It slipped out like mercury, swift and glinting.

Cosimo rose and stood in front of Stella. They braced themselves.

In one sad, demented try at care, Puffin took aim.

"Puffin! Puffin!" Temple called him.

Puffin looked around at each of them, then held on Temple's eyes.

Somewhere behind her, Claire heard a mournful shriek. It was Temple Fortune.

Puffin smiled wistfully at his old friend then plunged the sword into his own lost heart. Off the portico he dropped. The magpie was startled and flew, a quick shadow, into the wind. Over the hills you could hear the clouds lift and swallow the sound of the wings, free as the pealing of bells.

9

————•◆•————

Claire checked her room one last time, then closed her suitcase for good. Blacky and Dirk would be downstairs any moment to drive her to the station. She was taking the train with Otto von Auto to Hamburg, where he would be placed on board a liner, and she would take a plane. It had all been arranged by Blacky with typical German precision. She looked out the window. There they were, Dirk and Blacky. Rupert would come home for summer vacation. Blacky had decreed it would be better for Dirk to stay home from now on. She had to smile. They really were quite perfect for each other, those two.

Evangelika tugged on Dirk's knotted hair with a comb. Dirk argued hotly and ran off. Evangelika tripped him neatly and started wearily in again.

Blacky puffed on a beedi. The new Mill keeper, Blacky. He looked expansive and disheartened at once. The phone rang and Claire picked it up.

"Coming home?"

"Jupiter! I told you for the last time. I am not shooting cigarettes. Not for you or for anyone."

"Calm down, calm down. I wouldn't think of asking you to waver in your moral sanctimoniousness. Remember Matt McGee?"

"The fellow with the big bucks."

"Right-o. Well, he thinks it's a great kick that you refuse to do tobacco. Thinks it's a great angle. The whole agency has to give up all tobacco accounts."

Claire looked out the window for the last time at the uprooted magpie circling the hill, looking none the worse for wear. "What happened, he lost the tobacco account?"

"Better than that. He's got emphysema."

"Jesus."

"So you may come home to a relatively forgiving Manhattan."

"Ah. Thank you."

"You are welcome, my dear. Tell me, was it really wretched? That business with the loony?"

"Anything else on your mind, Joop? Because I have to catch a train."

"A *train*?" He said "A train" the way someone else would say "An elephant?"

"Just till Hamburg, then I put the car on a liner, and I take a plane to Queens."

"Uwww, how unfortunate for you, dear. But that's life, isn't it?"

"So have you got something for me when I get back?"

"Mmm. There's an all-star ballgame out in East Hampton. That will freshen you up. Put you back on your toes."

"I've got to go."

"Call me when you get in. Maybe I'll have something better."

"All right."

"I hear Johnny's been hanging out at your parents' house. Meek as a lamb. What about him?"

"What about him what?"

"Is he drinking?"

"If he is, he can leave until he sobers up. Anything else?"

"Maybe a small bottle of schnapps for me? *A bientôt*," he said, and they hung up.

*   *   *

Claire dabbed Chanel behind both ears and holy water on her Ajna Chakra, took a deep breath and crossed the threshold from her room.

Hans von Grünwald's bedroom door stood open. Claire walked slowly toward it. Isolde sat in there, her back to her, at the elaborate, and once Kunigunde's, Biedermeier mirror. It hadn't taken Isolde long to have it hauled down from the attic. Friedel the gardner had done it for her. Everyone had had a raise in pay. Not much, but a raise. Blacky ran a tight ship. So Friedel was in a good mood. And now that Stella was clearly out of not only his reach, but all mankind's, Gaby, the plump little serving girl who came to and from work on her bicycle, was looking better and better.

Isolde lined her lips, eyeing Claire in the mirror with reproach. "You should have gone to Corsica with Mara. She asked you to go with her. All the world is there now. How can you go back to the States? It is utterly devoid of culture."

"Sez you."

"Tch. Everyone knows."

"You only say that because when you're there you go to all those trendy places. You've never even had dinner in a typical American home."

"That's because there's no such thing. And no one's ever invited me."

"Is that right? I thought that was how this whole thing started. My inviting you to come stay with me in my home."

"You always have to have the last word."

"I'm glad marriage hasn't destroyed your sanguine temperament."

Isolde piled her hair up on her head. "My marriage suits me very well."

272

"I can see that. Are you coming to the station?"

"I would, but I'm contemplating a headache. You won't mind?"

"No. You hate the train station."

"You remember. Thoughtful Claire. How will I get along without you?"

"Very well, I'll bet."

"So you never found your treasure."

Claire shrugged. "Time will tell." She'd decided to look at this philosophically.

Isolde peered at her shrewdly. "If you had found a treasure, it would be legally mine now anyway."

"Gee. Good thing I'm still poor."

"You're not poor," Isolde said sulkily. "You always think something wonderful is going to happen to you."

"Good-bye, Isolde." She hugged her tenderly. Isolde tensed up, then remembered this was it, she was leaving. She threw her arms around Claire in a perfumy crush.

"Auf Wiedersehen," she said huskily, then let her go with a dashing wave of bracelets. Claire saw only the back of her head as she closed the door.

Stella came up behind her. "I'll help you with your things."

"Just these two." She handed her the lovely woven basket Evangelika had given her for shopping in America. She followed Stella to the end of the hall and down the stairs.

"Temple left this morning?" Claire asked her.

"Yes," she said gently. "For Ireland."

Claire nodded and checked again for her lens cap.

"I won't come all the way out," Stella said. "I'll bid you adieu right here."

"All right."

"I have something for you, though. Something you must choose."

"Time to go." Blacky, coming in the door, smacked the

palms of his hands together and rubbed them back and
forth. "What's that?" Blacky said. "Cosimo?"

"Oh, it's Beethoven's 'Appassionata.' " Stella Gabriella
clapped her hands. "He used to play that all the time. He
hasn't played it in years."

Claire listened. She found it difficult to move.

"Come on, come on." Stella pushed her into the kitchen.
"No time yet for sentiment. You have to choose a pot to
take home with you."

"Oh no!" Claire laughed. Stella had set up three bowls,
each half full with water, on the long kitchen table.

"What, now we have to wait for her to choose a direction?" Blacky cried. "She couldn't do that in all the time I
was with her. We'll never make the train!"

Dirk, never far from Blacky, mirrored his apprehension.
He was looking forward to the train station. It was always
milling with Turks.

"Yes, we will," Claire assured them. "I already made my
decision anyway. We've been down this road before."

"Never mind, never mind," Stella teased her, "every day
is a new day. Are you so sure you want the same path?" She
took hold of the table edge.

Claire looked again at the bowls. Puzzled, she looked
closer. They were different. These were not the tea bowls
she had chosen from the first time. These were much larger.
She looked to Stella. Her eyes told her nothing. Stella Gabriella shrugged. "It's up to you," she said in her breathless,
detached way.

Claire chose the middle bowl. Then it was really time to
go. She made sure she had Stella's address at the convent,
hugged and kissed Evangelika, and went out into the yard.

Evangelika wiped the headlamp with a corner of her holiday lily-print apron.

Claire climbed in and rolled down the window. "Remember." She stuck her head out and warned Evangelika,

"Iris is expecting you with Cosimo and Stella in October."

Evangelika nodded back with apprehensive eyes.

"Push over." Blacky invited himself to drive.

"I'll pick you up at the airport," Claire called shrilly across his lap. Dirk climbed in on her other side. Otto von Auto started grudgingly up. Claire gripped the formidable bowl on her lap.

Evangelika waved them away with one fist heaving to and fro.

As they pulled off, Claire saw Stella Gabriella watching her from her upstairs window. She was grinning, no longer fingering her beads in her usual way. All the small, shiny hinges and facets which hold a rosary together lay, unhinged and unfastened, on Stella Gabriella's pink marble tabletop. She would have a new pair from the convent soon anyway. And Kunigunde's ghost, she felt sure, could at long last rest easy.

They were just climbing the hill behind the chapel when a taxi came from the other direction. It stopped in front of them, cutting them off. It was Temple Fortune. Claire got out of the car. There was the moon.

"I couldn't leave without saying good-bye again," he said. Evangelika's clean white sheets flapped around them in the wind.

They walked into each other's arms, holding on for the last time, feeling each other's strange, familiar forms.

Blacky complained from the car. Dirk reached over and honked the horn long and hard.

Finally, they let go. She still had Stella's bowl in her hand, pressed between them painfully.

"Look what I've done! I've gone and cracked your fine bowl," he said.

"It doesn't matter," she said. "Now I have something of you."

She turned and climbed into the old rumbling car. They

275

pulled away, leaving Saint Hildegard's Mill, rolling past the chapel, the band of foresty trees. Temple stood beside his taxi, his hands down at his sides. He watched for a good long while, until the car was just a dot. Claire sat, a little squashed, between Blacky and Dirk.

A precious bright series of tears dropped into her bowl, dazzling the spot where Temple had chipped it.

Something winked excitedly beneath, revealing at last the spell unbound and baked into its just seams.